A Thousand Ships

A Thousand Ships

A Novel

Natalie Haynes

HARPER

An Imprint of HarperCollins*Publishers*

HarperCollins books may be purchased for educational, business, or sales promotional use. For information, please email the Special Markets Department at SPsales@harpercollins.com.

Originally published in Great Britain in 2019 by Mantle, an imprint of Pan Macmillan.

FIRST U.S. EDITION

Library of Congress Cataloging-in-Publication Data has been applied for.

ISBN 978-0-06-306539-0

21 22 23 24 25 LSC 10 9 8 7 6 5 4 3 2 1

For Keziah, of course

Her excellent reputation will never be lost;
the gods will create a song to delight mortals
about clever Penelope.
So unlike my wife, who did awful things . . .

Agamemnon, *Odyssey* Book 24.196–9

List of Characters

The House of Atreus

AGAMEMNON, king of Mycenae, near Argos, on the Greek mainland. Son of Atreus, husband of:

CLYTEMNESTRA, queen of Mycenae, and mother of:

IPHIGENIA, ORESTES, ELECTRA

MENELAUS, brother of Agamemnon, husband of:

HELEN of Sparta, later known as Helen of Troy. Helen was both sister and sister-in-law to Clytemnestra. She and Menelaus had a daughter:

HERMIONE

In addition:

AEGISTHUS, son of Thyestes (the brother of Atreus), was cousin to Agamemnon and Menelaus

The House of Odysseus

ODYSSEUS, king of Ithaca, son of ANTICLEIA and LAERTES. Husband of:

PENELOPE, queen of Ithaca, weaving expert, mother of:

TELEMACHUS

ix

Their household also contained:

EURYCLEIA, Odysseus' nurse

EUMAEUS, a loyal swineherd

Odysseus was delayed on his way home from Troy by (among many others):

POLYPHEMUS, a one-eyed giant or Cyclops. Son of POSEIDON, the god of the sea

CIRCE, an enchantress who lived on the island of Aeaea (pronounced Ai-ee-a)

THE LAESTRYGONIANS, some cannibal giants

THE SIRENS, half-women, half-birds, with a song that drew sailors to their deaths

SCYLLA, a dog-woman hybrid. Lots of teeth

CHARYBDIS, a ship-destroying whirlpool

CALYPSO, a nymph who lived on the island of Ogygia (pronounced Oh-gi-jee-a)

The House of Achilles

PELEUS was a Greek king and hero who married:

THETIS, a sea nymph. They had a son:

ACHILLES, the greatest warrior the world had ever known. His closest friend and perhaps lover was:

PATROCLUS, a Greek warrior and minor noble. During the Trojan War, they captured:

BRISEIS, princess of Lyrnessus, a smaller town not far from Troy

Achilles also had a son:

NEOPTOLEMUS

Other Greeks embroiled in the Trojan War include:

SINON, a warrior

PROTESILAUS, king of Phylace, a small Greek settlement. Husband of:

LAODAMIA, his queen

TROJANS

The House of Priam

PRIAM, king of Troy, father of countless sons and daughters and husband of:

HECABE, also called Hecuba by the Romans and later by Shakespeare. Mother of:

POLYXENA, heroine of Troy

CASSANDRA, priestess of APOLLO, the god of archery, healing and disease

HECTOR, the great Trojan hero

PARIS, Trojan warrior and seducer of other men's wives

POLYDORUS, the youngest son of Priam and Hecabe

List of Characters

Hecabe and Priam were also parents-in-law of:

ANDROMACHE, wife of Hector, mother of ASTYANAX

Other Trojans embroiled in the war include:

AENEAS, a Trojan noble, son of ANCHISES and husband of:

CREUSA, mother of EURYLEON (later known by the Romans as Ascanius)

THEANO, wife of ANTENOR (an adviser to Priam) and mother of CRINO

CHRYSEIS, a Trojan girl and the daughter of CHRYSES, a priest of APOLLO

PENTHESILEA was an Amazon princess, sister to HIPPOLYTA. She was not a Trojan, but fought as their ally in the last year of the war

OENONE (pronounced Oi-no-nee), a mountain nymph, lived near Troy

DEITIES

CALLIOPE, muse of epic poetry

ZEUS, king of the Olympian gods. Father of countless other gods, goddesses, nymphs and demi-gods. Husband and brother of:

HERA, queen of the Olympian gods and disliker of anyone Zeus seduces

APHRODITE, goddess of love, particularly the lustful variety.

Married to the blacksmith god, HEPHAESTUS, and occasional lover of the god of war, ARES

ATHENE, goddess of wisdom and defensive warfare. Supporter of Odysseus, patron goddess of Athens. Loves owls

ERIS, goddess of strife. Troublemaker

THEMIS, one of the old goddesses. Represents order, as opposed to chaos

GAIA, another one of the old goddesses. We think of her as Mother Earth

THE MOIRAI, the Fates. Three sisters – CLOTHO, LACHESIS and ATROPOS – who hold our destinies in their hands

A Thousand Ships

1

Calliope

Sing, Muse, he says, and the edge in his voice makes it clear that this is not a request. If I were minded to accede to his wish, I might say that he sharpens his tone on my name, like a warrior drawing his dagger across a whetstone, preparing for the morning's battle. But I am not in the mood to be a muse today. Perhaps he hasn't thought of what it is like to be me. Certainly he hasn't: like all poets, he thinks only of himself. But it is surprising that he hasn't considered how many other men there are like him, every day, all demanding my unwavering attention and support. How much epic poetry does the world really need?

Every conflict joined, every war fought, every city besieged, every town sacked, every village destroyed. Every impossible journey, every shipwreck, every homecoming: these stories have all been told, and countless times. Can he really believe he has something new to say? And does he think he might need me to help him keep track of all his characters, or to fill those empty moments where the metre doesn't fit the tale?

I look down and see that his head is bowed and his shoulders, though broad, are sloped. His spine has begun to curve at the top. He is old, this man. Older than his hard-edged voice suggests. I'm curious. It's usually the young for whom poetry is such an urgent matter. I crouch down to see his eyes, closed for a moment with the intensity of his prayer. I cannot recognize him while they are shut.

He is wearing a beautiful gold brooch, tiny leaves wrought into a gleaming knot. So someone has rewarded him handsomely for his poetry in the past. He has talent and he has prospered, no doubt with my assistance. But still he wants more, and I wish I could see his face properly, in the light.

I wait for him to open his eyes, but I have already made up my mind. If he wants my help, he will make an offering for it. That is what mortals do: first they ask, then they beg, finally they bargain. So I will give him his words when he gives me that brooch.

2

Creusa

A deafening crack awoke her, and she caught her breath. She looked around for the baby, before remembering that he was no longer a baby, but had seen five summers come and go while the war raged outside the city walls. He was in his own room, of course he was. Her breathing slowed, and she waited to hear him cry out for his mother, terrified by the thunderstorm. But the cry did not come: he was brave, her little boy. Too brave to cry out at a lightning bolt, even if it was hurled by Zeus himself. She wrapped the coverlet over her shoulders, and tried to guess what hour of the night it was. The pitter-patter of rain was growing louder. It must be early morning, because she could see across the room. But the light was peculiar: a fat yellow colour which caught the dark red walls and painted them an ugly, bloody shade. How could the light be so yellow unless the sun was rising? And how could the sun fill her rooms when she could hear the rain falling on the roof? Disorientated by her recent dreams, it was several moments before she realized the acrid tang was in her nostrils, not her imagination. The crash had not been thunder, but a more earthly destruction; the pitter-patter was not rain, but the sound of dried wood and straw crackling in the heat. And the flickering yellow light was not the sun.

Realizing the danger she was in, she leapt from her bed, trying to undo her previous slowness. She must get outside and away from the fire. The smoke was already coating her tongue with its greasy soot. She called for her husband, Aeneas, and her son, Euryleon, but they made no reply. She left her small bedroom – the slender cot with its red-brown coverlet that she had so proudly woven for herself when she was first married – but she did not get far. She caught sight of the flames through the small high window just outside her bedroom door, and all speed slid away from her feet into the floor. It was not her home which was ablaze. It was the citadel: the highest point of the city of Troy, which only watch-fires or sacrificial flames or Helios, god of the sun, travelling overhead with his horse-drawn chariot, had ever lit before. Now fire was jumping through the columns of stone – so cool to the touch – and she watched in silence as part of the roof caught, and a sudden shower of sparks flew from the wood, tiny whirling fireflies in the smoke.

Aeneas must have gone to help battle the flames, she thought. He would have run to offer assistance to his brothers, his cousins, carrying water and sand and anything they could find. It was not the first fire which had threatened the city since the siege began. And the men would do anything, everything, to save the citadel, site of Troy's most prized possessions: the treasury, the temples, the home of Priam, their king. The fear which had driven her from her bed ebbed, as she saw her own house was not ablaze, she and her son were not in danger, but – as so often during this endless war – her husband was. The sharp fear for survival was replaced instantly with a familiar pinching anxiety. She was so used to seeing him go out to fight the pestilence of Greeks who had been encamped outside the city for ten long years, so used to the dread of watching him leave, and the crippling fear of waiting for him to return, that now it settled on her almost comfortingly, like a dark bird perching on her shoulder. He had always come home before, she reminded herself. Always. And she tried to ignore the thought which the bird squawked unbidden into her mind: why should the past be any guarantee of the future?

She jumped as she heard another monstrous crash, louder surely than the one which had woken her. She peered around the edge of the window, looking out over the lower parts of the city. Now she saw that this was not a fire like other fires save for the importance of its location: it was not confined to the citadel. Pockets of angry orange light were flickering all over the city. Creusa murmured a prayer to the household gods. But it was too late for prayers. Even as her tongue formed the sounds, she could see the gods had abandoned Troy. Across the city, the temples were burning.

She ran along the short dark corridor which took her towards the front of the house through the courtyard room she loved with its high and ornately patterned walls. No one was here, even the slaves had gone. She tripped over her sheath, then twisted her left fist into the fabric to shorten it. She called again for her son – could Aeneas have taken him to collect her father-in-law? Was that where he had gone? – and opened their large wooden door onto the street. Now she could see her neighbours running along the road – none carrying water as she had imagined Aeneas would be, but only bags with whatever they had managed to gather up before they fled, or nothing at all – she could not suppress a cry. There were screams and shouting coming from every direction. The smoke was sinking into the streets, as if the city was now too ruined, too shamed to meet her eyes.

She stood in the doorway, unsure what to do. She should stay in the house, of course, or her husband might not be able to find her when he returned. Many years ago, he had promised that if the city ever fell, he would take her and their son and his father, and any other Trojan survivors, and sail away to found a new city. She had put her fingers on his lips, to stop the words from coming out. Even saying such things could invite a mischievous god to make them come to pass. His beard tickled her hands, but she did not laugh. And nor did he: it's my duty, he had said. Priam commands me. Someone must take on the mantle of founding a new Troy, if the worst should happen. She again tried to crush the flurry of thoughts that he would not return, that he was already dead, that the city would be razed before dawn, and that her home – like so many others – would not be here for anyone to return to.

But how could this have happened? She pressed her head against the wooden door, its black metal studs warm against her skin. She looked down at herself and saw oily black dust had already settled in the creases of her shift. What she could see happening across the city was not possible, because Troy had won the war. The Greeks had finally fled, after a decade of attrition on the plains outside the city. They had arrived with their tall ships all those years ago and had achieved what, exactly? The battles had been waged nearer the city, then further away; advancing right up to the beached vessels, then closing back towards Troy. There had been single combat and all-out war. There had been sickness and famine on both sides. Great champions had fallen and cowards had sneaked away with their lives. But Troy, her city, had stood victorious in the end.

Was it three days ago, four? She could no longer be completely sure of time. But she had no doubt of the facts. She had watched the fleet sail away herself, climbing to the acropolis to see it with her own eyes. Like everyone else in the city she had heard the rumours several days earlier that the Greek army was packing up. Certainly they had withdrawn to their camp. Aeneas and his fellow men – she would never think of them as warriors, for that was their role outside the city, not within it – had debated the merits of a raiding party, hoping to discover what was going on as much as to cause mayhem. But they had held themselves back within the city walls, watching patiently to see what might happen next. And after another day or two with no spears thrown nor arrows fired, people began to hope. Perhaps another plague was ravaging the Greek camp. It had happened before, a few moons ago, and the Trojans had cheered, making thankful offerings to every god. The Greeks were being punished for their impiety, for their senseless refusal to accept that Troy would not fall, could not fall to mortal men. Not to men like these, these arrogant Greeks with their tall ships and their bronze armour, glinting in the sun because not one of them could tolerate the notion that he should labour in obscurity, unseen and unadmired.

Like everyone else, Creusa had prayed for plague. She had not thought there was anything better to pray for. But then another day passed and the ships began to move, the masts quivering as the men rowed themselves out of the bay and into the deep waters of the ocean. And still the Trojans stayed quiet, unable to believe their eyes. The camp had been an eyesore to the west of their city, behind the mouth of the River Scamander, for so long that it was peculiar to see the shore without it, like a gangrenous limb finally amputated. Less horrifying than what had been, but still unsettling. And a day later, even the last and slowest of the ships was gone, groaning under the weight of the men and their ill-earned treasure, ravaged from every small town in Phrygia, from everywhere with fewer men and lower walls than Troy itself. They rowed themselves into the wind, then unfurled their sails and floated away.

Creusa and Aeneas stood on the city walls, watching the white froth churning up on the shore, long after the ships had disappeared. They held one another as she whispered the questions he could not answer: why have they left? Will they return? Are we safe now?

*

A loud, distant thud jerked Creusa back to the present. She could not now go up to the acropolis to look for Aeneas. Even from her house, she could see that the citadel roof had collapsed in a rush of smoke. Any man who had been underneath it would be dead. She tried not to think of Euryleon darting past his father's legs, trying to help quench an insatiable fire. But Aeneas would not have taken their only son into danger. He must have gone to collect Anchises, to lead the old man to safety. But would he return for Creusa or expect her to find him in the streets?

She knew Aeneas' heart better than she knew her own. He had set off to find his father before the fire had reached its fullest extent: Anchises lived closer to the acropolis, where the flames were burning most fiercely. Aeneas would have known the journey to his father's house would be difficult. He would have anticipated returning, but now he would see that it was impossible. He would be making his way to the city gates and trusting her to do the same. She would find him on the plains outside; he would head towards what had recently been the Greek camp. She paused on the threshold for a moment, wondering what she should take with her. But the shouting of men was coming closer and she did not recognize the dialect. The Greeks were in her city and there was no time to search for valuables, or even a cloak. She looked across the smoke-filled streets, and began to run.

*

Creusa had been caught up in the festival atmosphere that spread through the city the previous day: for the first time in ten years, Troy's gates were thrown open. The last time she had walked out onto the Scamandrian plains which surrounded the city, she had been little more than a child, twelve years old. Her parents had told her that the Greeks were pirates and mercenaries, sailing the glittering seas to find easy pickings. They would not stay long in Phrygia, everyone said. Why would they? No one believed their pretext: that they had come to claim back some woman who had run off with one of Priam's boys. The idea was laughable. Countless ships, as many as a thousand, sailing across oceans to besiege one city for the sake of a woman? Even when Creusa saw her – saw Helen with her long golden hair arranged over her red dress, matched by the gold embroidery which decorated every hem and the ropes of gold she wore around her neck and her wrists – even then she did not believe an army would have sailed all this way to take her home. The Greeks took to the seas for the same reasons as anyone else: to fill their strongboxes with plunder and their households with slaves. And this time, when they sailed to Troy, they had over-reached. In their ignorance, they had not known that the city was not merely wealthy but properly defended. Typical Greeks, Creusa's parents had said: to Hellenes, all non-Greeks were alike, all were barbarians. It had not occurred to them that Troy was a city surpassing Mycenae, Sparta, Ithaca and everywhere they themselves called home.

Troy would not open her gates to the Greeks. Creusa had watched her father's brow darken when he spoke to her mother about what Priam had decided to do. The city would fight, and they would not give back the woman, or her gold or her dresses. The Greeks were opportunists, he said. They would be gone before the first winter storms battered their ships. Troy was a city of fabled good fortune: King Priam with his fifty sons and fifty daughters, his limitless wealth, his high walls and his loyal allies. The Greeks could not hear of such a city without wishing to destroy it. It was in their nature. And so the Trojans knew this was why they had come, with the retrieval of Helen as their pretence. The Spartan king – Trojan wives muttered as they gathered by the water to launder their clothes – had probably sent Helen away with Paris deliberately, to give him and his fellow-Greeks the excuse they needed to set sail.

Whatever their reasons, when the Greeks had first made camp outside Creusa's home, she had been a child. And the next time she walked outside, she held the hand of her own son, who'd had a whole city for his nursery, but had never run across the plains outside. Even Aeneas, battle-wearied after years of fighting, had a lightness to him when the gates creaked open. He was still wearing his sword, of course, but he had left his spear at home. Scouts had reported that no soldiers had been left behind. The coast was empty of men and boats. Only a sacrificial offering remained, a huge wooden thing, they said. Impossible to know who the Greeks had dedicated it to, or why. Poseidon, for a safe voyage home, Creusa suggested to her husband, as their little boy tore off across the muddied ground. The grass would grow again, she told Euryleon when they first walked outside. Thinking of her own childhood, she had promised too much. She had not thought of all those studded feet trampling, all those chariot wheels churning, all that blood draining.

Aeneas nodded, and she caught sight of their son's face in his, just for a moment, beneath the thick dark brows. Yes, Poseidon was surely the divine recipient of their offering. Or perhaps it was Athene, who had protected the Greeks for so long, or Hera, who loathed the Trojans no matter how many cattle they slaughtered in her honour. They walked around the edge of what had recently been a battlefield towards the bay. Euryleon would finally feel sand beneath his feet rather than dirt and stone. Creusa felt the change already, as the mud became grainier and clumps of thick sea-grass sprouted around her. She felt tears warm on her cheeks as the soft west wind blew into her eyes. Her husband reached out a scarred hand and pressed her tears away with his thumb.

'Is it too much?' he asked. 'Do you want to go back?'

'Not yet.'

*

Creusa felt tears on her face once again but they did not come from fear, although she was afraid, and although Aeneas was not there to comfort her. Billowing smoke filled the streets, and it was this which made her eyes track sooty tears down her cheeks. She turned down a path which she was sure would lead her to the lower part of the city where she could follow the wall around until she came to the gates. She had spent ten years locked inside Troy and had walked its paths countless times. She knew every house, every corner, every twist and turn. But though she had been sure she was heading downhill, she suddenly found her way blocked: a dead end. She felt panic rise in her chest and she gasped for air, spluttering at the greasy blackness which filled her throat. Men ran past her – Greek, Trojan? She could no longer tell – with cloths tied around their faces to hold off the smoke. Desperately she cast around for something she could use to do the same. But her stole was at home, and she could not return for it now. Even if she knew the way back, which she was no longer sure she did.

Creusa wanted to pause and try to find something familiar, something which would allow her to work out exactly where she was and calculate the best route out of the city. But there was no time. She noticed that the smoke looked thinner at her feet, and crouched down for a moment to catch her breath. The fires were spreading in every direction, and although the smoke made it difficult for her to judge, some looked to be very close. She retraced her steps until she came to the first crossroads, and peered left, which seemed a little brighter, and then right into the deepest darkness. She must move away from the light, she realized. The brightest parts of the city must be where the fires raged most strongly. So Creusa would go into the dark.

*

The sun had dazzled her as she and Aeneas approached the promontory which had held the Greek encampment on the low plains. Only from the highest point of Troy – the citadel and the watchtowers – had the camp been visible. Creusa had climbed up to see it every time her husband fought outside the walls. If she could see him fighting on the plains, she had told herself, even if she couldn't identify him in the midst of mud and gore and glinting blades, she could keep him safe. And now here he was, walking beside her with his hand on her arm. She had expected to feel the strongest relief, when she saw the bay vacated and the camp abandoned. But as she and Aeneas turned the sandy corner, she barely noticed the missing boats or the detritus on the shore. Like the other Trojans ahead of them, their eyes were drawn upwards, to the horse.

It was the largest sacrificial offering any of them had ever seen, even those Trojan men who had sailed abroad to Greece before the war. It was another way in which the Greeks sought to distinguish themselves. Their offerings to the gods were extravagant beyond measure. Why offer one cow when you could offer a hecatomb? The smell of burning meat from outside the walls had filled Troy in the early days of the war, when Creusa had eaten nothing but a small cup of barley with a little milk. The Greeks were doing it on purpose, she knew: flaunting their carcasses in front of a besieged city. But it would take more than hunger to break Trojan spirits. And as the war dragged from one year to the next, she thought the Greeks must regret their earlier largesse to the gods. If they had only saved some of those cattle, they might have had quite the herd by now, grazing on the sea-grass perhaps, and sustaining the soldiers who grew leaner every year.

But this offering was so large that it tricked the eyes. Creusa looked away for a moment and was shocked anew when she turned them back to its huge wooden planks. It towered above them, three or four times the height of a man. And though the design was rudimentary – what else could you expect from Greeks? – the figure was perfectly identifiable as a horse: four legs and a long grassy tail; a muzzle, though it lacked a mane. The wood had been cut with a clumsy axe, but the panels had been nailed together neatly enough. Ribbons had been tied around its brow to convey its sacrificial status.

'Have you ever seen anything like it?' she breathed to her husband. He shook his head. Of course not.

The Trojans approached the horse warily, as though it might come to life and snap its teeth. Foolish to be fearful of a simulacrum, but how could this be all that was left behind by an invading army? The men began to discuss what should be done, and their women stood back, murmuring to one another about the strange beast. Perhaps they should draw long grasses and twigs into a pile beneath the creature's feet, and burn it? If it was an offering to a god for a fair wind back to Greece – as seemed likely, though Creusa had heard of them making uglier sacrifices in the past – then could the Trojans inflict one last blow on their enemies by destroying it? Would that divert the good will of the god away from the Greeks? Or should they take the horse and dedicate it to the gods for themselves?

What began as a whispered conversation soon developed into shouts. Men who had fought alongside one another, brothers in arms and blood, were snarling at their kinsmen. The horse must be burned or saved; driven into the sea or dragged up to the city.

Creusa wished she could simply call for silence so she could sit on the dunes and lie back, stretching out her arms and legs, feeling the sand on her skin. It had been so long since she had been free. What did the Greeks' offerings matter to the Trojans now? She grabbed Euryleon's hand, and scooped him close to her legs as Aeneas stepped forward, squeezing Creusa's arm as he walked away. He did not want to be drawn into an argument, but he could not shirk his duty as one of Troy's defenders.

The men had experienced a very different war from the women who waited for them, nursed them and fed them at the end of each day. To Aeneas, Creusa realized, the place where she now stood – from which she wished the Trojans would disappear so she could enjoy it in peace with her husband and her son – was still a battle-field.

Suddenly, the clamour fell silent and a shuffling figure made his painful way past Creusa, his dark red robes tangling around his gnarled feet. Priam walked like the old man he was, but he still held his head upright like a king. His proud queen, Hecabe, moved beside him into the centre of the crowd. She would not hold herself back, as the other women did.

'Enough!' Priam said, his voice quavering a little. Euryleon began to tug at Creusa's dress, wanting her attention for something he had seen – a beetle digging its laborious way through the sand-dune at their feet – but she shushed him. Nothing about this first day outside the city was matching her imagination, which had brought light into her darker moments. She had yearned for the day to come when her son saw for the first time the animals which lived along the shore. And now she was quieting him, so the king could speak to his furious subjects.

'We do not fight among ourselves,' Priam said. 'Not today. I will hear your thoughts, one after another.'

Creusa heard the arguments in favour of every possible fate for the horse, and found she did not care particularly what Priam chose to do. Burn the horse, keep the horse: what difference would it make? The last man to speak was the priest, Laocoon, a fleshy man with oiled black curls who was always too fond of the sound of his own voice. He was determined that the horse should be torched where it stood. It was the only way to placate the gods, he said, who had punished Troy for so many years. Anything else would be a catastrophic mistake.

*

Smoke from countless fires billowed around her and Creusa stumbled as she tried to make her way along the path to the city walls. She thought she was going in the right direction, but she could not be sure. Her lungs were screaming as though she were running uphill. She could see nothing ahead of her, and she stretched out her hands, one in front to break her fall if she tripped, one to her right, so she could try to trace the buildings she passed. It was the only way she could be sure she was moving forward.

Creusa tried not to let the thought become words, held it only in its haziest form before hurling it away from her, but it could not be denied: the city was beyond salvation. So many fires raging in every direction. More and more wooden roofs had caught and the smoke was only growing thicker. How much fire could one stone city make? She thought of everything in her own home which would burn: her clothes, her bedding, the tapestries she had woven while she was expecting Euryleon. The sudden sense of loss seared her, as though she had been caught in the flames. She had lost her home. Ten years of fearing that the city would fall, and now it was falling around her as she ran.

But how could this be happening? Troy had won the

war. The Greeks had sailed away, and when the Trojans found the wooden horse, they had done exactly what the man told them they must do. And in a terrible rush, Creusa knew what had set her city ablaze. Ten years of a conflict whose heroes had already made their way into the songs of poets, and victory belonged to none of the men who had fought outside the walls, not Achilles nor Hector, both long since dead. Instead, it belonged to the man they had found hiding in the reeds, near the horse, who said his name was – she could not remember. A hissing sound, like a snake.

*

'Sinon,' the man wept. Two spears were pointed at his neck, and he had fallen to his knees. The Trojan scouts had found him hiding in the low shrubs, on the far bank of the Scamander just as it opened out to meet the sea. They had driven him – one on either side, armed with knives as well as spears – into the midst of the Trojan men. The prisoner's hands were bound at the wrists and there were angry red welts around his ankles, as though ropes had bitten him there too.

'We might not have seen him,' said one of the scouts, prodding the prisoner with the tip of his spear. The man suppressed a cry, though the spear had not broken his skin. 'It was only the red ribbons which caught our eyes.'

The prisoner was a strange sight: his mousy hair curled into his neck and out again, and if it had ever been oiled, it was now matted with the mud which covered so much of his bare skin. He wore a loin-cloth but nothing else. Even his feet were bare. And yet, around his temples, bright ribbons had been tied. It did not seem possible that so dirty a man – more like an animal than a man, Creusa thought – could have any part of him so clean and pretty. The prisoner let forth a piteous howl.

'What was meant to kill me then is the cause of my death now!'

Creusa could not hide her disgust at the filthy, weeping Greek. Why had the scouts not killed him where they found him?

Priam raised two fingers of his left hand. 'Silence,' he said. The crowd stilled, and even the prisoner's racking sobs diminished.

'You are a Greek?' Priam said. Sinon nodded. 'And yet they left you behind?'

'Not intentionally, king.' Sinon raised his hands to wipe mucus from his face. 'I ran away from them. The gods will punish me, I know. But I could not stand to be . . .' His speech dissolved again.

'Take control of yourself,' Priam said. 'Or my men will kill you where you kneel and your blood will feed the gulls.'

Sinon gave one last juddering sob and took a breath. 'Forgive me.'

Priam nodded. 'You ran away from them?'

'I did. Though I was born Greek and I have fought alongside Greeks all my life,' Sinon replied. 'I came here with my father when I was still a boy. He died in the fighting many years ago, killed by your great warrior, Hector.' A ripple passed through the Trojan crowd. 'Please,' said Sinon, looking around him for the first time. 'I mean no disrespect. We were on opposing sides. But Hector did not kill him with malice. He cut him down on the battle-field, and took nothing from his corpse, not even my father's shield, which was finely wrought. I bear no grudge against Hector's family.'

The loss of Hector had been so terrible, and so recent, that shadows settled on Priam's face, and he seemed to Creusa's eyes to lose himself for a moment. Standing before her, before them all, was no king, but a broken old man whose ancient neck could scarcely support the gold chains he still wore. The prisoner might have noticed the same thing, for he swallowed and when he spoke again, his voice was quieter, speaking to the king alone. Creusa had to strain to hear him.

'But my father had enemies, powerful enemies among the Greeks,' Sinon said. 'And we were unfortunate enough to incur the hostility of two men in particular, though I swear to you neither my father nor I did anything to deserve it. Still Calchas and Odysseus were set against him, and so against me, from the outset.'

At the hated name of Odysseus, Creusa could not suppress a shudder.

'An enemy of Odysseus holds some common ground with us,' said Priam slowly.

'Thank you, king. He is the most hated of men. The ordinary Greek soldiers detest him, the way he swaggers around as though he were a mighty warrior or noble king. He is a far from exceptional fighter and Ithaca – his kingdom, as he calls it – is nothing more than a rocky outcrop that no man would envy. Yet our leader Agamemnon and the others, they have always treated him as a hero. And his arrogance has only grown in consequence.'

'No doubt,' said Priam. 'Yet none of this explains why you are here, or why your countrymen have all disappeared so unexpectedly. And the name of Calchas is not familiar to me.'

Sinon blinked several times. He could see, Creusa thought, that he must make his point quickly, or lose his chance to speak forever.

'The Greeks have known for some time, king, that they must leave. Calchas is their chief priest, and he has appealed to the gods for happier news. But their answer has been the same, since last winter: Troy will not fall to a Greek army camped outside the gates. Agamemnon did not want to hear it, of course, and nor did his brother, Menelaus. But eventually they could no longer argue their case. The Greeks are sick of being far from home. The war could not be won, so it was better to take the booty they had acquired and set sail. This argument was put forward by many men –'

'Including you?' Priam asked.

Sinon smiled. 'Not at the formal discussions,' he said. 'I am no king, I would never be permitted to speak. But among ourselves, the ordinary soldiers, yes: I agreed that we should leave. I believed we should never have come. And that made me unpopular. Not with the rank and file, who were of the same mind. But with the leaders, the men who had staked their reputations on the war, with Odysseus. Still, they could not argue with a message coming directly from the gods. Reluctantly they agreed to sail home.'

'And they left you behind as punishment?' Priam asked. His scouts had relaxed their spears a little, so

Sinon no longer saw them right at his throat as he spoke.

'No, king.' He sucked in his tear-stained, mud-smeared cheeks for a moment. 'You know the story of the Greek voyage to Troy? How we massed our fleet in Aulis, but then could not sail, because the winds disappeared?'

Around him, the Trojans nodded. It was a tale they had all heard, and told: how the Greeks had offended the goddess Artemis, and she had taken the wind from them until they appeased her. Horrifyingly, they had done so by conducting a human sacrifice. What Trojan did not know of this terrible, typical cruelty?

'When it came to the time to return to Greece, Calchas and Odysseus hatched their plot together,' Sinon continued. 'The king of Ithaca could not resist an opportunity to rid himself of me.'

Creusa looked again at the red ribbons around the prisoner's head and felt a prickling behind her eyelids. Surely he was not saying such a dreadful thing.

'I see you understand my meaning, king,' Sinon said. 'Calchas announced at the assembly of Greeks that the gods had chosen their sacrifice, and that it was my blood they wished to drink from a makeshift altar. There was a little criticism from the soldiers but better me than them.'

'I understand,' said Priam. 'They intended to sacrifice you like an animal.'

'They did more than intend it; they prepared me for it. They bound me at the wrists.' Sinon raised them to show the grimy ropes which still held his hands together. 'And at the feet. They oiled my hair and tied fillets around it.

Everything about this sacrifice had to be perfect, of course. But the bonds around my ankles were not quite as tight as these,' he shook his hands, 'and when I was left out of sight of the guards, I wrenched myself free.' This explained the angry weals around his feet.

'I knew the guards would soon drag me to the altar. So first I crawled and then I ran as fast as I could away from the camp. By the time I heard the shout go up I had made it almost to the reed banks and I lay down and hid.'

The tears began to flow from the man's eyes once again, and a corresponding dampness appeared on the face of the Trojan king. Creusa knew that she too was weeping. It was a horrific story, even to those well-versed in the barbarity of the Greeks. Priam's wife, Hecabe, looked on without comment: her mouth in a short, thin line, her grey brows drawn.

'I heard the men searching for me,' Sinon said. 'I heard them cutting at the grass with their whips and spears. I was desperate to run further, but I knew I couldn't risk being seen. So I waited for the longest night of my life, praying to Hera who has always been my protector. And the next morning, my prayers had been answered. The Greeks had decided to fashion this wooden offering to the gods, instead of sacrificing an unwilling victim. They built it, dedicated it, and then set sail without me. So in spite of my bad fortune, I have lived a few more days than I was allotted. Now you will kill me, king, and rightly: I am one of the men who came here to raze your city, and I deserve to be treated as your enemy, even if I was only a boy when I was brought here. I have no family who can ransom me. So I do not beg you to send my body home to grieving relatives. I have none. I have but one request to make of you.'

'What is that?' Priam asked.

'Take the horse.'

*

Creusa had fallen heavily and she could feel the blood inching down her shinbones as she pulled herself upright. She could see almost nothing ahead of her now, though the heat on her back made her certain she was taking the only possible route. Was everywhere behind her in flames? She could not bring herself to look, knowing that if she did, the brightness of the fire would blind her when she turned back towards the darkness. It was this – thinking of the practical things she could and could not do – which was keeping her on her feet, when nothing in her life had prepared her for what was happening. Although she wanted to hitch up her dress and run, she took small, quick steps to minimize the likelihood of crashing into anything else.

She was glad of it when she found herself at what she thought was another dead end. About to give in to despair, she stared into the smoke and thought she might see a smaller path to the left, running between two houses. She was trying to remember whose homes they were, and work out where she might be, when a gang of soldiers erupted from the one furthest away. Creusa shrank back against the front wall of the building opposite the men, but they did not see her. They laughed as they ran down the alleyway which Creusa planned to use. She did not need to hear their words to know that the men had killed whoever they had found inside. Creusa waited for the men to disappear before she dared follow. Having tried so hard to remember whose house she was passing, she was grateful that she had failed. She did not want to know whose throat the men had just slit.

She dragged her fingers along the wall beside her, making her way more slowly now, to be sure that the men would not see her behind them. When the passageway finally opened out into the street again, she saw that she had done it. She had found her way to the city walls.

*

'Take the horse,' Sinon said. 'In so doing, you will take its power from them. They built it here and dedicated it to Athene, protector of the Greeks. They believed it to be so large that you Trojans would have no chance of dragging it away into your city. They saw the distance across the plains, the height of your acropolis, and they laughed at the notion that you could take it for yourselves.'

'How do you know?' asked Hecabe. Her Greek was rudimentary, but clear.

'Forgive me, queen, I do not understand,' replied the prisoner.

'How do you know what they thought about the horse?' she repeated. 'If you were hiding in the reeds, fearing for your life. You say they built the horse after you had run away. So how do you know what was said?'

Creusa thought she saw a flicker of annoyance cross the man's face. But when he spoke again, his voice was still quavering with sorrow.

'It had been their original plan, my lady. Before Calchas

and Odysseus cooked up their plot against me. The Greeks wanted to build a giant horse and invest it with all the sacred power they could. Then they wanted to leave it outside your city to taunt you: a sign of the goddess guiding them home safely. It is the kind of arrogant gesture that Agamemnon cannot resist.' Hecabe frowned but said no more.

'So please, king,' he added. 'Rob them of their safe voyage home. Take their horse to your citadel before night-fall. It could be dragged by your men. I will set my own shoulder to the ropes if you will only permit me. Anything to punish those impious Greeks who would have taken my life without hesitation. If you let me help you drag the horse into your city and up to its highest point, I will fall on the sword of any of your men the moment the task is completed. I swear it.'

'No.' Laocoon the priest could keep himself in check no longer. 'I beg you, king. The horse is cursed and so shall we be, if we allow it in our city. The man speaks with a false tongue. Either he deceives or he is deceived. But the horse must not come inside our city walls. Let us burn it, as I proposed.' He lifted his meaty arm and flung the spear he held into the horse's flank. It vibrated for a moment, humming in the shocked silence which followed his words.

Creusa could not be sure what happened next. She didn't see the snakes for herself, though many others claimed to have done so. She wasn't looking at the reeds. She was looking at the man, Sinon, and his filthy, unreadable face. The only sign that he could understand Laocoon's words was the shiver of his biceps against the ropes which still held him. She thought Laocoon's children had simply run out into the water. Why wouldn't they? They had long since tired of hearing the men argue and – like all the other children of Troy – they had never been down to the shore before, never played in the sand. So of course they had wandered off, following the river a little way until they reached the waves on the beach. The two of them had waded out into the shallows before anyone noticed they were gone.

The seaweed grew in huge fronds, Creusa knew. As a child, her nurse had warned her never to enter the water in search of the dark green tentacles. While the seaweed's fingertips were thin enough for a child to tear, the body of the plant was thick and fibrous. It would have been all too easy to stumble and lose her footing. And that was surely what had happened to Laocoon's children. One of them must have caught his foot in a loop of seaweed and fallen. Unused to the current, he panicked and, writhing, entangled himself further. The other, ploughing over to help his brother who had slid right under the water, found himself in the same predicament. His thin cries for help were carried away by the shore breeze.

But by the time Laocoon had run – too late – to save them, the seaweed had taken on a malevolent form. Giant sea-snakes sent by the gods, someone said, to punish the priest for defiling their offering with his spear. As soon as the words had been spoken, they had believers.

As the priest wept on the sand, cradling the bodies of his drowned children, Priam's choice could hardly have been different. The gods had punished the priest, so the Trojans must heed the warning and follow the words of the prisoner, Sinon. They laid logs beneath the horse and dragged it across the plains, the men taking turns to heave on the ropes. They rolled it through the city, though it barely fitted into the indentations of cart-tracks which cut through the streets. They drew it up onto the citadel and cheered when it reached the highest point and the men rubbed their aching arms and rolled up their ropes. Priam declared a sacrifice must be made to the gods, and a feast would follow. The Trojans cheered again as the fires were lit and the meat cooked. They poured wine first for the gods and then for themselves. Troy had won the war at last.

*

And Creusa turned and looked back at her burning city. She had made it to the walls but now she could see that the fire had reached them before her. She could not follow the walls around to the city gates as she had planned: the paths were ablaze. If she could have climbed the wall where she now stood, she could perhaps still have escaped. But it was too high, too sheer, and she had nothing to cling on to. The men she had followed were no longer a threat to her: choked on the thick smoke, they had lost their lives in the pursuit of carnage. She could see their bodies on the ground ahead of her, already being claimed by the fire.

She understood her predicament far more quickly than the birds which were singing overhead – on roofs which had not yet burned – though the sky was black, the moon obliterated by thick grey smoke. The fires across the city were so bright, they thought it was morning, and Creusa knew she would remember this oddity – the fire and the birds and the night made day – for as long as she lived.

And she did, though it mattered little, because she was dead long before dawn.

3

The Trojan Women

The women were waiting on the shore, gazing blank-eyed at the sea. The tang of dried green seaweed and bent brown reed stalks fought against the stench of smoke which filled their clothes and matted hair. After two days, the Greeks were finally completing their systematic looting of the blackened city, and as the women waited to find out who they now belonged to, they huddled around their queen as though her last embers might keep them warm.

Hecabe, a small, leathery figure with half-hidden eyes, sat on a low rock worn smooth by water and salt. She tried not to think of her husband, Priam, cut down by the vicious Greek as he clung to an altar, his dark blood trickling down his chest as his head drooped back from his murderer's blade. Something else she had learned as the city fell: the old did not die like the young. Even their blood was slower.

Her mouth hardened. The thug who slaughtered him – an old man pleading for the protection of a god – would pay for his cruelty, his disrespect, his impiety. It was the only thing she could cling to, now everything else was lost: a man could not expect to disregard the sanctity of a god's temple and continue to live and thrive. There were rules. Even in war, there were rules. Men might ignore them, but the gods would not. And to slaughter a man as he bent his stiffening knees to seek sanctuary? Such behaviour was unforgiveable and the gods – as the queen of the smoking remains of Troy knew all too well – were rarely prone to forgive.

She bit the inside of her cheek, welcoming the metallic taste. She began the list again in her mind, the sons who had died in combat, the sons who had died in ambushes, the sons who had died two nights ago, in the sacking of the city. With the death of each one, another part of her dried up, like animal skins left too long in the sun. Eventually, she had thought, when Hector died, when the butcher Achilles took her bravest warrior-son, there was nothing of her left to shrivel up. But one of the gods – she dared not say Hera's name – must have heard even that hubristic thought, and decided to punish her further. And all because of a woman. All because of that conniving Spartan whore. She spat the blood out, onto the sand. Her desire for revenge was total, and futile.

She caught sight of a bird, turning on the wind, and flying back towards the shore. Was it a sign? The flight of birds was known to carry messages from the gods, but only skilled priests could read the language of wings. Still, she was sure this message was a simple one, reminding her that there was one boy – one, of all her beautiful sons, so tall, so strong – one still left alive.

And only because the Greeks did not know where he was, or even that he was. Her last, youngest son, bundled out of the city under the cover of night, and hidden away with an old friend in Thrace. A friend whom they had paid handsomely. Even allies needed encouragement to support a losing side, Priam had said. And Troy had been the losing side for so long: only strong walls and obstinacy had kept her firm against the Greeks for ten long years.

She and Priam had wrapped the boy's belongings around four twisted gold circlets, and tied the pack closed before he left. 'Give two to your host when you arrive,' they said. 'Hide the other two and never let on to anyone that you have them.' 'Then what good are they to me?' he asked, a ready, trusting boy. 'You will know if you need them,' she had answered, resting her fingers on his shoulder so she could look him in the eyes, tall as he was. 'Men will do more for a stranger if he has a nub of gold to offer.' She showed him how the soft metal branches would give beneath his hands, allowing him to snap off a smaller bribe if need be.

They said nothing to the slave who accompanied their son: the lure of gold would be too strong, and her boy would have a knife between two ribs before he was a day's ride from home. Secrecy was vital, and she prayed to the gods that her son would realize that his life was at stake if he could not keep quiet. Her husband had warned him, and so had she. He was not her last surviving son when he kissed her the final time and set out through a little-known passage on the north side of the city. But she had known, even as she wept and bid him farewell, that he would be.

She felt a brief shudder run through her, and tightened her stole around her shoulders. The Greeks were taking their time in the city. Picking over every corner in case they had missed something bright; as grasping as jack-daws. Gold and bronze had been pilfered from every hiding place, piled up on the sand to be divided up among the men. Carefully, since the inequitable distribution of booty had caused them no end of trouble in the past year. There would be some trickery, of course. Men had already been caught stuffing small pieces of precious metal into their clothing. One Greek, she had heard, had been found by his comrades with a gold ring wedged between his cheek and his teeth, and had been slashed across the face for his deception. He would hide nothing in his cheek now. Not even his teeth.

The women were waiting, powerless and broken. What happened after the end of the world? Polyxena sat at her mother's feet, absently rubbing her hand up and down her mother's calf like a small child. Andromache sat slightly apart from her mother-in-law. She was not born a Trojan, but had married Hector and become one of them. Her baby nestled beneath her chin, grizzling a little – the noise and panic had disturbed his sleep. And Cassandra faced the ocean, her mouth moving soundlessly. She had long since learned to keep quiet, even if she could not halt the stream of words flowing from her lips.

None of the women wept. The dead husbands, fathers, brothers and sons were fresh wounds to them all. They had mourned through the nights and torn their hair and garments. But the Greek men who guarded them had little time for lamentation. Polyxena nursed a blackened bruise on her eye socket, and now the women were silent. Each promised herself and the others that they would grieve in solitude when they could. But all knew that they would never know solitude again. When a war was ended, the men lost their lives. But the women lost everything else. And victory had made the Greeks no kinder.

Polyxena issued a low, guttural cry, which merged with the chatter of the cormorants and went unheard by their captors. No matter how hard she tried to suppress her grief, she could not help herself. 'Could this have been avoided?' she asked her mother. 'Did Troy have to fall? Was there no point when we could have been saved?'

Cassandra's shoulders quivered with the effort of not screaming. She shook with the force of her desire to shout that she had told them a hundred, a thousand, ten thousand times. And that none of them had listened, not once, not for a heartbeat. They didn't hear, they couldn't see, and yet she could see nothing but the future, all the time, forever. Well, not forever. She could see her own future as clearly as she saw everything else. Its brevity was her one consolation.

Hecabe looked down at her daughter and ran her fingers over Polyxena's hair. She did not notice the thin film of soot it left behind on her palm. She could not look at her hands touching her daughter, knowing as she did that the hands of a Greek would be defiling her before the night came. The only question was which man would have each of her daughters, her daughters-in-law. Who, not if or when.

'I don't know,' she said. 'The gods know, you must ask them.' And as she looked out at the sea, over the heads of her battered retinue, she realized that one of the Trojan women was missing. 'Where is Theano?' she asked.

4

Theano

Theano, wife of Antenor, mother of four sons and one daughter, bent over to light the candle and blinked in its small, smoky flame. Mother of four sons who would not bury her, when her time came. Four sons who had not survived the war. Sons obliterated by the folly of another woman's son. Her tears came from the smoke, and also from the anger which burned at her core, like the wick of the candle she carried to the table and placed in its centre. Her husband sat opposite her, his head in his gnarled hands. She had no pity for him: the war was raging through its tenth year outside the city walls and he was too old to fight. She would have given his remaining life – lived uncomplaining as a widow – to spend a single moment with one of her dead sons.

'You have given Priam every chance to heed your warnings,' she said, as Antenor shook his head. His thick grey eyebrows pushed their way out from behind his fingers, and she reached around the candle and pulled his hands down to the table. 'Every chance,' she repeated. His filmy eyes met hers, and she wondered if she looked as old and feeble to him as he looked to her: snowy hair, creased skin, etched grief.

'He refuses to listen,' her husband said. 'He cannot see past her.'

His wife spat on the ground. There was only ever one 'her' in Troy, and that had been true for ten long years. Ten years that had taken her four most precious jewels.

'You have served him well,' she said. 'Years have passed since you first advised him to return the whore to her husband.'

'Years,' Antenor echoed. They had conducted this conversation so many times in the past that it had come to seem to him like a song, in which he no longer had to remember his words, any more than a man had to remember his way home. It was simply a part of him.

'Priam has been too prideful,' his wife continued. 'The goddess has told me, more than once.'

Her husband nodded. Theano had been a priestess of Athene when he first saw her, with her parents in the temple precincts. How many years ago was that? He couldn't recall. She had been a lithe girl, he remembered, bright-eyed with a sharp intelligence which had, over the years, attenuated to impatience.

'I made the offering of the robe,' she reminded him. The women of Troy had embroidered an ornate ceremonial robe for the statue of the goddess, and his wife had dedicated it to her the previous summer. It had done nothing to win Athene's support away from the Greeks and in favour of the Trojans. They might as well, Theano had whispered as the body of their youngest son was carried back from the battlefield, have offered her a pile of rags, for all the good it had done. Her husband had begged her not to blaspheme, but with only one child – their daughter

Crino – left, his wife was in no mood to be told. The goddess was quite clear, Theano said: return Helen to Menelaus. Purge the pollutant from our city. Send ten gold kraters – Priam's largest and most highly decorated – and ten finely worked red and gold tapestries along with her. Send Paris to abase himself before the man whose wife he had stolen, and beg his forgiveness. If it was unforthcoming, his wife had added, Priam's over-indulged son would have to pay for his folly with his life. It was not an unreasonable price for taking a man's wife from her home, overturning generations of tradition, which rightly said that a guest must respect his host.

'Priam will not force his son to lose face,' Antenor said.

'Lose face!' she snapped. 'Reputations can only be lost if they have not already been trampled in the mud. Only a deluded man could think Paris has any reputation beyond that of a philanderer and the woman who shares his bed will always be known as a whore.'

'The king cannot see it.'

'He will have no choice.' Theano paused. 'But you do have a choice.' The conversation had never turned this way before. She watched her husband's eyes flicker to hers, barely able to see her expression. 'You have heard the message, Antenor. You know they will act tonight.'

'They may not,' he said, his voice quavering. 'The message only said that they are lying in wait somewhere nearby.'

'You know where,' she snorted. 'They are inside the horse. They must be.'

'But how many men would fit inside a few planks of wood, Theano, even if your suspicions are correct? Five?

Ten? It is not enough to overthrow a city like Troy. It is nothing like enough. We are proud citizens who have withstood a ten-year war. We cannot be overthrown like children from a wooden fort.'

'Quietly,' she chided him. 'Crino is asleep.'

He shrugged his shoulders, but spoke more softly. 'You know I'm right.'

'We only know half of the story,' she replied. 'The Greeks have made a big show of sailing away. What if they have not? What if they are waiting for a few warriors to be smuggled into the city inside their votive horse? What if those men open the city gates to a whole army?'

His face contorted in pain. 'Troy would be destroyed,' he said. 'They would loot it and burn it.'

'And kill the men and enslave the women.' She continued his thought. 'All the women. Your wife, Antenor. Your daughter.'

'We must warn them,' he said, looking around himself, agitated. 'I must hurry to Priam now, and warn him before it is too late.'

'It is already too late,' she said. 'The horse is inside the city now. There is only one thing you can do to save us.'

'What is that? What have you planned?' he asked.

'Go down to the city gates now,' she said. 'Open them yourself.'

'You're mad,' he said.

'The guards will have left their posts long ago. They believe the Greeks have sailed away. They think there is but one Greek left on Trojan soil, and that is the snake, Sinon.'

Her husband rubbed his right hand against his left

arm, as though it pained him. 'He will unlock the gates if you do not,' she said. 'And they will reward him for his bravery, instead of you.'

'You want me to betray our city? Our home?' he asked.

'I want our daughter to live,' she said. 'Go now, before it is too late. And quickly, husband. It is our only chance.'

The old man returned carrying an animal skin and a stark message. He must nail the panther's hide to the door of their home, and the Greeks would pass it by.

5

Calliope

Sing, Muse, the poet says, and this time he sounds quite put out. It's all I can do not to laugh as he shakes his head in disappointment. How does his poem keep going wrong? First he had Creusa, and she filled him with confidence. All the epic themes covered: war, love, sea-snakes. He was so happy taking her through the city, searching for Aeneas. Did you see how much he enjoyed the descriptions of the fire? I thought he might choke on his epithets. But then she lost her way when he was barely past the proem.

I took him straight to the shore so he could see what happened to the women who did escape the fires and he didn't even notice that the survivors were hardly any better off than poor Creusa. I'm not sure I could have made it more obvious, but he hasn't understood at all. I'm not offering him the story of one woman during the Trojan War, I'm offering him the story of all the women in the war. Well, most of them (I haven't decided about Helen yet. She gets on my nerves).

I'm giving him the chance to see the war from both ends: how it was caused, and how its consequences played out. Epic in scale and subject matter. And here he is, whining about Theano because her part in the story is completed and he's only just worked out how to describe her. Idiot poet. It's not her story, or Creusa's story. It's their story. At least it will be, if he stops complaining and starts composing.

6

The Trojan Women

The black cormorants wheeled above them, diving one by one to the surface of the dark sea, their feathered throats throbbing with fish when they rose again. Hecabe shifted her weight from one leg to the other. Her whole body ached from sitting on the rocks, pain spreading out from the base of her spine to her every bone. She was hungry, but she said nothing to her women. They must all be hungry too. Foolish, to think that hunger and thirst would disappear, just because their lives lay in ruins. Even slaves needed to eat.

Hecabe looked around at the women and children who surrounded her, trying to count them all. She hoped there were a few missing families, a handful of Trojans who might have slipped away in the smoking chaos. She counted her daughters and daughters-in-law before moving on to the other women. She realized that soft-tempered Creusa wasn't there. Her husband Aeneas had survived ten years of conflict; had he died when the city was set ablaze? Or had he escaped with Creusa and their son? Hecabe issued a quick prayer to Aphrodite that it was so. Perhaps, even as she watched the birds feasting on the water, Aeneas and his wife were sailing out across the horizon to find a new home, far from the ravaging Greek soldiers.

'Who else is missing?' she asked Polyxena, who lay on the sand nearby, her back to her mother. Her daughter did not reply. Perhaps she was asleep. Hecabe counted again. Creusa, Theano and Theano's daughter, Crino. All gone.

A young woman with hollow eyes and pale skin, sitting near Polyxena, holding a small comb in her hand – wood, not ivory, so perhaps she would be allowed to keep it – answered for her. Hecabe couldn't find the young woman's name in her mind. The upheaval was too great. She was the daughter of . . . No. That too had gone.

'Theano's family was spared,' she said.

'Spared?' Hecabe looked at the girl in astonishment. The Greeks had not appeared to her to be in the mood for sparing anyone. 'Why?'

But even as she said it, she knew. She knew that Antenor had betrayed them. His cautious counsel to appeal to the Greeks and ask for terms on which the Trojans could return Helen had not been advice for the benefit of his city, but for the benefit of himself.

The young woman shrugged. 'I don't know. I just saw the soldiers pass their house by. There was a leopard skin nailed to the door. The Greeks saw it and they took their swords and their torches to the next house. It was a sign.' She stopped. The next house had been the one before her own.

Hecabe snorted. The double-faced traitors, friends to their enemies, enemies to their friends. But even as she opened her mouth to express her contempt for such treachery, she paused. Antenor's behaviour was despicable, certainly, but there was no denying that he had won a better fate for his women than Priam had for his own family. Theano and Crino: free women; Hecabe and her daughters: enslaved.

She saw that Andromache, her son Hector's wife (Hector's widow, she corrected herself again), was listening to her conversation. Andromache did not speak, however. She had not spoken since the day before, when the Greek soldiers brought her out of the city, pushing her between themselves, grabbing at her breasts and laughing, before shoving her into the circle of Trojan women. Andromache had held her baby tightly in her arms as she fell forward onto her knees. She did not notice when her ankle, scraped along the sharp edge of a rock, began to bleed. Hecabe had glared at the men, and one of them made a sign to ward off the evil eye. Hecabe snorted. It would take more than a gesture to combat the bottomless sea of sorrows she was wishing upon them all.

Hecabe wondered if Andromache was doing the same thing as she was, stacking up the names in her mind. Creusa was dead or had escaped somehow. But Theano, Crino: their names would be added to the curses Hecabe ran through every morning when she woke and every night before she slept. She was not so foolish as to believe that she herself would have the chance to punish all the traitors and murderers and wrongdoers who had contributed to the downfall of her city. But she would have the gods remember who they were. They would take vengeance on the oath-breakers. It was all she could wish for.

She would have been startled to discover that her daughter-in-law was doing precisely the opposite thing in her mind.

Creusa, Theano, Crino: three Trojan women at least who were free, either in death or in life. Andromache marked each one with a silent joy. Everywhere she looked she could see only women in her own condition: fallen into slavery, the property of soldiers and thugs. But there were three who belonged to no one.

Polyxena awoke with a sudden cry. No one chided her, though the Greek soldiers who had been charged with keeping the women together looked over in annoyance. They all had nightmares now. Hecabe watched her daughter's breathing slow again, as she saw where she was. Still living in a nightmare, but a lesser one than the one in her sleep. Polyxena moaned quietly as she sat up at her mother's knee. 'I keep dreaming that the city still stands.'

Hecabe nodded. She had already learned that the worst dreams were not the ones where the flaming walls were crashing down on you, or where armed men were chasing you, or where your beloved menfolk were dying before your eyes. They were the ones when your husband lived again, when your son still smiled, when your daughter looked forward to her wedding.

'When did you know they would take Troy?' asked Polyxena.

Her mother thought for a moment. 'We knew this day would come when the Amazon fell,' she said. 'Your father and I guessed before then. But the day the Amazon died; that's when we knew for sure.'

7

Penthesilea

They were so alike, the Amazon girls, that when Hippolyta died, Penthesilea felt she had been deprived of more than a sister. She had lost her own reflection. For as long as she could remember, she had known what she looked like by looking at someone else: every shift in her own skin, every line, every scar almost, was matched on the body of the one she loved the most. And so as Hippolyta fell – her face creased with pain, the arrow piercing her ribs – Penthesilea knew that she was losing her sister and herself at once.

They had always used weapons. Long before she could walk, Hippolyta had taught Penthesilea to sling stones across their mother's halls. The older they grew, the sharper the blades became: wooden swords and soft-wood spears were soon exchanged for the real things. And she had revelled in it. They both had. There was something so immeasurably delightful about being young and strong. The girls would ride for hours on near-identical horses: gentle trotting and then cantering and then galloping through the lower reaches of the mountains, their hair plaited tightly to hold it in place, pinned beneath their bright leather caps. They would dismount in the outskirts of the forest, and leave the horses, running until they collapsed on the ground, too breathless to groan at the pain in their lungs. They would lie amid the pine cones and look up at the sky between the upper branches of the trees, and know there was no one alive who was happier than them.

And the games they used to play. Running up the slopes, picking up white pebbles, or an abandoned birds' nest, running back to the bottom of the hill to add it to a pile of woodland treasures, each one eyeing the other's growing hoard with envy, marvelling at her swiftness and strength. And the speed test, which Hippolyta always won. The two girls would stand beside one another on open ground, and count themselves down: ready, steady, go. Penthesilea would fit an arrow to her bow, and shoot it high in an elegant parabola. At the same time, Hippolyta would begin to run, laughing at her own ability to cover so much ground so quickly that by the time the arrow began to descend, she was waiting, ready to catch it in her hand. She never failed, until the last time.

And so Penthesilea had lost her sister, dearer to her than life itself. Not only that but she had killed her. An accident, the others said, trying to comfort her. As though there could ever be any consolation for this. And because she had lost the thing she held most dear, and because she had not merely lost it but had herself destroyed it, and because there was no possibility that she could go on living without Hippolyta, Penthesilea resolved to die.

Death itself would not be enough, however. For the terrible crime she had committed she could face only one death: that of a warrior, in battle. Which battle it was did not matter particularly. The only requirement was that there must be a warrior skilled enough to kill her. Most men (Penthesilea was not arrogant, merely aware of her talents) did not have the capacity to beat an Amazon in combat. There was one man, however, that even the Amazons spoke of in whispers. Quicker even than them, one had heard. The fastest warrior ever to fight. And so Penthesilea took her women on the long journey south to the fabled city of Troy.

The journey was not arduous for the Amazons, who were a nomadic people. Their horses were strong and they rode from dawn to dusk without ever growing tired. They slept only briefly during the hours of darkness and began their journey again as the sun rose the next day. If her women wished to stop their princess – to beg her to reconsider her plan to die – they respected her too much to do so. They rode alongside her, and they would fight alongside her. If she was resolved to die, they would die alongside her too.

Their arrival was not a complete surprise to King Priam, whose scouts had heard a rumour that the women were coming south. Two Trojans rode out to meet Penthesilea, and ask her intentions. Whose side did she intend to take, in this, the tenth year of war on the Scamandrian plains? Greek or Trojan? Were the women aggressors or defenders? Priam had sent two large gold tripods and jewel-encrusted bowls to try and win an alliance with the Amazons. Penthesilea accepted them without a second glance. She cared nothing for trinkets – what use were baubles for a woman who lived on horseback? – but she did not wish to give offence by refusing them.

'I'll fight for your king,' she said. 'Ride home and tell him the Amazons will fight the Greeks, and that I will fight Achilles, and I will kill him, or die in the attempt.' She did not add that these two outcomes were equally desirable to her. The scouts bowed and sought to flatter her with desperate thanks. But she bustled them away. She did not need to know that Priam was grateful for her support. Of course he was. The story of what had happened to his son, to brave Hector, the Trojans' greatest warrior, had penetrated even the northern reaches of her Scythian home: how Hector had defended his city for ten long years, and how he had led his men in many famous victories. Penthesilea knew, everyone knew, how he had once fought a man dressed in Achilles' armour and killed him; how for a brief moment the Trojans believed that Achilles himself was dead, and how they pushed the Greeks all the way back to their camp, the greatest day of fighting in the whole war. But then Hector stripped the armour from the fallen Greek to discover – incensed – that it was not Achilles, but rather another man, Patroclus, wearing Achilles' arms and fighting in his stead. The rage of Achilles when he heard of the death of his friend was instant and implacable; she knew how he had roared like a mountain lion and sworn his revenge on Hector and any Trojan who crossed his path. He was as good as his word, and stalked through the battlefield, mauling every man he saw, until Hector stood before him. Penthesilea knew how he slaughtered Hector – thick, black arterial blood spattering on the mud beneath their feet – and screamed his savage joy. How he mutilated the corpse of his enemy, and tied leather thongs through his feet, turning man into carcass with no thought for the impiety of his actions. How he drove the body of the Trojan prince around the walls of his own city, dragging the battered corpse three times past the eyes of his broken parents, his pitiful wife, his uncomprehending infant son.

Of course Priam was grateful for a friend in the Amazons. The man had nothing else left.

Penthesilea and her women made camp by the River Simois, slightly to the north of Troy: their tents were sparse and plain, animal skins tied round wooden stakes. They contained nothing beyond the hides on which the women slept, and the armour they would wear in battle. Even their food supplies were meagre: Amazons disdained the luxury of their Trojan friends. Plain food, as little as they could thrive on, and that was all. Anything else would only slow them down. She did not send an embassy to the Greeks: she had no desire to make a formal announcement of her presence. They would know she was there soon enough when she led her women into battle the next morning, beside the Trojans.

Although the ground was rock-strewn and hard, Penthesilea slept an unbroken night, for the first time since her sister had died. It would be her last night of sleep, she knew, so perhaps Hypnos had decided to make it a pleasant one. When she awoke before dawn, stretching out her long limbs in preparation for her armour, she yearned for the battle to begin. She ate with her women, a warm, nutty porridge cooked over the embers of last night's fire. They spoke little, and only of tactics.

Then she returned to her tent and put on her warrior

garb. First, the dark yellow chiton, a short tunic, tied at the waist with a thick brown leather belt, which also held her sword sheath. Then she added her prized leopard-skin cloak, which gave her warmth and ferocity in equal measure. These men, these Greeks would see they could not scare her, a woman who could outrun a leopard and cut him down mid-stride. The creature's paws hung below the tunic, its claws stroking the front of her thighs as she moved. She bound the straps of her leather sandals around her finely muscled calves and reached for her helmet. Hippolyta's helmet, with its high plume of blackest horse-hair and its inlaid snakes, curling around her cheeks. When the Amazon queen rode into battle, she would ride as her sister, as the greatest warrior of them all. She picked up her round shield, hard red leather bound to five layers of calf-skin. She placed her sword in the sheath, and picked up her long spear, testing its weight and its sharp point. She was ready.

Her horse, a tall grey mare with a vicious bite, stood patiently as she plaited its mane into a neat row. No warrior would grab her horse from under her by the hair, and if he tried, she would likely take off his fingers. When everything was prepared to her liking, Penthesilea turned and looked at her women, these imperfect reflections of herself. Her Amazons were bright jewels of the mountainous north, glittering in these lowlands. They would defend a city none had ever set eyes upon until yesterday, and they would protect women and children they had never met. She felt a surge of something in her breast, and it took her a moment to identify the feeling of pride beneath the ever-present grief. Hippolyta was beyond help, but Troy could be saved, and her women would be its saviours.

She took the reins in her shield-hand, so her throwing arm remained unencumbered. She had dropped her bow when Hippolyta died and, even after the funeral pyre, when she remembered it was lost, she had not returned to the ground where it fell, knowing she would never fire another arrow. But her women were all fine archers, and they strapped their quivers to their backs, and balanced their bows across their shoulders. What match could any Greek be for them?

The Amazons mounted their horses and began to ride the last few stades towards the field of battle. As they left the lower ground on the southern banks of the Simois, they heard distant trumpets sounding the opening of the gates of Troy. Penthesilea's women were soon across the flank of the Trojan warriors, and then in front of them, where they belonged. The Trojans were, Penthesilea noticed, a ragtag gang of fighters now. Where were the heroes she had heard about in the bard's song? Hector was dead, of course, but where was Paris, or Glaucus, or Aeneas? She frowned as she scanned the men, and saw none of towering height or obvious strength. Their biceps were no match for her own. The heroes must be among them, but they were not such men as she had expected to find.

When the Greek warriors approached from their camp in the west, she felt her breath quicken. These men were scarcely any greater in number than the Trojans. Was this all that remained of the fabled thousand ships which had carried their men to the sandy shores of the Troad? How many had died, she wondered, and how many had simply given up and sailed home again? Still, among the Greeks she could see a few men of significant stature, their armour and ornate shields declaring their nobility. Surely somewhere was the man who would bring her the death she craved.

And then she saw the light glinting off the red and black plumes of his helmet. He carried no shield because – she had heard – these days, he feared no one but the gods. No Trojan had bested him in battle for years, and the only man who had offered the slightest resistance was poor Hector: dead and defiled, belatedly buried. And once he had killed Hector, he no longer cared whether he lived or died, just like her. This man, surely, was the one Penthesilea sought. Achilles, king of the Myrmidons, their black shields fanning out behind him. This was the man who carried her death in his hands.

The combat between these two great warriors was – for all its importance to the people of Troy – shatteringly brief. No one, not even her women, could say whether Penthesilea had ridden into battle to die rather than to kill. But the result was the same either way. Achilles was the fastest creature alive, faster than the lynx that roamed the mountains, faster than Hermes who carried messages from Zeus to men. And faster than Penthesilea.

She and her Amazons made straight for the Myrmidons, who scurried aside, like ants. But after ten years of war, they were battle-hardened: they knew the terrain as though it were their home. The Amazons, who were used to fighting on the hard mountains of the north, were less sure-footed. But their horses soon understood that broad, soft mud was as treacherous as narrow, stone-strewn paths. The archers took aim and picked off the ant-men on the right-hand flank. Achilles whirled around to see who was targeting his men – after he had spent so long being feared and shunned on the battlefield, who could be so audacious as to bring their attack to him?

These new riders were fresh but they were not so large in number. His men – he scanned quickly, automatically, and shook his head as he noted that ten had been felled already – were pulling back, fear running from one to the next, like the plague which had picked off so many Greeks last summer. Achilles would not see his men routed. The one riding behind the archers, sword drawn. Was that their king? He believed so: the others rode around him, as though they were protecting him for single combat. Well, Achilles would give him what he asked for. In less time than it took to blink, he hurled his short spear. His aim was unerring. The shaft humming in its neck, the king's horse fell, its forelegs buckling. But the king was not afraid: he leapt nimbly from his collapsing steed and landed squarely on his toes. Over the heads of their men, the two leaders' eyes met, and both knew it was a fight to the death. Achilles barked orders and his men stopped their retreat and readied themselves against the next barrage of arrows.

As he had done so many times before, Achilles moved through the battlefield, impervious. He was not so much stronger or braver than other men. A little, but any man can be lucky on his day, and cut down a better soldier.

Yet no one ever laid a hand on Achilles, because they could never get close enough to try. Every man on the plains knew what the Amazons did not, which was that Achilles' true strength lay in his astonishing, impossible speed.

And so one moment he was hundreds of feet from Penthesilea, and the next he was beside her with his sword buried in her neck. He gave it a small shake, like a hunting-dog with its prey, and watched with only the mildest interest as wine-coloured blood spurted from her throat and sprayed across his tunic. He had worn so many men's blood over the years, what difference did one more make? He wrenched his sword free and watched the king stagger to his knees. Penthesilea's head slumped back and her helmet fell to the ground. And only then did the greatest warrior alive realize that he had killed a woman.

He felt a sudden wrench of shame. Not because he had never killed a woman before. He had only a hazy recollection of most of the people he had killed: one death was so much like another, after all. But the Myrmidons had devastated so many towns in surrounding Phrygia throughout this war, he must have killed dozens of women as he went. Not all of them had offered themselves up as slaves or concubines; some must have refused to abandon their husbands, or chosen to try to protect their children, whom he would also have killed moments later. He could picture none of them. Even the face of Hector, the one man he had killed in rage rather than because slaughter was what he was for, even that was sliding away from him now as the months wore on. But the face contorted in pain in front of him was like nothing he had ever seen, and he knew that he had finally committed the one act he would regret. This woman was his mirror image, just as Patroclus had once been. He gasped as the blood bubbled up between her lips. He, who had never shown hesitation or fear. He watched her eyes cloud, like cataracts forming. He saw her open her mouth and say a single phrase, and then he saw the light darken. He looked up at the sky, filled with horror, and heard a coarse voice laugh behind him. He turned and stabbed the man without thinking: he would never know who it was he had killed. He saw other Greeks back away from him, afraid he would turn on them too. He gave it no further consideration, thinking only of the woman and her blood-filled mouth.

He wondered if anyone else had ever died saying the words, 'Thank you.'

8

Penelope

My dearest husband,

Can it really be ten long years since you sailed from Ithaca to join Agamemnon and the other Greek kings in their ignoble quest to bring Helen back from Troy? Was it a thousand ships which sailed, in the end? That's what the bards sing now. A thousand ships, all sailing across the perilous oceans in hope of finding one man's wife. It remains, I'm sure you agree, an astonishing state of affairs.

I don't blame you, Odysseus, of course I don't. I know you did your best to avoid leaving me, still a young bride, our son just a few months old. Playing dead might have worked a little better, perhaps, but playing mad was a good idea too.

I still remember that snotty Argolid's face when you ploughed the fields with salt. He thought you quite insane. In my recollection, you were pulling the most hideous faces, and the man looked at me with such pity. A baby with a madman; no woman should endure such a fate. How close you came to dodging their draft. So close to staying with me, leaving the other Greeks to indulge in their oath-bound folly.

But of course it would be Agamemnon who forced your hand. I will never forget him ordering his man to snatch Telemachus from my arms and place him on the damp ground in front of you. Testing your madness by endangering your son: would you plough on regardless, and slice right through him, right through the chubby limbs of your own child? Or would you see the infant, know him, and stop? You will forgive me for saying that I'm not sure I have ever wished anyone dead with quite such enthusiasm as I did Agamemnon that day. And bear in mind that I grew up in Sparta, so have spent more time than most with Helen.

Sometimes, when the mood takes me and the wind blows through our draughty halls from the north, I offer a little prayer for the death of Agamemnon. I used to wish he would die in battle, but now I hope for a more ignominious end for the man: a falling rock, perhaps, or a rabid dog.

You couldn't keep feigning the madness in the circumstances, I understand that. To protect your son, our child, you had to stop, and in so doing reveal the truth. And though I wept to see you sail away the following morning, I felt sure you would be home again before the end of the year. How many moons can it take to track down an unfaithful wife, after all?

First the days dragged by, then the months. Then the seasons and finally the years. Ten years, now, and still Menelaus can neither persuade his wife to come back home, nor accept that he is a red-faced bore and find himself a new wife, one less exacting than Helen.

It seems impossible that you have been gone so long.

You have never seen your son walk, or heard him speak, or watched him swing from the low branches of the old pine tree that grows beside the east wall of our palace. He looks like me more than you, you know. He has my build: tall and slender. And though I love him from the very depths of my heart, I have nonetheless found myself thinking of the other children we might have had, if you had killed him that day. We would have lost our first child, but we might have had four more.

It is unworthy of me even to think such thoughts, I know. But the seasons have turned so many times, husband, and I am no longer a girl. I have begged the gods to bring you home before I turn barren with age. And perhaps now my prayers have been heard, because there are rumours flying across Greece, even to our craggy outpost, which say that the war is finally over. Is it true? I can hardly bear to ask. But the watchmen have lit their beacons and the news races from one hilltop to the next: the Greeks have won at last. I know you will have had a hand in the victory, Odysseus. I tell Telemachus that his father is the cleverest man to walk the earth. Cleverer than Eumaeus? he asks. He does not mean to be insulting, by the way. He is fond of Eumaeus. I say yes, you are cleverer than the swineherd. Cleverer than you, Mama? he says. No, precious, I tell him. Not quite as clever as me. And then I tickle him, so he doesn't ask how I know.

But if he were to ask, and I were to answer that question, I would say this. I would not have let them see I was not mad, and I would not have hurt my child, my beautiful boy. I would have swung the plough into my own feet, and cut them into ribbons before I hurt our son

59

or let the Argives take me away from here. The pain would have been terrible but fleeting. They would certainly have thought you mad if you had slashed at your own flesh. And even if they had their doubts, they could hardly have taken you on board their ships with your feet spewing blood. A man who cannot stand cannot fight.

Still, it is easy to be wise after the event, isn't it? I said I didn't blame you for what has happened, and I don't. You did the best you could with a phalanx of men watching your every move. And it was nearly enough. But you have been gone too long, Odysseus, and it is time for you to come home.

Your loving wife,
Penelope

9

The Trojan Women

Hecabe was squinting at the sun as the tide came in. Her women thronged around her still: she remained their queen until they were separated and taken away. The guards had allowed them to walk across to the river and scoop water into whatever battered receptacles they had. Who knew, when she fled her house in the night and the smoke, that stopping to pick up a dented old cup would mean the difference between thirst and comfort? When she saw Hecabe had nothing to drink from, one of the younger women gave her own cup to the queen, sharing silently with her sister. Hecabe took it without thanks.

Hecabe demanded the guards bring food for the women and they laughed at her. But after a while, a bag of meal was brought over, with a battered cauldron and a few sticks to make a fire. Andromache, having tied the baby to her chest, built the fire. The flames soon caught beneath her quick hands. Polyxena was allowed to fetch more water, as the guards knew she would not try to escape. How could she, with her aged mother sitting on the shore? The women made a thin broth, flavoured with nothing more than the salt tang of the thick damp ropes of seaweed which coiled along the shore. They ate it without complaint. The guards said there would be grain later, so the women could cook bread on the embers of their fire. Hecabe wanted to ask the men how much longer they would keep her women stranded on the shore with no shelter but the rocks next to which they sat, and their torn garments, but she knew there was no answer she would want to hear.

This was the last time she would ever see her women. When the Greeks had finished looting the city, they would return to their camp, a short distance along the shore. They would debate among themselves, or perhaps one of the elders would decide, and the women would be allotted to the leaders of the different Greek tribes, in order of status. And then each woman would be separated from her family, her friends, her neighbours, and given to a stranger whose language she didn't speak. Hecabe knew a little Greek, though she would prefer it not to be known. Perhaps one or two of the others did. But when a city was sacked, everything within it was destroyed, right down to its words.

Hecabe's mind played tricks on her: if you could choose to stay with one of these women, who would you pick? As if she would be granted any such wish. She looked at her women and admitted to herself that she knew the answer, even so. Andromache was not her blood, so she would not pick her, even though she was fond of the girl, who had been such a good wife to her favourite son, and borne him a son in turn. And Cassandra was a torment, like a gadfly biting at her mother, every day since the madness came upon her. She had been such a lovely child, Hecabe remembered. Soot-black hair and deep-set eyes like rock pools. She had run about the broad stone halls with her brothers and sisters, always the centre of attention. And then one day it happened. She appeared in the mouth of the temple of Apollo, her clothing torn and hair caught up in knots. Cassandra could not speak for days, only stammered and juddered as though the words were desperate to escape her lips but could not find their way past her teeth. And then when she did talk again, to the nurse who had cared for her since she was a baby, the words were gibberish. She spoke of one terrible thing after another, one disaster to befall them and then one more and one more. No one could bear to hear her speak, predicting death and destruction everywhere she looked. Hecabe had her shut up in her chamber, hoping she would quieten down over time: no one needed to hear her screaming about flames engulfing the city, and so many men dying outside the walls and inside their homes. But soon the slaves would not wait on her, not even under threat of being flogged. Cassandra would tell them of their own impending deaths, and those of their parents or children. And even though it was nonsense – no one believed a word the deranged girl said – it disquieted them. One day, Cassandra was screaming and crying about . . . Hecabe paused. She couldn't remember. Her daughter had been hysterical, as usual. The details scarcely mattered – and Hecabe had reached across and slapped her hard, across the face. Cassandra had grabbed her hand and held it, shrieking. And Hecabe had slapped her with her left hand until there were bright red fingermarks on both of her daughter's cheeks, with deeper indentations on the right side, from Hecabe's thick gold rings.

From that day onwards, Cassandra had at least muttered her curses and madness more quietly. Her family and slaves still made signs against the evil eye when they saw her, but she was easier to ignore. Even now, as the women waited to find out where they would go and to whom they would belong, Cassandra barely spoke above a murmur. She did not dare.

So Hecabe knew that if she could have kept one of her women with her, over the months and years to come, it would be Polyxena. Her most beautiful daughter. The youngest, with golden hair quite unlike any other Trojan woman. People used to say that a goddess must have favoured her with such beauty and yet Polyxena was never conceited. She was a kind and thoughtful girl, everyone's favourite. Hecabe shuddered, thinking which Greek would take her. The butcher Neoptolemus, who had cut down Priam, Polyxena's father, as he clung to the altars and pleaded for sanctuary? The devious Odysseus? The idiot Menelaus?

She said nothing, but Polyxena suddenly grew restless, as if she could sense her mother's thoughts. She stretched her arms above her head and sat up on her heels. 'I don't think it was the Amazon,' she said. Her mother bit back her irritable retort. She already had one daughter whose every utterance was meaningless, she had no need for another.

'You don't think what was the Amazon?' asked Andromache quietly. She had found her tongue again at last. But the baby still slept and she hoped to keep him that way. When he awoke, he would be ravenous, and she had only a little milk-softened grain to give to him.

'Troy didn't fall because of the death of Penthesilea,' Polyxena said. 'It fell because the gods willed it so. We were almost saved before, remember? But the gods must have changed their minds. Even an Amazon could have made no difference then.'

'Before?'

'When they took the priest's daughter, Mama. And the girl from Lyrnessus.'

10

Briseis and Chryseis

No one ever needed to ask which priest's daughter, although Troy had plenty of priests and they had plenty of daughters. If someone was talking about the daughter of a priest, they always meant Chryseis, daughter of Chryses. Who else would have been sufficiently cunning to escape a besieged city, and sufficiently careless to be captured by the Greeks?

They stabbed the shepherd boy she had been sneaking outside to meet, who tended his flocks on the lower slopes of the mountains. He had been mortally afraid that the Greeks would catch sight of him on a moonlit night, and kill him, taking his flock to sate their hunger. But he never shared his anxiety with her, because he was shy and he did not wish to appear afraid in front of a girl who seemed entirely without fear. And so, when the night finally came that a pair of Greek scouts – hunting around the edges of the city like weasels looking for birds' eggs – found them, she was entirely unprepared for what would happen.

They killed him exactly as he feared they would. But she didn't see his blood flow out from his chest, because it was too dark, and she had dropped her torch when the men attacked and knocked it from her grip. The ground was damp, and its flame was extinguished straightaway. She felt the men's greasy hands on her flesh and on her clothes as they dragged her back to the camp. She was frightened, but she did not cry out, because she was still more worried that the Trojans would find her than that the Greeks would kill her, even though she realized this was ridiculous. She thought of the sweet soft mouth of the shepherd boy, and felt a sudden twisting hurt in her side that she would never kiss it again.

As the men pulled her towards the shoreline, away from the city, she caught sight of the sacred flames burning in the temple of Apollo, on the citadel of Troy. Her father would be serving the god at this hour. The pain she had felt at the loss of her shepherd boy redoubled when she acknowledged to herself that she had abandoned her father.

Chryses was a broad-backed, black-haired servant of Apollo, whose wife had died giving birth to their daughter. Her lifeblood had ebbed out with the baby and had never stopped. Wan and grey, with matted locks of hair stuck to her pale cheeks, she died before her daughter was a day old. Her heartbroken widower had no appetite for fatherhood, and gave the child, still unnamed, to a wet-nurse with no instruction as to whether she should be fed or left to die on the slopes of Mount Ida. By the time his grief had subsided and he could bear to have the girl in his presence, his daughter had been named by others: Chryseis, daughter of Chryses.

Chryseis took after her mother. Dark brown hair flowed over her shoulders and her eyes were almost black. Her skin was golden, and she took small, neat steps, like a dancer. But where her mother had been a patient, obedient woman, always where she should be, shuttle in one hand and wool in the other, Chryseis was as headstrong as a donkey. People said the troublesome spirit had entered her when she was a baby, because they could think of no other explanation for why, if there was any trouble inside the city, Chryseis always seemed to be involved.

And now she had found herself in trouble outside the city. The youngest Trojans had grown up under a siege: they knew no other life. For Chryseis, only sixteen years old in this tenth year of the war, the city was her home and her prison alike. But unlike the daughters of Priam – Polyxena and the others – she refused to be contained. The city was riddled with secret pathways which could take an adventurous girl out into the plains below, if she was only daring enough to find them. It never occurred to her that the other sons and daughters of Troy might not have been looking to escape the city, or that the pathways went unused from fear rather than ignorance.

There was one such path, which tunnelled beneath the city walls, behind the temple of Apollo where her father spent his days. It was this one Chryseis had used to escape and meet her shepherd. She felt a fresh pang of sorrow for the soft-mouthed boy, and then a sharp jab of anger at her father who had left his bored, resourceful daughter alone for hours outside the temple while he tended to the god's needs. He knew she would get up to mischief; she often did. She had been beaten once, by a senior priest, for playing with the goat kids which were kept outside the precincts for sacrifices. They were not pets, he had shouted as his large square hands slapped her face and arms, they were sacred animals. How dare she pollute them with her childish touch? Her father stood by and watched the man hit his daughter. It took time for her to unpick his expression, but eventually she concluded he had been embarrassed that she had brought shame on him. And yet he had left her to amuse herself, knowing she would get into trouble. Another emotion assailed her: perhaps he had not cared what happened to her. Perhaps she had tried his patience too often, embarrassed him too profoundly.

She had been wondering if she might try running from the Greek scouts, neither of whom looked as if he had the speed she knew she could produce. But the thought of her father's disappointed face when he saw her and the memory of his mortification when she had been caught for other, lesser infractions kept her from making her escape. It distracted her and she did not notice her pace was slowing, until one of the Greek soldiers prodded her waist, grabbing at her flesh and laughing when she screamed.

Fear of upsetting her father had been a much greater influence on her behaviour than anything else, she realized. Since she had discovered the tunnel, she had explored the edges of the plains and the lower reaches of the mountains many times, hiding behind the trees and the rocks so that she wouldn't be seen by the Trojan watchmen or anyone else who might tell Chryses. It had never occurred to her that she might be caught by Greek soldiers and slaughtered where she stood, her blood staining the grassy nubs in the sand beneath her feet. It had also never occurred to her that being captured by the Greeks might be worse than being killed by them.

When she arrived at the camp, she heard a great deal of shouting and jostling, but she understood very little of what the men said. Was it a different language they spoke, or simply a thick dialect? She could not tell. All were armed and armoured: the clanking of metal on metal was so loud it made her teeth ache. Eventually, she was man-handled towards a tent and pushed inside. She blinked in the guttering torchlight, and pulled her cloak around her body. The tent was full of women, other prisoners, huddled together with arms round one another, as though protecting each other from the cold. Chryseis scanned their faces, in the hope of seeing someone she knew. But all her friends and relatives were safe behind the city walls, where she should have been. These women were strangers, and none of them spoke to her.

Her gaze was drawn to the bright blue eyes of a tall, slender woman who stood with the others but was somehow apart from them. The woman's hair was extra-ordinary, like gold in firelight, and her skin was pale. She resembled the chryselephantine statue of Artemis that dwelt in the temple near the shrine of Apollo where her father served. But the statue was the work of craftsmen, gilding the stone, painting the robes, coating the face with thin layers of ivory and the eyes with lapis. Chryseis had always thought she would never see anything so beautiful in her life until now, when she saw that the statue was a pale copy of this woman, or someone who looked very much like her. The priest's daughter found herself thinking that so long as she stayed near this gold and ivory woman, everything would be alright, so she walked towards her and tried not to reach out and touch the woman's hair.

'Where did they find you?' asked one of the other women. The light flickered behind her, and she was nothing but a silhouette. It took Chryseis a moment to realize that she understood what this woman was saying. Her accent was thick, but they spoke the same tongue.

'On the edge of the plains,' she replied. 'At the bottom of the mountain.'

The tall woman's expression did not change. The woman in shadow turned her head to Chryseis and stared at her. Chryseis could only see the torchlight glinting off the woman's pupils but she could feel her annoyance. 'You're no shepherd-girl,' the woman said. 'Anyone can see that from looking at you. You've come from inside the city, haven't you? How did you get caught outside?'

Chryseis had no answer. 'Where did they find you?' she asked instead.

'Lyrnessus,' said the woman. 'We were all taken from Lyrnessus and Thebe.'

Chryseis paused. 'Are they nearby?'

The woman snorted. 'You've never been outside Troy before tonight, have you?' Chryseis did not explain her previous excursions around the city. None of these women would be impressed by her adventurous spirit, the way her peers in Troy were.

'Yes,' the woman continued. 'Lyrnessus is a day's hard ride from here. The Greeks have been out raiding. All this time trying to crack open the nut of your home with no success. They need other places to feed them. They've ravaged every town between here and Lyrnessus already.'

Her voice softened. 'No wonder you haven't heard of the places they're taking now. They cast their net wider with each passing year. They're never happy unless they're taking what doesn't belong to them, and burning everything they can't carry with them.'

'Is that what they did to your town? Looted and burned it? Couldn't your men fight for you?' Chryseis asked. Who were these poor women whose menfolk had abandoned them? The Trojan warriors, her father among them, were far braver than these women's husbands and sons.

'What men?' said the woman. 'They killed all our men.'

'All of them?' Chryseis said. She had been told many times by her father that the Greeks were no better at fighting than any other men. No braver, no stronger, no more beloved by the gods. Had he lied to her?

'You don't see much inside your city walls, do you?' said the woman. 'That is what the Greeks do. They kill the men, they enslave the women and children. They have done it across the peninsula. And it's what they will do to Troy, when the Fates compel it.' Chryseis shook her head. The day would not come. Her father sacrificed to Apollo and made offerings every morning, and he was one of many priests in temples to all the gods across the whole city. The gods would not abandon Troy, so full of willing servants. Of course they would not. 'Your walls cannot keep them out forever,' the woman added. 'You may be the first Trojan woman they've captured, but I promise you will not be the last. And when they come for your sisters and your mother' – Chryseis did not trouble to correct her – 'your menfolk will be no more help than ours were. A soldier can't fight if he's dead on the ground, and the Greeks outnumbered us by so many that we never had a chance. They are not an army, these Greeks. They're a pestilence.'

'I'm sorry for what you have lost,' said Chryseis, using the formulation she had heard her father say so many times.

The woman nodded curtly. 'Our losses will be shared,' she said. 'You should save your sorrow for yourself.'

Chryseis looked away and found herself staring at the tall woman with the blue eyes. 'I'm sorry for what you have all lost,' she said.

At last the golden-haired statue looked down and seemed to see her for the first time. 'Thank you,' she said. Her voice was low and soft, her accent less guttural than the other woman's.

'May I sit beside you?' Chryseis asked her.

The woman in shadow replied on the statue's behalf. 'You can sit where you like, Trojan. The men will divide us up in the morning. It will make no difference then.'

'Just for tonight, then,' Chryseis said. She had convinced herself that if she could have this one wish granted, her lot would improve. 'I have no one else,' she added.

The statue patted the ground beside her, and they sat down together. 'I have no one else either,' the woman said quietly.

'No one?' asked Chryseis. An inappropriate feeling of warmth began to creep over her. If this woman was alone too then Chryseis, paradoxically, felt less alone. The woman shook her head. She looked less like a statue up close, now Chryseis could see the tiny golden hairs on her skin.

'He killed them all,' she replied. 'My husband, my father,

my three brothers. They were fighting to defend our home, and he cut them down as if they were stalks of wheat.' Her voice was strangely melodic, so even as she told her terrible story, Chryseis half-imagined it was a poem, a song about another woman, another lost family. She could not bear to think of this woman experiencing anything so terrible.

'It was so quick. One moment they were there, armed and ready to attack. And then they were on the ground, all of them at once. I thought they were playing a trick at first. There's a pause, you know, before the blood starts to flow out beneath them.'

Was this what had happened with the shepherd boy? Had his blood paused like that? Chryseis could not bring herself to interrupt the woman, when she had lost so much and Chryseis so comparatively little: just one boy, just tonight, the memory of whose fingers wrapped round her wrist still made it feel warm. She felt her eyes prick but she would not allow herself to be overcome, because she did not want to distract this woman from her own tale.

'For a heartbeat before that happens, they could still be alive. But then it pools beneath them, so much, more of it than you can imagine. He'd killed them all, just like people said he would. And I thought I had lost everyone when I saw a grey-haired woman, mad with grief like a Maenad, hurl herself at the legs of his horse. She didn't have a weapon. I don't know what she was trying to do. Unseat him, kill him, kill herself? His horse didn't even break its stride. He just leaned a little to his right, it looked like he barely moved his sword arm, and then she was on the ground too, cut right through at the neck. I didn't understand at first that it was my mother he had killed. My mother lying there on the hard dry earth next to the men she had lost. So when I tell you I have nothing, you know I speak the truth. They took me before I could throw a handful of earth on any of them, so I don't even have that.' Chryseis gazed at the woman, whose eyes were not puffy, whose hair was not torn and whose tunic was not ripped. The woman saw her looking and nodded. 'They will not see my grief,' she said. 'They have not earned it. I will grieve for my family when I am alone.'

'What if you never are?' Chryseis asked.

'Then I will weep for them in the darkest hours of the night,' the woman replied, 'when no one can see. What is your name, child?'

'Chryseis,' said the priest's daughter. 'What's yours?'

'Briseis,' said the blue-eyed woman.

*

Chryseis huddled up against Briseis' back, as the sky began to lighten. She had not slept. She had never been in such close proximity to so many women; her mother's untimely death meant she had grown up in an often-empty house. She had always longed for a sister, almost as much as she had wished for her mother. She had spent the night thinking of Briseis' family, their bodies lying unburied while their souls must be wandering the banks of the River Lethe, with nothing for the ferryman, no way to cross and enter the Underworld, until someone took pity on them and threw a few grains of dust over them. How long would they wait?

But Briseis was as good as her word. She did not weep or wail. She merely spread her cloak on the ground beneath her. She patted it: there was room for Chryseis here too. The girl curled up beside her and felt the warmth radiate from the woman's body. Her golden hair smelled of grassy herbs and something Chryseis could not name. An animal smell, comforting.

The talkative woman from the night before – Chryseis never did find out her name – had been given meal and water by the Greeks. She made a warm, flavourless broth for the women, which Chryseis ate, nonetheless. By the time the flaps of the tent were flung open and two men ordered them all outside, it was a relief, because the waiting was over.

The women were placed in a line by the guards, in an order which was meaningful to them but not to the women. Every now and then they would stand for a moment, arguing about whether someone should be to the left or the right of her neighbour. The older women were furthest away from Chryseis, and she wondered if they were ordering them by years. But that did not look quite right: Briseis remained right next to her, though there were two other girls who were visibly closer to her age. After more pulling and shoving, she found herself at the end of the line. She understood some of what the men said, but the guttural speed made it difficult to follow.

She focused instead on the camp, which extended on both sides and in front of her all the way to the sea, and the tall ships which had sailed to Troy all those years earlier. The tents were clustered together, dirty and weather-beaten, with hungry-looking cattle in small pens here and there.

She turned to look behind her and saw the fortifications on the north edge of the camp, sharpened wooden stakes pointing at the city, at her city, like arrows. One of the men grabbed her arm and jerked her back to face the same way as the others. She did not cry out, and felt sure that Briseis was impressed with her self-control. If a woman who had lost so much could remain calm, Chryseis could too.

They stood in the line, waiting, as the sun broke through the early-morning cloud and caught them in its pitiless glare. Chryseis looked along the row of women and saw fear behind their eyes. Some were not even troubling to hide it: they wept openly, clawing at their skin and tugging out their hair. Chryseis almost wished she could do the same: wail for her absent father and for the loss of her poor shepherd boy. But she would not let these men, these enemies of Troy, see her afraid. She was her father's daughter and no Greek would see her cry.

Finally, a herald raised his horn to his lips and sounded a call. The men did not appear all at once, but gradually, from every direction, they began to gather in front of Chryseis. The soldiers came in gangs with others who shared the same clothing, the same weaponry, the same home. Chryseis tried to remember the list of Greeks that her father had prayed to Apollo to curse: Boeotians, Myrmidons, Argives, Aetolians. They looked battle-weary, she thought, like the men of Troy. So many flaming scars across faces and arms. So many more limping from injuries she could not see.

She stared over the taunting faces of the Greek soldiers as they massed in front of the women. She looked up at their ships. Would she be bundled onto one of them and carried away to Greece? The idea seemed both absurd and inevitable. She knew she could not afford to think about the possibility of being taken from Troy and never seeing her home or anyone she knew again. She focused on the ship, and what it would be like to sail across the ocean. She had never been on water, had no memory of even touching the sea. Had her father brought her down to the shore when she was an infant? The idea of her father in his priestly robes standing over a child as she played in the shallows was preposterous. As he had told her many times, Chryseis had been born to disappoint him, and she had never let him down.

She heard a murmur rush across the crowd of men. The last of them were arriving now, the leaders of each tribe, she supposed. These men seemed taller than their soldiers; thick-necked and thick-armed. Perhaps they just carried themselves more confidently, she thought. And their clothes were fresher, not covered in so many patches and repairs. It must be one of these men who had killed Briseis' family: the story she had told described a great warrior, a man of prodigious speed and cruelty. It could not have been an ordinary soldier. She scanned the crowd to see if she could guess which one. But as she looked, she remembered that every one of these leaders had killed a man she knew over the past nine years: a cousin, an uncle, the father of a friend. It came into her mind in a rush, that there was no sense wishing to be given to one man or another, when they were all equally bad. She would wish for Briseis instead, she thought. Wish that she would avoid the man who had taken everyone from her.

But if the gods were nearby, they were not minded to listen to Chryseis. The herald spoke more slowly than the other Greeks, shouting to make himself heard by those at the back of the crowd. The booty would now be awarded to the commanders who had excelled in the recent raids, he explained. The men cheered.

'First to the king of Mycenae,' cried the herald. 'To Agamemnon.'

His words were lost in a sea of shouts, not all of which, Chryseis thought, were approving. A heavy-set man, his greying hair in a sharp widow's peak, was standing directly in front of Chryseis. This was the most powerful of all the Greeks, she knew. The king of kings, and brother of Menelaus, whose wife was now ensconced in the citadel of Troy with her lover, Paris. Agamemnon was the one who had assembled the Greeks for their campaign against Troy. He quieted the roar from his Argive soldiers with a small wave of his hand, and stepped forward.

'To Agamemnon,' repeated the herald, 'the Greeks award the first choice of the slaves.'

Agamemnon barely looked at the line of women in front of him.

'I'll take that one,' he said, jerking his head at Chryseis. A man's hand grabbed Chryseis from behind and thrust her at the Argive king. Men laughed as she stumbled but she managed to stay upright. She felt a jolt of pain in her foot, and she was grateful, because it distracted her briefly from looking at the fat old man who had just made her his own.

'Come,' said Agamemnon. 'No, wait.' He turned to the herald. 'Allot all the women and then we shall take them to our quarters. I want to see what the others pick first.' His men roared again. Chryseis stepped back into her place.

'Second,' cried the herald, 'to the greatest warrior among us, Achilles.'

The noise was deafening. This was the man whom these soldiers loved the most. Chryseis watched Agamemnon's expression as he too realized that the shouts for him had been cursory. His old man's face – Agamemnon was older than Chryseis' father, and she tried not to feel sick – was consumed with jealousy. Chryseis allowed her eyes to flicker to where the noise was loudest. That must be Achilles, scourge of the Trojans, stepping out of a line of black-clad warriors. Golden-haired and golden-skinned, like a god. The Trojans said he was the son of a goddess, a sea nymph, and now she could see why. He was beautiful, even with his mouth set in a cruel line. He did not bother to silence his cheering soldiers. He simply opened his mouth, knowing they would fall quiet of their own accord.

'I'll have the one next to her,' he said. He turned to the man who stood beside him, slightly shorter, slightly less muscular, a darker reflection of himself. The man nodded. 'The yellow-haired one,' Achilles confirmed. His men cheered again, and Briseis made the smallest sound. No one but Chryseis – her ears level with the woman's lips – could have heard her. But she knew at once that the gods had shunned her prayers for her new friend. It was this man, Achilles, who had killed Briseis' family as she watched. And now she belonged to him, and there was nothing either of them could do. Still, Chryseis would not cry. And nor would Briseis, although the two women were taut, like bowstrings. They would not snap.

The distribution of the rest of the women, and of a towering pile of gold and silver objects which had also been looted from their homes, took a long time. But Chryseis heard little of what was said. She pushed her fingers against the back of Briseis' hand, and the two of them stood together in the blistering sun, metamorphosing from people into property. When it was all over, the guards shouted at her, taking pleasure in making her jump.

'If you have anything in the tent, now's the time to fetch it,' one of them said. She was about to say she had nothing to collect when Briseis took her hand and nodded to the guards. The two of them walked back to the tent where they had spent the night.

'I don't have anything,' Chryseis said.

'You do. Here.' Briseis dug into the cloak on which the two women had slept and produced a small leather bag. 'Take these. You must put them in his wine when he asks you to pour it out for him.' Chryseis looked at the bag dumbly. 'Are you listening?' Briseis said, reaching out and shaking her friend's arm. 'Put a pinch of them in his wine. He drinks it sweetened with so much honey, he won't taste them. It's important.'

'What will happen?' Chryseis whispered. 'Will it poison him?'

Briseis shook her head. 'It will leave him . . .' She paused. 'Leave him uninterested in you. Or unable. He may become angry when it happens. He might hit you. But he will still be incapable, do you understand?' Chryseis nodded. Briseis knew her darkest fears before she knew them herself. A strand of hair fell in front of her face and Briseis reached out, unthinking, and tucked it behind her ear.

'If he becomes very angry, you should ask him if he has a daughter,' Briseis continued. 'He becomes melancholy when he thinks about his daughter. It will make him less likely to hurt you.'

'Thank you,' Chryseis said. 'But what will you do? Don't you need these for yourself?'

Briseis shrugged. 'I will manage,' she said. 'You don't need to worry about me.'

'Will I see you again?' Chryseis asked.

'Of course. The camp is not as large as all that. The men will be away fighting many times, we will find each other then. In the mornings. By the water. Will you remember?'

Chryseis nodded again. She would never forget anything Briseis said to her.

*

Briseis walked five paces behind the man who had killed her family. She watched his smooth calves – impossibly unmarked after all these years of fighting – bulge as his feet touched the ground. He was tall, broad across the shoulders, narrow across the hips. His biceps were thick like the haunches of a bull. But he stepped so lightly that the leather of his boots did not even creak as he moved. The man who walked beside him was not quite so tall, or so broad, or so muscular. His hair was darker, a mousy brown, and his skin was covered in the small tattoos of war: the crimson lines of long-healed wounds. He had to extend his stride a little beyond its natural length to keep in step with Achilles. Briseis watched his hips twitch as he tried to maintain the pace. It was this man who looked back, every few steps, to check that she was behind them. He could not have thought she would run away: the Myrmidons – Achilles' men – surrounded her. Yet still he turned to look at her, and then back to Achilles.

'Pompous old fool,' Achilles was saying. 'His desperation disgusts me, I can smell it on him.'

'Of course he's desperate,' the smaller man said. His tone was soothing, as though he were calming an anxious horse. 'He knows what they all know: that you are the greatest of the Greeks. It sickens him, the envy. It bites at him from within.'

Achilles nodded. 'How many more lives must I take?' he asked, and suddenly he was plaintive, like a child. 'Before they give me my due?'

'The men give you your due,' his friend replied. But he spoke slowly, his tone that of consolation rather than contradiction. 'It is not surprising that Agamemnon will not acknowledge your superiority. What would that leave him with?'

'His own shallow pride,' Achilles snapped. 'Which is everything he deserves. He is not the son of a goddess, he has nothing in his ancestry but cursed blood and good luck. Instead of which he walks around, puffed up with his misplaced sense of self-worth, taking first pick of the treasure won by my sword and mine alone.' His friend said nothing, but Briseis still felt the tension spring up between them. 'Not alone,' Achilles corrected himself.

'The majority of booty was won by your sword,' his friend murmured.

'By my Myrmidons, under my command,' Achilles agreed.

Briseis had watched him scythe through her city, his sword swinging down from the back of his horse, culling anyone who could not move out of his way. Her elderly father, her strong husband, her young brothers, her demented mother, cut down one after another, with no pause to consider their worthiness as his opponents, their fitness to fight. He slaughtered the Lyrnessans as easily as drawing breath. His men had been needed for one thing and one thing only: gathering up the treasure, the women, the children that this one-man killing spree had won for them. Achilles was trying to console this man about his lesser martial prowess, Briseis realized, at the same time as his friend was trying to calm him down. How curious, she thought. Two warriors determined to be so kind to one another.

'He picked the wrong girl,' the smaller man smiled.

Achilles looked across at him. 'Of course he did,' he said. 'He picked the one on the end. Once the guards had placed her there, he was always going to. As soon as other men had judged her the most beautiful, he followed them. He is a follower of men, in all things. Even women.'

'I can't imagine how they ordered the women like that,' the second man replied. 'A blind man can see she is the most beautiful woman we have ever captured. Helen herself could not be more perfect.'

Achilles smiled, his face transforming into a sweetness

which Briseis knew to be false. 'You can't imagine?' he asked.

The man stopped dead, but Achilles did not, and his friend had to run a few steps to catch him up again.

'You bribed them!' he said.

Achilles laughed. 'Of course I bribed them. You said she was the one you wanted, and I wanted you to have her. I would rather have picked her first, as was my right. But I knew you would prefer me not to argue with Agamemnon about that again. So I rigged his choice in your favour. I knew he wouldn't realize, because the other one was younger. But you liked this one better.' The man said nothing. 'You're not angry, are you?' Achilles said, and again Briseis heard the child behind the man.

'Of course not,' said his friend, patting the warrior's arm. 'I'm surprised. I didn't think you had such a mind for subterfuge.'

'It was Nestor's idea,' Achilles replied. 'The wily old man will do anything to keep the peace, you know. Even if it means cheating his king of the first pick.'

'Agamemnon chose first,' the second man said. 'He'll never be able to say he didn't.'

'Imagine his face when he looks at that girl by torch-light tonight, and sees she is scarcely more than a child,' Achilles said. 'You should send your girl to collect water as close to his quarters as possible every day, so he can see what he missed out on.'

'I will,' the man said. 'I'll take her there myself, so I can see his expression and report it back to you in every detail.'

'That alone would make the bribe cheap,' Achilles said. And, saying nothing, her eyes on the ground in front of her, Briseis kept walking behind them.

*

Chryseis was sitting on a low stool outside the tent of the Argive commander, gulping in the clean, salt-washed air. Agamemnon's tent reeked, like a filthy stable. The man seemed unable to discern the thick staleness which caught in her throat. And none of his advisers seemed willing to say anything. They laughed at him behind his back, Chryseis had seen. The short, stocky one with the cunning eyes – Odysseus – and the young one like a stout tree – Diomedes – pulled faces at one another when Agamemnon's back was turned. They found his personal quarters as disgusting as she did.

But at least Chryseis had the herbs which Briseis had given her. She had followed the older woman's instructions and dropped a few small leaves in Agamemnon's wine as soon as the sun began to dip over the sea. Every night, the commander had lurched at her, grabbed whatever of her he could reach, but he had fallen into a deathlike unconsciousness before he could do more than pull in-effectually at her clothing. Chryseis wondered if she was giving him too high a dose. She was not especially worried about poisoning him, though she sensed that she would be in trouble if Agamemnon was found dead with small flecks of foam around his lips. But she looked into the small leather bag every day, trying to calculate when the herbs would run out. Could Briseis supply her with more, or direct her to the plants she needed to find? Or, as seemed more likely, had she brought the mixture with her from Lyrnessus? Chryseis felt a twisting in her stomach at the thought that the bag she was holding contained all there would ever be.

Sitting behind the tents, it took her a moment to notice the flurry of activity at the front of the Argive camp, the sound of men and hooves hastening across damp ground. She heard shouts and muffled whispers and more shouts, and eventually Agamemnon's voice, demanding to know who was asking for an audience with him.

Chryseis preferred to stay out of sight of the soldiers, keeping herself to the places where other captured women and camp-followers congregated: near the cooking pots and the stream where they washed their clothes. But curiosity overwhelmed her, and she crept round the edge of the tent, holding herself close beside it, in the hope that she wouldn't be noticed.

Of all the humiliations which had rained down upon her in the last few days – the proprietary hands, the lascivious looks, the mocking laughter – this one was (she thought afterwards) the worst. Because as she looked around the corner of the tent, to see what all the fuss was about, she saw her father, standing in front of the Argive king, his staff in his hand and his ceremonial headdress covering his hair. He was probably a year or two younger than Agamemnon, she thought: he and her mother had tried for many years to have a child, but they had always been unlucky. Chryseis had been their last chance, her mother's final stroke of luck. But he looked old, and small among these Greeks. A sullen crowd of Argive soldiers had gathered behind him.

Chryseis was almost paralysed with fear and shame. She felt her enslavement more keenly now than she had during the days when she washed and skivvied for the Greek king, and the nights when she drugged him and slept on the furthest side of his tent, on the hard ground. That her father – who had barely seemed to tolerate her – should have come to ransom her. It contradicted everything she had believed of him: he would not come begging to a Greek for anyone, least of all Chryseis. And now he was so close that she could call out to him and apologize for all the mistakes she had made which had led them both to this moment, the father she had believed she would never see again. Her eyes itched with an unfamiliar sensation, and she realized that tears were on the verge of spilling down her face. And at the same time, she felt an acute shame that her father looked so small. In her mind, he was a match for any, for all of the Greeks. But as he stood among them, she could see he was only a man. Only a priest.

But he was a priest who knew his worth to the god he served. Humility had never been in Chryses' character, and although he was a suppliant for his daughter's freedom, he would not beg. As Agamemnon stood before him, he bowed his head, but only briefly. He did not drop to the ground. Instead, he spoke as though they were transacting business.

'King Agamemnon, I ask you to return my daughter,' said Chryses. His tone was reasonable, mild even. But Agamemnon – as Chryseis knew but her father did not – would not respond well to quietness. He was a man to whom shouting came more readily than talking, and he distrusted anyone who behaved differently.

'I don't have your daughter, priest. Who told you I do?'

'Apollo told me.'

A murmur ran through the crowd. Some of the men were openly derisive of her father, a crazy old priest with an inflated view of his own importance and his safety. But some of them stood still, trying to hear more.

'Then you misread Apollo's message, old man,' said Agamemnon. 'Sacrifice another goat or two and see if it improves your accuracy.' Again, men laughed. Everyone knew that Troy had few animals left for sacrifices. A besieged city was limited in her offerings, which only added to the Greek belief that the gods favoured them over the Trojans.

Chryseis felt the shame on her father's behalf. Her cheeks flushed red, she could feel the heat creep up her face. Why could he not be more – she searched in her mind for the word but could not find it. Why could he not be less like himself? That was what she wanted to ask. He had demanded that she change her behaviour countless times (though she had rarely obeyed). But he – she saw it with the newfound clarity of an outsider – was the same. The same as her. She held her fingers up to her cheek. Perhaps not all of the heat came from shame.

'You cannot deceive the Archer and you will not deceive me,' replied her father, anger shading into his calm voice. Chryseis had heard this tone many times before. 'You have Chryseis, and I demand her return.'

At the mention of her name, the Argive soldiers looked less comfortable in their derision. Agamemnon did have a Trojan girl, didn't he, from that last division of spoils? And hadn't someone called her by that name?

'You dare to demand anything of me?' Agamemnon laughed. But there was no mirth in his voice, and though she could see only the back of his head, Chryseis knew there would be no merriment in his eyes. 'You are an unwelcome guest in this camp,' Agamemnon continued. 'It is thanks to my good will to your god that you do not already lie dead on the ground. Do not try my patience further.'

'Apollo will punish any man who injures his servants,' Chryses said. Chryseis found herself almost pitying Agamemnon, having been faced with her father's immovable nature many times before. She knew that, desperate as she was to leave the Greek camp and return to her home, the punishment from her father would be so terrible that she could not imagine what it would be. He had beaten her for disobeying him in the past when the scale of her misdemeanours had been relatively minor. What would he do if Agamemnon suddenly softened and allowed Chryseis to leave with him? Chryseis wanted nothing more than to return to Troy. But she could not deceive herself about the consequences her father would demand for this humiliation of his priestly self before an invading army.

'Apollo will not punish any man who has you marched out of this camp for your impudence and folly,' Agamemnon said. 'No man can offend the patience of his enemies in this way, and expect nothing to happen in return.'

'Very well,' said Chryses, standing a little taller. He looked almost relieved, Chryseis thought. Her father preferred conflict to compromise, preferred a battle to a discussion. 'That is your answer? You will not return my daughter, as Apollo demands?'

'I will not return your daughter. I think you blaspheme,

old man: you are not as pious as you would have us all believe. They are not Apollo's demands you throw around my camp, they are your own.'

'If you prefer to believe that, of course I cannot convince you otherwise.' Her father was almost whispering now. This quiet part of his anger had been the most frightening for Chryseis as a child. 'I cannot. But Apollo will.'

Agamemnon barked orders at two of his men. 'Take him to the other side of the fortifications. I will not kill a priest, even when he deserves it. Do you hear that?' he shouted at Chryses. 'You will leave my camp unharmed, even though your arrogance is intolerable.'

Chryses stood for a moment, until the two soldiers came up behind him and seized him by the arms. As they manhandled him away, his eyes suddenly flicked to Chryseis, almost hidden behind the fabric of the tent. She felt the colour suffuse her cheeks once again, as surely as if he had slapped her. 'I will take you home,' he said to her, and in that moment it sounded (even in her humiliation) not like the threat of a chastising parent to his wayward child, but like the promise of a father to a daughter. When she thought of it at night, as the Greek king slept like the dead across his filthy tent, she could not have explained how Chryses had known she was there, or how she could hear him, when no one else seemed to notice that he had spoken.

*

Briseis sat on the low couch, and combed her hair. Achilles' friend, Patroclus, was staring at her, as he had every night since she arrived in the Myrmidons' camp.

'I've never seen hair that colour,' he said quietly. 'It looks like honey being poured from a jar.'

Briseis had heard these compliments – and many more like them – since she was a child. Men and women alike had stopped in their tracks to touch her hair and remark upon its extraordinary colour. She had her beauty to thank for her husband, her enslavement and her life, she knew. If her husband had not sought her hand, if the Greek men had not noticed her, she might have remained a free woman. Or she might have been slaughtered where she stood.

'Did you always look so sad?' he continued. She repressed the urge to scream.

'Do you have a sister?' she asked instead. He shook his head. 'A mother, then?' she suggested.

'She died when I was young,' he said. 'I don't remember her.'

'Who do you love most?' she asked.

He thought for a moment. 'Achilles.' He shrugged. 'We have been close since we were children.'

'Can you imagine for a moment how you would feel if he were taken away from you?' Briseis asked.

'I'd like to see someone try,' Patroclus smiled. 'It would be a swift death at his hands.'

'What if someone took you from him?' she asked. 'Your sword hand is not quite as fast as his, perhaps?' She thought the man would colour when she reminded him of his inferiority, but he did not. His devotion to Achilles precluded envy.

'Then I would feel as you feel,' he said. 'Deprived of my greatest happiness.'

'I watched your beloved friend slaughter my greatest

happiness,' she said. 'I watched them bleed into the sand. How can you ask me if I was always sad?'

'I didn't ask if you were always sad,' he corrected her. 'I asked if you always looked sad. You have a face which is enhanced by suffering. You have a hollowness here.' He reached out and touched her cheekbones and then her collar-bones, one after the other. 'I wondered if you had always looked like that, or if it is a consequence of your enslavement.'

'Freedom matters less to me than grief,' she said. 'I would gladly have given up my freedom to keep my husband and my brothers safe.'

'But you lost everything instead,' he said. 'The gods favour Achilles. Your city should have acknowledged its place in his story, and surrendered. Now, all that is left of Lyrnessus will be half a line in the bard's song about this war.'

Briseis glared at him but saw he was not trying to goad her. The Greeks were all the same: they saw no worth in any but their own. 'The lives of my family cannot be measured by their deaths. And your friend should hope the bards treat him so kindly. Many men would see no glory in the murder of an old man and his wife. Perhaps they will sing of his senseless cruelty and lack of honour.'

Patroclus laughed. 'They will call him the greatest hero who ever lived,' he replied. 'What are the lives of your kin, against the hundreds he has killed already?'

'Is that the only measure of greatness? Killing so many that you have lost count? Making no distinction between warriors and unarmed men and women?'

'You argue well for a woman,' Patroclus said. 'Your husband must have been a patient man.'

'Don't speak of my husband,' she said. 'Or I will not speak to you at all.' The silence lay between them, as they both wondered what Patroclus would do in the face of her anger. He sat in silence for a moment, then jumped to his feet and strode across the tent. He took the comb from her hands and placed it on the couch beside her.

'I don't know what Achilles gave those guards, to prevent Agamemnon from claiming you,' he said. 'But it would have been worth double.'

Briseis did not reply.

*

The following day, the first goats died. This was not so unusual, as the goats on the Trojan peninsula were scrawny things, with none of the sleekness or sturdiness of their Greek counterparts. So no one thought it was anything important. But the next day, the pens held more dead goats than live ones, and the heifers – which the Greeks had stolen from every smallholding nearby – were sickening too. The cows were made of sterner stuff than the goats, and it took them correspondingly longer to die. In fact, the first Greek soldier was dead almost half a day before the first cow collapsed to the ground and sputtered its last foaming breath.

The fever came on so suddenly it was hard to detect. By the time a man understood he was ill, and not simply hot because the sun beat down on them from above and there was so little shade in the camp, he was moments from death. Even the healers could do little. They were battle-trained, and their skills were in binding cuts and cauterizing wounds. Their herbal concoctions had no effect on this blight, which swept across the camp like the hot south wind. Men scratched at phantom insects which crawled over their skin, tearing weals into their arms and ulcerating their legs. Blisters formed in their mouths and on their eyelids, and sharp nails soon opened these up into raw wounds. Like the goats, the cattle and even the few dogs which had made the camp their home, the men were dying. First their comrades prayed, and then they wept. When neither of these helped, they went to their king.

*

Chryseis was sitting in her usual hiding place, behind Agamemnon's tent, when the men made their appeal. She knew something was wrong, some illness. One of the women who washed clothes at the river in the mornings had died the previous day, and now another was ill. No one had seen Briseis or any of the women from the Myrmidon camp for several days. The thought of her beautiful friend lying stricken was more than Chryseis could bear. After everything she had lost – everything they had both lost – were their lives the next thing to be taken from them? She wanted to send a message to Briseis, but there was no one she trusted to take it. Besides, the rumour among the other women at the water's edge was that the Myrmidons were refusing to meet with the other Greeks. No one in the Myrmidon camp had yet been afflicted, so people said. The blight must be like the swords of his enemies: nothing touched the godlike Achilles.

Agamemnon at first refused to see the men who gathered outside his tent demanding an audience. But they did not disperse, and the hum of the crowd grew louder as they waited. Chryseis knew he would have to face them sooner or later, but she had already noticed that Agamemnon was a coward. He was desperate to avoid arguments with his men because he could rarely best a man with words; but his petulance forced the arguments into being, just the same. Chryseis' only first-hand experience of living with a man was with her father. And although she had often thought him cold and inflexible, she now realized that he was also a strong, principled man who did not shirk his responsibilities.

Agamemnon, she could see, was not. He spent a great deal of time telling everyone about his unparalleled importance, but he rarely wished to make the choices that a king must. How such a weak and petty man had risen to such a position of authority, she had wondered more than once. She had concluded that the Greeks' selfishness was the cause: every man looked out for himself first and his men second, and the other Greeks after that, if at all. Merit was decided by what a man had, not what he did. Chryseis contrasted the Argive king with her father, who would never permit such shallowness in himself or his daughter. So although she was afraid of Agamemnon's pawing hands and his vicious temper, she found herself feeling oddly superior to the man who now owned her.

From within the tent, she heard the frantic murmurs of his advisers cease. Agamemnon walked out to angry jeers from the men who had been waiting in the suffocating heat to hear him speak. But he was not in a conciliatory mood.

'Go back to your tents,' he shouted. 'We have seen the summer fever before: this is no different. In a day or two it will all be over.'

'It's not the summer sickness,' a man called out from the middle of the crowd. 'This is something else.'

The murmuring increased, like the chatter of frightened birds. 'Go back to your tents,' Agamemnon said again.

'Tell him what you told us,' another man shouted, and with that Chryseis could no longer wait out of sight. She needed to see what was happening. She crept on her knees to the space between two tents so she could see. 'Tell him,' more voices were saying. Finally, someone stepped forward. A priest, Chryseis knew immediately. She saw the arrogance behind his eyes and the ornate robes he wore in service of the god, which also served to emphasize his own importance.

'What is it, Calchas?' Agamemnon said. 'What would you have me sacrifice today?'

It was an odd turn of phrase, Chryseis thought. He must have known that only a few meagre calves were left in the pens: a choice of sacrificial victims belonged to happier men than this mottled band of Greeks.

'I have spoken with the gods,' Calchas said. 'And the men are right: this is no ordinary sickness. It is a punishment sent to us by Apollo.'

The chattering was growing ever louder, until Agamemnon raised his fist.

'A punishment from Apollo? Then sacrifice a hecatomb,' he said to derisive snorts. If the men gathered every cow in the camp, they would not have a fifth of the hundred required.

'We could sacrifice two hundred cows and it would have no effect,' said Calchas. 'The Archer has one demand, and that is for you to return the daughter to her father, the priest.'

Chryseis felt a thickening in her throat. Had her father done what he had threatened and called down the wrath of Apollo on the Greeks?

Agamemnon's face flushed a bright, sickly red. 'Give away my prize?' he said. 'Never.'

'It is the only cure for the blight,' Calchas replied. 'The priest wants his daughter back and he has called down the curse of the god he serves. The plague will not be lifted until we return her.'

'We?' shrieked Agamemnon. 'She doesn't belong to us. She belongs to me. And why would Apollo demand that only one man gives up his prize? Why should that man be me, king of all the Greeks? Why shouldn't Odysseus give up his prize, or Ajax?'

There was a long pause. 'Because your prize is the daughter of Apollo's priest,' said Calchas.

'You have always been plotting against me,' Agamemnon said. 'Even before we sailed from Greece. Your conniving ways have already cost me my daughter, my oldest child.' His voice cracked, and suddenly Chryseis understood why Briseis had advised her to mention his daughter when he seemed likely to harm her, all those nights ago. The man had lost his own child, and he could not stand to think of it. 'And now you would take away my prize. Mine, out of all the leaders of the Greeks. Get out of my sight, or I will kill you myself.'

'I assure you, king, that I do not mean to be the bearer of ill tidings,' Calchas said, and Chryseis was immediately certain that the man enjoyed nothing more. He was almost smacking his lips together. 'But the girl must be returned to her father, or the Greeks will all pay the price.'

'Give her back,' shouted someone. 'Give her back.' The cry was taken up by others, and soon spread across the crowd. Agamemnon looked from one group of men to another, but could not see any hint of disunity. They were of one mind, and that mind was set against him. And Chryseis saw that her time in the Greek camp was at an end. Her father had done exactly as he had sworn he would do. She should have known that he would force even an invading army to bow to his will.

'I will not be left without a prize,' he said. 'You!' He pointed at Odysseus. 'Go to Achilles and tell him that I claim his girl. If mine is taken from me, then I will have his.'

The shouts turned to silence. The king could not mean what he had just said, could he? Odysseus was leaning against the trunk of a long-dead tree, his brow creased in confusion. 'Are you quite sure that's what you want me to do?' he asked, straightening his back slowly.

'Of course.' Chryseis could hear the doubt behind the bluster. So could his men, she was sure. But he would not back down. 'Fetch me his girl, and someone escort mine back to her cursed father.'

*

Briseis had once promised the Trojan girl that she would not let these Greeks see her weep, and it was a promise she kept far longer than she had anticipated. She had not wept for her family, and she had not wept when Achilles chose her as his reward for looting her town.

She did not weep when Patroclus took her to his bed, even though the memory of her husband was still so raw that she could sense his presence, hovering behind her, refraining from judgement. Her husband had always been a kind man. And so would Patroclus have been, in other circumstances.

She did not weep when Odysseus arrived in the Myrmidon camp and told Achilles that Agamemnon had claimed his girl. Achilles wept, from impotent rage, and Patroclus wept to see his friend so angered. But Briseis, carried away to another man's tent, and another man's bed, did not. She also did not resent Chryseis, whose father had the ear of the god and who had taken her back to Troy. What would be the point in that?

The Myrmidons' war came to an abrupt halt on the day she was moved to Agamemnon's tent. In fury at the Argive king's behaviour, Achilles withdrew himself and his warriors from the battlefield. Briseis listened to the other tribal leaders – Diomedes, Ajax, Odysseus, Nestor – counsel their king. Don't worry, they said. His wrath cannot last long. He will miss the killing, the warmth of blood on his hands. Agamemnon did not care what the Myrmidon prince did or did not do, he claimed. The Greeks did not need him when they had so many heroes who fought on their side, and the gods, who understood that a man could not seize another man's wife and expect to go unpunished. They did not need him, for all his speed and the sharpness of his sword.

Briseis also heard the counsellors when they left Agamemnon's quarters, as they murmured to one another that Achilles would never soften his rage against their leader. He had sworn not to fight and he would not. They did have many other warriors, all anxious to return to battle, now the blight had passed over. But the men saw Achilles as more than a warrior; he was a talisman, a figurehead. First the plague and now the loss of their greatest fighter: it was not clear to everyone that the gods were still on their side.

Nonetheless, they returned to the plains with their spears and their swords, and they fought. Every day they came back blood-spattered, carrying their comrades on makeshift stretchers. After sixteen days of the worst losses the Greeks had known in more than nine years of war, Agamemnon's advisers told him he must act. The Greeks needed a wall built to protect their ships. Without it, there was a grave risk that the Trojans, emboldened by Hector's recent victor-ies, might push the Achaeans back into their camp, back to the water's edge, back to their tall ships. If the Trojans reached the ships, they would set them ablaze. And this was the greatest horror of every Greek who marched out each morning to fight for Agamemnon. If the ships were burned, no one would ever return home.

At first, as was his habit, Agamemnon refused to listen. But then his brother Menelaus arrived, red hair turned sandy by the sun, red face turned purple by the embar-rassment. He could no longer guarantee his own men – the Spartans – if the Greeks did not build a wall. No quantity of threats nor bribes could persuade them to stay if there was a chance they might end up stranded on the Trojan peninsula, to be picked off by their enemies. His men had not set sail ten years ago to die far from home. He could not promise that they would not rise up against him and the war, and set sail for Sparta without him. At this, Agamemnon wailed like a child whose favourite toy had been smashed. But he gave in and agreed to build the wall.

A day after building was completed, Hector and his Trojans pushed the Greeks back so hard that they nearly lost the wall, and their lives, and their ships. The men were now openly mutinous and many were gathering their few belongings, ready to sail home at last, and dismiss the past decade as an unfortunate mistake. Nestor, the oldest man in the camp, and the one who held the greatest sway over Agamemnon, persuaded him to send an embassy to Achilles. Return his girl, the men urged. Give him ten more girls. Beg him to return to the battle.

Agamemnon resisted this too, but not for long. Even his monstrous vanity could see that the Greeks were asking for the only thing that could save them. Achilles sent away the men who went to plead Agamemnon's case. Eventually, they sent Nestor, thinking that a young man could not spurn the pleas of an old one. But he continued to refuse to fight, even while the greatest of the Greeks were begging him on bended knees. Nestor turned his attention to Patroclus, whose rage was not so terrible as that of his friend. Eventually, he persuaded the lesser man to step back onto the battlefield in Achilles' stead, if Agamemnon would return Achilles' prize. No one was happy, but some professed themselves content.

After eighteen days in the tent of Agamemnon, witness to every twist in his temper as he was overcome first by the advances of the Trojans and then by the advice of the Greeks, Briseis was relieved to be sent away from the vicious, petulant commander. She was returned to Achilles, and therefore to Patroclus, the night before the latter went to battle the Trojans. Patroclus combed her hair for her carefully, almost lovingly.

The following evening, when Patroclus' body was returned, stripped of the armour which had once belonged to Achilles but had been stolen from his friend's still-warm body by Hector, Briseis was waiting for him. While Achilles raged with grief, she washed Patroclus, and laid him out in his finest clothes. She was able to do for this man, her captor and her owner, what she had not been permitted to do for her husband. But she did not weep.

She did not weep when Patroclus was placed on his funeral pyre. Nor did she weep when Achilles, raging like a mountain lion deprived of its young, returned to battle to avenge his dead friend, although everyone knew that the tide of the war had now changed: you could smell it in the air, like a storm coming in from the sea. And she did not weep when Achilles returned from the battlefield with a battered corpse tied to the back of his chariot wheels, having dragged the body of the slain Hector around the walls of the city three times.

Achilles left the Trojan hero rotting outside his tent and Briseis thought of sneaking out in the early hours to wash Hector's body and prepare him for burial, or the funeral pyre, but she did not dare. Three nights later, she was listening when the aged king of Troy, a man she had heard of but never seen, came begging Achilles to return his son's body to him. She heard Priam's voice crack as he pleaded for mercy from this most merciless killer, and she was astonished when Achilles softened and let the old man buy back his dead son with a pile of treasure.

Having held off for so long, she thought her eyes would not remember what to do. But many days later, standing in front of the funeral pyre of Achilles – cut down in battle by Apollo, they said – she did weep. And she wept for everyone but him.

11

Thetis

Tears did flow for Achilles, but they mingled imperceptibly with the seawater which surrounded them. Thetis wept for her son at his death as she had done countless times during his life. Indeed she had wept long before he was born. The other sea nymphs had always mocked her propensity for tears: the deep, green waters of Ocean himself were replenished by Thetis and her endless sorrows. Had she been a wood nymph, another Nereid spitefully remarked, her forest grove would have soon become a bog.

She had first wept when Peleus, a mortal man and nowhere near the equal of a Nereid, had claimed her hand in marriage. She sobbed again when it became clear that Zeus would not save her from the degrading union. A prophecy had foretold that Thetis' son would be greater than his father and, mindful of his own impervious hide, Zeus was determined that the boy be half-mortal.

She had always known that her son would cause her grief. Greater than his father? What man would not be? She despised the mortal blood of her husband, loathed to think of it running through the veins of her son, where ichor should flow instead. She longed for him to be a god, so she bathed him in the waters of the Styx to thicken his thin human skin. And she tried to keep him safe when the war came. She knew, had always known, that if Achilles went to Troy he would not return home; Zeus was not the only one to hear prophecies. She hid Achilles away when the Greek commanders came for him, but they rooted him out nonetheless. The pestilent Odysseus was too clever to fall for her tricks. It was a grudge which she would nurture in her breast for as long as Odysseus lived. The sea would never be safe for the king of Ithaca, not while she dwelt in its murky depths.

But through nine long years Achilles had stayed safe. The list of his dead grew longer and more glorious, but he remained unhurt. She had let a brief moment of hope flare up when Achilles withdrew himself from battle in the tenth year of the war, some trivial dispute over a mortal girl. But whenever he asked for her advice, she could not refuse to tell him. She left the warm dark sea and told her son what she had always known: that he must choose between a long life and brief renown, or a short life and eternal glory. Only half of him was a god, after all. He could not have both.

She knew as soon as her damp words dripped into his ears that the decision was already made. Her son would never choose life over fame. His godly heritage rejected any such notion. And so she persuaded Hephaestus to forge new armour, a new shield for Achilles, after his had been stolen by the filthy Trojans from the body of his friend. With the protection of the gods, she thought, Achilles would have a little longer to carve his name into stone.

Still, she knew that once Hector was slaughtered, and once Penthesilea was added to the long list of heroes whom Achilles had left on the cold ground, her boy would soon follow them across the River Styx. And when her son was cut down by Apollo (his disguise as the adulterous Paris might fool some, but not Thetis), she wept even though she had known the day was coming. His body was so lovely that she had scarcely believed he was dead. A tiny wound, a single arrow from the toxic Archer was all it had taken to kill her beloved son. And now he dwelt on the Isle of the Blessed, and she knew that he wished he had made the other choice. One day, Odysseus would find him in the Underworld and he would ask him what death was like, and her son would reply that he would rather be a living peasant than a dead hero. And this filled her with anger and shame. He truly was mortal, her son, if he valued his precious life more than anything else. How could he be so stupid, so ungrateful, when she had given him so much? Sometimes the thought slid into her that she could not truly know her son's mind, because she would never die. But this only made her despise him more: the blood of his father ran through his veins more thickly than she had believed. And so she wept, but her tears tasted of nothing.

12

Calliope

If he tells me to sing one more time, I think I might bite him. The presumption of these men is extraordinary. Does he believe I have nothing else to do with my time than sit around being his muse? His. When did poets forget that they serve the muses, and not the other way around? And if he can remember new lines of verse during his recitations, why can't he remember to say please?

Does everyone have to die, he asks, plaintive like a child. Perhaps he thought he was writing about one of those other wars. Devastation is what happens in war: it is its nature. I murmur to him in his dreams sometimes (I do have other things to do, but I like how he looks when he sleeps): you knew Achilles would die. You knew Hector would die before him. You knew Patroclus would die. You've told their stories before. If you didn't want to think of men cut down in battle, then why would you want to compose epic verse?

Ah, but now I see the problem. It's not their deaths he's upset about. It's that he knows what's coming and he's worrying it will be more tragedy than epic. I watch his chest rising and falling as he grabs a fitful rest. Men's deaths are epic, women's deaths are tragic: is that it? He has misunderstood the very nature of conflict. Epic is countless tragedies, woven together. Heroes don't become heroes without carnage, and carnage has both causes and consequences. And those don't begin and end on a battle-field.

If he truly wants to understand the nature of the epic story I am letting him compose, he needs to accept that the casualties of war aren't just the ones who die. And that a death off the battlefield can be more noble (more heroic, if he prefers it that way) than one in the midst of fighting. But it hurts, he said when Creusa died. He would rather her story had been snuffed out like a spark failing to catch damp kindling. It does hurt, I whispered. It should hurt. She isn't a footnote, she's a person. And she – all the Trojan women – should be memorialized as much as any other person. Their Greek counterparts too. War is not a sport, to be decided in a quick bout on a strip of contested land. It is a web which stretches out to the furthest parts of the world, drawing everyone into itself.

I will teach him this before he leaves my temple. Or he will have no poem at all.

13

The Trojan Women

The high tide was shifting the seaweed fronds against the sand, as the women continued to wait on the rocks. The Greek guards had disappeared a while ago, after one of them had run up to the others from further down the coast, insisting they follow him immediately. But the women didn't think of trying to escape. What would be the point in gathering their feeble belongings and running? There was nowhere for them to go. The Greek ships lined the bay, drawn up and ready to leave. All they could see that wasn't now in Greek hands were the smoking remains of their city.

'You know Achilles would still have fought, even if it hadn't been for Briseis,' Hecabe said. 'He lived to kill, to torment and to torture. It wasn't enough for him to slaughter my son.'

No one asked her which son. She always meant Hector, even though Achilles had killed many of his brothers too. 'He had to defile him. Had to make Priam beg for the return of Hector's body on bended knee. An old man, begging on his knees. That is who Achilles was: he would have fought again alongside the other Greeks, even if

Agamemnon had taken his woman and slit her throat where she stood. Butchery was everything he was.'

Cassandra gazed up at the sky, where the gulls were starting to gather and wheel. She had watched them doing the same thing at the same time yesterday. Polyxena had noticed, years ago, that her troubled sister took comfort in repetitive things. The gulls would soon start diving, one after another, into a shoal of fish in the shallow waters.

Further along the shore, above the place where the guards had gone, another cluster of the birds were hovering, waiting. Cassandra already knew why.

'Do you think that's true?' Polyxena asked her mother. 'Achilles was destined to be a killer?'

Hecabe shrugged her shoulders, but the cool breeze coming off the sea turned it into a shudder. Polyxena unwound her stole – once a fine wool, dyed a bright, saffron yellow before it was smeared with grey streaks – and stood up to wrap it around her mother. She did not expect to be thanked, and Hecabe said nothing.

'If you think of him like that,' Polyxena said, 'it means he had no choice in what he did. So how can we hate him, if he was just acting as the Fates demanded? If he had no more say in his life than you or I?'

'He had a choice,' Hecabe replied. 'To butcher my sons or some other woman's sons. But slaughter was all he was good for.'

Cassandra nodded, and whispered her words into the sand. 'He's not finished, he's not finished, he's not finished.'

14

Laodamia

The heat was intense in Phylace, even this early in the day. Nestled in the lower reaches of Thessaly, between the Gulf of Pagasae to the east and the Phthiotis Mountains to the south and west, it was always hot. The sun burned down so relentlessly on Protesilaus' small kingdom that no trees ever grew tall enough or verdant enough to provide anything more than a spindly, ineffectual shade. The mountains in the distance climbed in sharp, straight zigzags, and Laodamia had often wished she could roam them like a she-goat. It must surely be cooler up there, where the trees grew more thickly. As it was, she felt sweat forming at her temples and on the back of her legs. Her parents had told her bedtime stories when she was a child, and the one that stuck in her mind even now was that of Helios, the sun-god, pausing to rest his horses every day right over the city she called her home.

Laodamia walked in a loop – out from the palace, down to the city walls, to the road which led away from Phylace towards the sea. There she would wait each day, until the sailors and traders who were coming inland had arrived. How many days did it take a man to sail from Troy to

Thessaly? Clipping the island of Lemnos, before crossing the dark Aegean and hugging the coast of Euboea into the Pagasean Gulf. She had the whole route fixed in her mind because in the days before he left, Protesilaus had talked of little else but how he would get home.

'Don't cry, little queen,' he said, as her tears flowed so freely that she thought they would drown her. He reached out his hand – long, slender fingers, better suited to playing the lyre than wielding a sword – and wiped them away with his thumb. 'I will be back before you have time to miss me. I promise.'

And she nodded, as though she believed him. 'You must promise me something more,' she said.

'Anything,' he replied.

'You must promise not to be first,' she said. His pretty brow – the thing she had loved about him from the beginning, the slight crease between his eyes – was the only sign of his confusion. His mouth continued to make soft, calming sounds, as though he were placating a scared horse.

'I mean it.' She wanted to tell him to stop stroking her arms and pay attention to her words. But the torchlight glittered on his golden skin, and she found she could barely pay attention to them herself. 'You must let your ship lag behind the others, when you land at Troy. Yours must not be the first to make its mooring.'

'I doubt I will be at the helm of the ship, my love,' he replied. He felt her stiffen beside him. 'But I will ask the helmsman to make no haste. I will distract him with talk of sea-monsters and whirlpools.'

'You aren't taking me seriously,' she said. She tried to

jerk her arm out of his reach, and remonstrate with him, but she could not. She longed for his touch, even when she had it. 'You must allow the other men to get off the ship before you. All will be well if you will just stand back a little and let another man off the ship first.'

'Ah,' he said. 'But perhaps the sooner I leave my ship, the sooner I can return to it, and then to you.'

'No,' she said. 'No, please. That's not it at all. You cannot be first off the ship, you cannot.' Her tears spilled out again.

Protesilaus smiled patiently, and ruffled her hair. 'I said, don't cry, little queen. Please stop.'

Their bedroom was not large or opulent by the standards of other palaces, she had no doubt. The kingdom was small, the palace was small, and she was small. Or delicate, as Protesilaus laughed. He always said that he would have married her even if she hadn't been beautiful, because she was the only queen who would fit in his low-roofed home. But the thick walls kept the palace cool: the only cool place in their hot little city. And so they could fill their bedroom with quilts and torches, even as the rest of the kingdom baked in the evening sun. She loved to be there more than anywhere else, tangled up with her husband in their private room.

But when the call came for the suitors of Helen to mass their ships at Aulis, her small, perfect happiness began to unravel. She knew that Protesilaus had once bid for Helen's hand in marriage, of course. It was before she had known him, so she bore only the slightest grudge. But oh, if only he had not. Because the suitors had all sworn an oath to bring Helen back – if ever she went missing – to whichever of them was named her husband. Otherwise, she could not have been married at all: every Greek king wanted her to be his own. There had to be some consequence for so many competing claims.

The man who eventually took her was no Greek and had sworn nothing. Yet the oath which bound Laodamia's husband could not be broken. So when Helen disappeared with the prince of Troy, Protesilaus received his orders to join his fellow Greeks and wage war for her return. Because the Spartan king had lost his queen, a hundred queens lost their kings. And Laodamia resented the Greeks at least as much as she resented the Trojans. She had asked for very little in her life: only that her husband be hers, and be safe, and be near.

And now he was none of those things. She knew the moment it happened, days before the messenger arrived with the news she had dreaded above all else. She had always known, she thought, even before she could have put words to the fear. The moment she met Protesilaus, she had somehow known she would lose him. She remembered the warring sensations when her father introduced them: immediate devotion mingled with a desperate presentiment of grief.

She had known as she closed her eyes in his embrace that final time, having travelled with him to his ship so she could wave him off. Again, she begged him to hang back from the sandy shores of Troy, to be last, to be second from last, to be anything but the first Greek to set foot on foreign land. She had hidden her tears from her husband so he would have her smile to take with him. But as soon as she thought he would no longer be able to see, she wept steadily and never stopped. She watched his outline until she could make him out no more, and then she watched his ship until it became a speck. Still, she could not bear to leave the water's edge, so strong was her sense that once she had turned away from the ocean she had turned away from all happiness. Eventually, slaves steered her back to the palace, her maidservant holding her around the waist so that when she stumbled (unable to see through her tears and the twilight), she would not fall. The poor girl could not see that Laodamia had already fallen and would never get up again.

Her parents consoled her: Protesilaus would return, the distance was not so great, the sea was calm. Too calm, it transpired. A few days after he had sailed from Thessaly, Protesilaus sent word that he – like the rest of the Greeks – was becalmed at Aulis. The fleet could not sail and Laodamia allowed herself to hope that the enterprise would be abandoned, and her husband would sail home again. That the image she kept seeing – of his beautiful feet, the long toes pointing outwards, left foot in front of right, perched on the prow of a ship – was Protesilaus disembarking on the Thessalian coast and not leaping to his doom at Troy. She could see it in such detail: his knees slightly bent, like a dancer, his weight moving forward with such deliberate precision.

But of course she knew it was hopeless. Agamemnon, the leader of the expedition, committed some atrocity to appease the gods and win back the wind for his ships.

The fleet sailed, as she had always known it would. It reached Troy safely and her husband, her beloved, so desperate to get the war underway so he could hurry back to his little queen, leapt from his ship into the shallow waters which lapped at the shore. The Trojans were waiting for them, but Protesilaus was no coward. She did not know – until the messenger arrived with the awful news – that her husband was such a fine warrior. If asked, she would have said that he was, of course. But if asked, she would have said, with equal pride, that he might fly. It was no consolation to her to find out that her husband was brave and skilled with both spear and sword. She would have preferred it if he had sat quivering behind a couch, refusing the call to fight. Who could love a coward, she had once heard a woman say. Laodamia knew the answer. Someone for whom the alternative is loving a corpse.

But though she took no comfort in his bravery, she knew others did. His fellow citizens were filled with pride for their late king. They sat beneath sun-bleached flax awnings, telling each other of Protesilaus' exploits. How he had leapt from his ship ahead of all his men, and killed three Trojans – no, four – before the Myrmidon ships had even landed. Swift-footed Achilles, people called the Myrmidon king. But their king had been swifter still. How they boasted of him: she heard it from the slaves who hoped to ease her suffering. And it had not been an ordinary Trojan who cut her husband down. It had been no less than Hector, the favourite son of Priam, the barbarian king. He was built like an ox, they said. Tall and strong, and fighting in defence of his city. All agreed that those who fought to protect what they valued fought more desperately than those on the attack. Such a man it had taken to fell their young king and make him the first of the Greeks to die.

After the news of his death had reached her, Laodamia had not known what to do. She tore her garments and ripped at her hair and cheeks, because she knew it was expected of her. She rent her skin with her sharp nails – nails which she had dragged down her husband's spine in moments of pleasure – and in the moment of causing the damage she felt a release. The physical pain was a shallow reflection of what she felt, but even a poor reflection was better than nothing. The dull soreness which followed was insufficient. The wounds healed, but nothing else did. Unable to bear the conversation of her parents or friends or servants, she found herself repeating the looped walk, across to the eastern side of the city where she sat under a thin tree and waited for no one to come, because there would be no news she ever needed to hear again.

The citizens of Phylace left her alone with her grief every day, until the blacksmith – whose forge lay opposite her tree – could bear it no longer. A tall, bulky man with huge, soot-blackened forearms and a gut which he restrained with a tanned leather belt, he had watched his queen sit opposite his smithy since the day the king had left. He had never considered himself to be a sentimental man: he had hammered out the king's spearheads for him, he knew what happened on a battlefield. But the sorrow which exuded from her like a stench – forcing others to turn away and hurry past, even when it was too hot to hurry anywhere – did not repel him. Rather, it reminded him of his wife, when she lost their second child a few months after birth. The baby had slept fitfully and cried often, and one morning when they awoke, he lay cold in his crib. There was no sign of sickness or injury; he was perfect. He looked more beautiful dead than he had looked alive, always gasping for breath. The blacksmith had taken the child and buried him in a pit he dug himself. His wife could not speak for days. The smith tried to remind her that they still had a son – toddling around their chair legs, tugging at her skirts – and that they would surely go on to have more. But grief stood before his wife like an immovable object around which she could not find her way. She grew paler and thinner from staying indoors, and after a day or two, he began to take his surviving son around the corner into the smithy each morning because he could see that if she was not feeding herself, she was not feeding the boy. He begged his sisters and his brothers' wives to talk to her. But no one could reach her. A month after the child died, he buried his wife.

The blacksmith was a good man and he could provide for his family, so he married again within a year. His second wife was ten years younger – broad-hipped and quick to laugh – and they had five more children in rapid succession. She never treated his eldest son as anything but her own, and it was this which made his voice still catch in his throat sometimes when he spoke about her. His friends would roar and laugh and raise their cups at the sight of the big man brought low by his own affection. But the laughter was never cruel.

Every morning, he watched Laodamia walk to her tree. And every afternoon, when he had finished his work for the day, he began to make something else. He was not usually a rich man, but he had sold a great number of weapons to the Greeks who were now waging their war on Troy. And he had a large chunk of bronze which was not spoken for, having arrived after the men had set sail. His wife did not complain when he came home a little later, nor did she ask what kept him at the smithy for the extra time. Instead she rubbed olive oil into the red weals under his arms and beneath his belt, where the salt deposits from his sweat had abraded his skin.

Two months after the king had sailed into the Pagasean Gulf, the blacksmith found himself waiting for the little queen to arrive as he was hammering a pair of greaves into shape. He had done this so many times before that he did not need to look down. The greaves would fit their owner perfectly around the calves when he came to collect them tomorrow.

When Laodamia arrived at her perch beneath the tree, the smith thought one last time about whether he was doing the best thing. But her birdlike frame had become so gaunt that he could not ignore it. He walked over to her slowly, because he was aware of his size and he did not want to scare her.

'Potnia,' he said, bowing his head slightly. He felt foolish, hoped it was early enough that his neighbours were busy with their own work and wouldn't see him. She showed no sign of having heard. He crouched down on his haunches in front of her. 'My lady?' he said again. She dragged her eyes from the middle distance to see what huge boulder had rolled in front of her. She was astonished to discover that it was a man.

'I cannot help you,' she said. Whatever he was asking for – food, water – she had none. Nor did she have the mental resources to find them. 'Forgive me,' she said. 'I cannot help.' Their eyes met and he saw the depths of his first wife's misery once again. He had not been able to save Philonome, but he would save this girl.

'I do not need your help, Potnia,' he said. She almost smiled to hear the word. Protesilaus had called her that, in the bedroom which belonged to them.

'Come with me,' he said, and she looked at him in confusion. He held out a meaty hand and she placed her own into it, as though he were her father and she were a child. He led her across the dirt track, steering her around the furrows made by carts laden with marble and stone.

'Now this way.' He took her into his forge: only low walls separated it from the street and she followed him past a set of hanging bellows made of calfskin, which had been polished to a hard shine with the blacksmith's sweat. Behind the battered anvil and the collection of small, sharp spearheads he had made with leftover metal shards as he worked on larger pieces, was a doorway which led into a storage room. Her eyes took a moment to adjust to the relative darkness, and she saw dented pots and split cauldrons, waiting to be reheated and hammered or spliced back together.

Behind all these, in the furthest corner, was a huge pile of cloth. No, not a pile, she realized. Just one piece of cloth covering something large. Something taller than her.

'Will you accept a gift from a stranger?' the smith asked,

and he whisked away the cloth with a deft tug. She felt the air leave her lungs, squeezed like the bellows outside. Because there, standing in front of her, was Protesilaus. She was not conscious of moving her feet, only following her hand which reached out to touch her husband's perfect face. The bronze was warm to the touch, as though his blood flowed beneath it. She opened her mouth, but could not find the sounds.

'I am truly sorry for what you have lost,' said the smith. 'If your ladyship would like it, I will wheel it up to the palace whenever you wish.'

She nodded. 'Yes. Yes.'

The smith looked at her, and shook out the cloth so he could cover his work once again.

'No!' she screamed. 'Please don't.' She threw her arms around the statue and grasped it tight. The smith smiled. 'Don't worry,' he said. 'My boys will be here shortly. You can stay with it and accompany them home with it, if you like.'

'With him,' she said. 'Thank you. I will.'

Over the days and months which followed, Laodamia did not let her bronze husband out of her sight. She refused to eat or drink unless the statue was present, and she could not be prevailed upon to leave her chamber. Her parents grew worried that their daughter could not continue in such a fashion. The slaves used to talk of her as a tragic figure, but as time passed, they grew scornful of a girl who could not accept her husband's death and marry again. She was young enough to bear any man children.

Her parents tried to reason with her, and when that

had no effect, they decided to act in her best interests. They waited for her to fall asleep one night, and had slaves remove the statue from her room. She awoke to find it on a funeral pyre, burning in place of the body which had never been returned to Greece. She issued a cracked howl, and hurled herself at the flames.

The gods saw this and, unusually, took pity upon her. As she was grabbed by her father and bundled back to her room, locked in for her own safety, the gods sent Hermes to negotiate with the lord of the Underworld. For the first and last time, Hades agreed to their request. As Laodamia wept her hopeless tears into a sodden pillow, she felt a warm hand on her upper back.

'Hush, little queen, don't cry,' said her husband. And at last she wept no more.

They spent a single day together before Hades' patience expired and Protesilaus was returned to the halls of the dead. Unable to live without what she had lost once before, Laodamia tied her bed-sheets into a noose and followed him. The gods remarked upon her devotion, and when the people of Phylace built a shrine to their king and queen, the gods smiled upon their prayers.

15

Iphigenia

Her father had sent word that she was to be married to Achilles, and her mother's servants had packed their things and bundled them out of the palace so quickly she had known that they were afraid the great man would change his mind. But why should Achilles be anything other than delighted to marry her? She was the daughter of Agamemnon and Clytemnestra, sister to Orestes and Electra, niece to Menelaus, cousin to Hermione. Whereas Achilles was who? Of course, they said he was the greatest warrior the world had ever known, but he had yet to fight in a war. And when he did strap on his greaves and unsheathe his sword, it would be for her family. The troops were drawing together at Aulis, ready to sail to Troy. But it was her father who commanded the Greeks, not Achilles – who commanded only his own men, the Myrmidons. And yes, perhaps he was more nimble than Apollo, swifter than Hermes, more destructive than Ares, as the rumours went. But he was not disgracing himself by marrying her. Her chin jutted forward as she berated her imaginary accusers for their ill-considered slight.

Iphigenia and her mother were on the road to Aulis

before she even knew where it was. Her infant brother accompanied them while Electra remained at home with the wet-nurse. They rode in a small cart which juddered along the stony paths, and when the going became too rough, she and her mother clambered out and walked so the horses had less of a burden. No one wanted to lose a horse in the mountainous region north of Mycenae. Even as she turned her ankle, stepping on loose sand which covered a treacherous rock, she consoled herself with the beauty of her saffron-coloured gown, packed into a box, safe from the bleaching sun and the billowing dust. She would make a spectacular bride, gazed at by every man in her father's armies.

But these thoughts consoled only her. By the time they arrived at Aulis, her mother was irritable from the heat and the dust and, most of all, the absence of her father to greet them. Agamemnon was somewhere in the camp, they were told by a gruff soldier who hastened them to their tent, but no one seemed sure where.

'The commander will wish to see his wife, his son and his daughter,' Clytemnestra declared to the men who bustled past carrying animal feed and weapons. But no one slowed down to listen. The queen of Mycenae was not important here.

Knowing her mother's temper was unlikely to improve, Iphigenia took her little brother away for a while, down to the rock pools so that he could prod for crabs with a small stick he had picked up on the journey, and she could inspect her reflection. Although she did not look her best when seen from below, which tricked her into thinking she had acquired a double-chin. She stood back and angled her neck to get a better view. Her dark hair was parted down the centre, its kinked rows pinned tightly along her scalp before foaming into extravagant curls at the crown of her head. It flowed down her back, and she knew it would be set off perfectly by the saffron wedding dress. But none of the soldiers she could see – talking and play-fighting with one another, testing their strength and guile – wanted to pay her any attention at all. Were they all so afraid of her groom that they would not flirt with a princess, and one sitting so prettily in the afternoon sun?

She had thought that Achilles would wish to present himself to her – officially, at her mother's tent, or approaching her here in private, while Orestes busied himself with the soft red arms of a starfish which curved up like flower petals when he touched them – but he did not. Perhaps he was nervous, she thought. Though he could not be a coward, this hero about whom she had heard such things.

When she took Orestes back to their tent, she found Clytemnestra in a slightly better temper, after a brief meeting with Agamemnon and Menelaus. Her mother was still vexed that no one had greeted their party, but she had been mollified by the suggestion that they had travelled more quickly than the men had imagined would be possible. Clytemnestra was a vain woman, and few things gave her more pleasure than men admiring her for having achieved something in the way a man might have done it. She considered herself a queen rather than a wife, and she never wished to be compared to other women, unless it was for the purpose of demonstrating her vast superiority to the rest of her sex.

'The wedding will be tomorrow at first light,' she told Iphigenia, who nodded happily. She did not share her mother's disdain for womanish things and hunted through her belongings for the make-up she wished to wear the next morning: red discs on her forehead and cheeks, each one surrounded by a little cluster of red dots, like tiny suns. A thick black line encasing each eye, and darkening her solid brows. She had delicate gold chains to wear threaded through her hair. When the wedding ceremony began, she would be ready. The perfect bride.

Before dawn, by the smoky light of a torch, Iphigenia prepared herself. She painted the lines and the circles, tied the sparkling metal strands into her carefully plaited locks. A servant arranged her hair exactly as she wished, making her glad that they had rehearsed the style at the end of every day's travel. This was the moment when everything had to be flawless. She had the slave examine her work, lifting her chin and tilting it left, then right, to be certain that the dots she had placed on each cheek were level, before she filled them out to the neat circles she desired. Her mother did not paint her own face, but she wore a bright red dress which Iphigenia had never seen before, and the two of them smiled, clutching hands for a moment.

'I look beautiful,' Iphigenia said. She could not quite bring herself to phrase it as a question.

'You do. The most beautiful bride these men will have ever seen, no matter which part of Greece they have travelled from,' her mother said. 'Here.' She produced a small pot of thickly perfumed oil, and Iphigenia smoothed the scent of crushed flowers onto her hands and then into her glistening hair. 'Perfect,' her mother said. 'You will make me proud today. My first daughter, married to the greatest warrior among all the Greeks.'

They heard the sound of heavy footsteps outside, and a small, low cry. The soldiers were here to accompany her to the altar on the shore. Orestes was still asleep and Clytemnestra vacillated for a moment about waking him to accompany her, so the prince of Mycenae would see its princess become queen of the Myrmidons. But the thought of a fractious infant was more than she could bear, and she left him behind with the slaves. They opened the flap of the tent to see a motley assortment of soldiers waiting for them.

'This is hardly the honour guard we might have expected,' Clytemnestra said. 'Do you not have more respect for Agamemnon and his family?'

The men mumbled their apologies but there was no sincerity in their voices. They were waiting to go to war, Iphigenia thought. They had not the least inclination to attend a wedding between a man most of them had never seen fight, and the daughter of the man who commanded them, but not yet in battle. It was too soon for pride and honour. Her mother could not see it.

The soldiers waited for her to adjust her sandal so the strap didn't rub, and then began the short walk towards the sea. She walked beside Clytemnestra in silence, imagining how she must look in profile with her perfectly straight neck. For just a moment, she wished her father was there to tell her everything would be alright. But he had not returned to their tent after she had missed him the previous day. Still, as they came around the high dunes near the shore, she could see him ahead of her, standing by a makeshift altar.

There were so many men lined up in front of the water, so many tall ships drawn up behind them. The city of Troy would never withstand such a force. Iphigenia felt a brief spasm of sadness, that her husband would be unable to distinguish himself in such a short-lived conflict. Perhaps there would be other wars. She continued to walk towards her father, so grand in his ritual garments, standing beside an ornately dressed priest. And as she felt the sand scratching the skin between her toes, she realized something was wrong.

The sails of the ships were completely still. It was too early to be hot, but there was a solidity to the air which stifled her. She had thought the same yesterday, when she was watching her brother play in the rock pools, but she had dismissed the oddity: they were in a sheltered part of the shore. But here were all these men, all these ships, and yet nothing was rippling in the breeze: every sail lay limp. The air was never so still this close to water. Was it an omen? She felt her breathing quicken. Were the gods warning her off this marriage? Or was it the opposite: they had calmed the winds in honour of the ceremony? She wished that she could ask her mother, but Clytemnestra had not noticed anything unusual. She marched forward as though walking to her own wedding. She seemed almost surprised when the soldiers placed themselves between her and her daughter, several of them leading Clytemnestra off to the side while four men continued towards the altar with Iphigenia.

It wasn't just the windless sky which was worrying

Iphigenia now. There was something else. She knew men were not perhaps so interested in weddings as their wives and sisters might have been. But the atmosphere was not at all celebratory, and she thought the prospect of a few wineskins later on would have been enough to provoke a little joy. Instead of which, the men seemed closed off, from each other as well as her. They frowned as she passed them, staring at the ground rather than revelling in her beauty. For a terrible moment, she thought she must have done something wrong: worn an ugly dress or applied her make-up inappropriately. But her mother's slaves had been unanimous in their praise of her. She was correctly attired for a wedding.

And then she saw the glint of her father's knife in the morning sun and she understood everything in a rush, as though a god had put the words into her mind. The treacherous stillness in the air was divinely sent. Artemis had been affronted by something her father had done, and now she demanded a sacrifice or the ships would not sail. So there would be no marriage, no husband for Iphigenia. Not today and not ever. She had perfect clarity of thought, even as her senses became blurred. She heard her mother's cry of rage, but distantly, as though it were echoing off the walls of a cave. The men stopped at the foot of the altar, and she climbed its three rickety steps towards her father. He looked like someone she had never met.

She knelt in silence before Agamemnon. Tears streamed into his beard, but he held the knife just the same. Her uncle stood behind him, his red hair glowing in the morning sun. She sensed his hand reach out to her father, offering strength for the ordeal he was about to undergo.

She looked out across a sea of leather armour and wondered which of them was Achilles. On Iphigenia's right she could see her mother, mouth gaping in a savage scream, but a buzzing sound had filled her ears, so she could not hear the words. She saw Clytemnestra was being restrained by five men, one of whom eventually forced his arm around her throat. Still her mother did not fall limply into their arms. She continued shouting and flailing, long after she could have had air left in her lungs.

Many of the men in the front ranks looked away when the knife came down. And even those who did not blanch rarely spoke afterwards of what they had seen. One soldier was sure that in the crucial moment, the girl had been spirited away and replaced with a deer. But no one listened to him, because even the men (the young ones who had not fought in many battles, and the fathers of daughters who had fought in too many) who had looked away as the blade cut – who had shut their eyes rather than see her blood pouring from her neck – even those men had seen her white, lifeless body lying at her own father's feet. And then they had felt the gentle breeze wrap itself around them.

16

The Trojan Women

That evening, it became clear that the Greeks intended to stay on the Trojan peninsula for one or two more days, as they distributed their illicitly won gains and divided up the last of the women. Many of them had been taken already, and now only the royal family – Hecabe, her daughters, her daughters-in-law – remained to be split among the men who regarded themselves as heroes.

As the sun began to drop again, two Greek soldiers appeared behind the women, half-shoving, half-dragging another woman between them.

'What are you doing?' she spat. 'Take me to Menelaus.' The men ignored her, laughing as they pushed her one last time into the circle of Trojan women.

'Menelaus will come and find you in the morning,' said one of the guards. 'When he finds out you're here. But until then, you can spend the night with the Trojans you like so much.' They hurried away to their camp, knowing that none of the other Greeks were likely to notice them in the half-light and that none of the women would be able to identify them the next day.

Cassandra focused her attention on making the fire burn

more vigorously, now the air was turning cool. Even Hecabe, quick to deride her daughter's uselessness, had to admit that the priestess had always had a gift for fire. Armed with her foreknowledge, Cassandra still dreaded the encounter she was about to witness. But even after all these years, she could not look away from the impossible beauty of the woman who lost none of her poise when she was abused by these Greeks.

Helen looked no different today than she had ten years earlier, when she stepped into the city beside Paris, who had returned with her from Sparta, declaring her his wife and Troy her home. They made a beautiful couple: him so dark with his perfumed black hair, and her so tall and fair that she seemed like a swan among ordinary birds. People said she had hatched from an egg, the daughter of Zeus and Leda. Poor Tyndareus, cuckolded by a god in the form of a swan. And there was something inhuman about her golden hair, her pale skin, her dark eyes, her shimmering clothes. She was hard to describe in her absence, as though the mortal gaze could not retain the memory of such perfection. It had long been a feature of life in the royal palace, that people would find excuses to be in the same room as her. Not just the men – although of course there were always men; they sniffed the air hungrily whenever she passed – but the women, too. Even the ones who loathed her – which was most of the Trojan mothers, wives and daughters – still could not bear to be away from her for long. They had to rest their eyes on her while they despised her.

'The Trojan whore: is that what they're calling you now?' Hecabe asked, her mouth twisting in disdain.

'I would think so,' Helen replied. 'They've never been a very imaginative group of people, my husband's soldiers. And Agamemnon's men are certainly no better. So let's say the answer to your question is yes.'

'I thought Menelaus would be clamouring for your return,' Hecabe said. 'It seems impossible that he could want to spend another night apart from you. After all these years.'

'I'm sure he will be able to wait until tomorrow. All he has ever wanted is to have Helen as his wife. He had her, he lost her, and now he has her again. My presence is scarcely required at all, so long as it cannot be said that I am with someone else.'

'You expect sympathy for having a boorish husband?' Hecabe snapped. 'You?'

'I, who destroy everything I touch, polluting and ruining with my very existence?' Helen said, eyebrows arched in annoyance. 'No, I expect no sympathy and nor do I want it. I was simply answering your question about Menelaus' indifference.'

'None of the Greeks seem to want you back,' Hecabe said.

'Why would they?' Helen replied. 'They blame me for the war just like you do.'

'Of course they blame you.' Andromache spoke so quietly that Cassandra could barely hear her over the sound of the waves. 'Everyone blames you, and Paris.'

'At least you don't make me the sole culprit,' Helen said. Hector had loathed Paris, but he and Andromache had always been kind to their unexpected sister-in-law. Andromache shook her head.

'I do,' Hecabe said. 'I blame you. Paris is a . . .' She paused. 'Was an immoral fool. But you were a married woman. You should have refused him.'

'Paris was a married man,' Helen said. 'Why does everyone always forget that?'

'He was married to a nymph,' Hecabe replied. 'She was hardly likely to besiege our city for his safe return.'

Helen looked around at the rocks and chose one, seaweed-strewn and jagged. She took a few steps and sat upon it. In that moment, it looked like a throne. The falling sun should have been in her eyes, but he did not dare.

'So why do you single me out for blame?' Helen asked. 'Paris came to me, remember? He came to Sparta, and to the palace of Menelaus, for one purpose only: to seduce me.'

'And your crime was to be seduced.'

'Yes,' Helen sighed. 'That was my crime. To give your handsome son everything he asked for, like everyone else did, because he was pretty and sweet and he enjoyed it so much.'

Hecabe was silenced by the truth. She had indulged Paris as a young man, because he was so easily pleased, his delicate face so ready to break into a smile. Her other sons had worked harder and been more dutiful, but she had loved Paris like a pet. No one could resist him, and so he was always spoiled. Had Priam even questioned him, when he announced that he needed a ship to sail to Greece? Had anyone asked him where he was going or why? Blood suffused her creased cheeks: she knew that no one had. They had recoiled when he arrived back in Troy with Helen, and his hazy smile – she would never forget it – had morphed into a petulant confusion. Paris was perplexed that his family did not rush to welcome him and his new wife home. He was less perplexed when the Greek fleet arrived in the bay, but still seemed to believe that the Trojans were withholding their approval from some malicious cause rather than a genuine horror at his behaviour and its consequences. Even as he watched his brothers, friends and neighbours fight and die in a war he had begun, he never offered an apology, never claimed responsibility. For Paris, the problem was not his behaviour but Menelaus' reaction which was, to him, entirely inexplicable. Everyone had always allowed him, encouraged him even, to take whatever he wanted. He had done that, and then suddenly there was a war.

'Why did Menelaus even accept Paris into his home?' Hecabe asked. 'What sort of man leaves another man alone with his wife?'

Helen rolled her eyes. 'A man like Menelaus,' she replied, 'who would never seduce another man's wife, so can't imagine that another person might behave differently. A man who would dutifully welcome a stranger into his home, but would soon tire of his perfumed hair, his effete clothes, his soft voice. A man who would not wish to offend the gods by asking the stranger to leave, but would be unable to face spending another day in his company. A man who would go on a hunting trip, begging his wife's pardon for burdening her with the tedious guest, promising to return in a few days when the coast is clear. A man who would not see the way his wife and her guest are looking at one another and realize that the hunt is taking place at home while he is away with his hounds.'

'But you could have refused Paris,' Hecabe said. 'To abandon your husband, your daughter . . .'

Helen shrugged. 'Which of us can refuse Aphrodite?' she asked. 'A god's power is far greater than mine. When she urged me to accompany him to Troy, I tried to resist. But she gave me no choice. She told me what I must do and then she withdrew, and in her absence, I heard a high-pitched noise, a distant scream. From the moment Paris entered our halls, it was constant. I thought I was going mad: no one else could hear it and it would not cease. I put wax in my ears but it did not block out the sound. Then when Paris kissed me and I took him to my bed, the shrieking grew fainter. When I stepped onto his boat, it disappeared altogether. That is what it means to refuse a god, it is to be driven mad.'

Hecabe gazed unblinking at Cassandra, who was scratching something into the sand with the end of a small stick, one sign on top of another, until the pattern was all churned up, illegible. 'Whatever you say.' She turned back to look at Helen. 'But if you had refused to accompany him, the noise might have disappeared of its own accord. Besides, if Menelaus was as unthinking as you imply, why did he marshal all these Greeks for your return?'

'Because my father Tyndareus had made them all swear,' Helen said. 'When the time came for me to marry, every man in Greece wanted to be my husband.'

'Of course they did,' Hecabe spat.

'I am only telling you what happened,' Helen said. 'Because you asked. Kings and princes travelled across Greece to ask my father for my hand in marriage. He soon realized that war might ensue, given that he would have to disappoint all but one of them. That's why he made them swear the oath that bound them all to defend whoever married me. If Aphrodite had given your son any other woman as his prize, the war would not have happened. Your grudge is with the goddess, it is not with me.'

Hecabe opened her mouth to respond, but Cassandra suddenly let out a curdling howl. 'Be quiet,' her mother hissed, raising her hand to slap her daughter across the face. Cassandra was blind to her, staring along the coast, where the light was already fading. Two Greek soldiers were walking back towards their camp, towards the women, carrying something heavy between them on a litter. Although Cassandra already knew that it was not something, but someone.

17

Aphrodite, Hera, Athene

The three goddesses would have said they had nothing in common, but each one had the same overwhelming dislike of any social occasion which did not revolve around her. And each had the same incapacity to conceal her disdain. So their collective ill-temper on the day of the wedding of Thetis and Peleus was assured before the sun embarked on his journey across the sky.

Of the three, it was perhaps Hera whose ill-temper was least appropriate. The goddess stood tall and stately, a small frown blighting her beautiful clear face, her huge brown eyes fixed somewhere above the hubbub which surrounded her. Thetis was a mere sea nymph, scarcely worthy of resentment from the queen of the Olympians. Not only that but Thetis had done that rarest of things, and rejected the overtures of Hera's husband, Zeus. Hera's usual reason for loathing someone – nymph, goddess or mortal – was Zeus' spree of infidelities. There were days when she thought he must have threatened or cajoled every person he had ever seen into his bed. And after a while, this had become annoying: demi-gods popping up all over the place, each one claiming Zeus as a father. It was the discourtesy, the vulgarity of it all which she minded most. And while she punished her husband as best she could, there were limits to the revenge which could be taken against the king of the gods. Zeus simply was more powerful than his wife, and there was little she could do about that. So she punished the girls, the mortal ones especially, tricking and torturing them whenever the opportunity arose. Even when Zeus had sworn to protect them, he rarely gave them his full attention for long, not least because his eye was caught by the next beautiful young creature. Hera's eye was not so easily distracted. But still, Thetis had done nothing to warrant her disapproval. When Zeus had shown his predictable enthusiasm for her, she had fled.

It was perhaps this rejection, more than the prophecy, which had persuaded Zeus to act. He had insisted on Thetis, against her will and beneath her status, marrying a mortal man. Hera could not even remember his name, some Greek king from whichever island they were currently on. It was impossible to keep track of every corner of the archipelago. If they didn't have a temple with a large, flattering statue of her inside it, Hera made no effort to remember them at all.

But the prophecy was the reason which was being murmured behind their hands: Zeus had been told, so the gods were saying, that Thetis' son would one day be greater than his father. It was what every man should wish for, and what every god should dread. In particular, the god who occupied the highest throne on Olympus after overthrowing his own father, Cronos, who had once overthrown his father, Ouranos. Fathering a son who would be marked with such a great and alarming destiny was not a risk that the all-powerful Zeus was willing to take. So it was decided that Thetis' son would be half-mortal, confining his greatness to be relative to that of a mere man. The risk was cauterized, and Thetis' unhappiness with the marital arrangements made no difference to anyone but herself.

Aphrodite, on the other hand, saw every wedding as a small defeat. She prized love, but not the marital kind. Never the marital kind. What kind of love was that: companionship? The precursor to children? It was all she could do not to snort. What was companionship, when you could feel all-consuming passion? Who would not exchange a husband for a lover who would thrill rather than comfort? Who would not prefer to have her child slink unnoticed from a room if it meant her lover could sneak in through another door? It was impossible to believe that anyone would choose marital love over the kind of single-minded desire which Aphrodite called her own. People always said they prized their spouses, their offspring (indeed Aphrodite had a son of her own, whom she liked perfectly well), but she knew the truth. In the small hours of the morning, when men and women whispered their secret prayers, they were to her. They begged not for health and long life, as they did during daylight hours. They begged for the blinding, deafening force of lust to be visited upon them, and they begged for reciprocation. Everything else – wealth, power, status – was just furniture placed around the thing they truly wanted, to obstruct or disguise it. And that had nothing to do with marriage. You could see it today, in that poor fool's face, as he gazed across at his bride-to-be, desperately trying to make eye contact and failing. He knew what it was to feel that desire. And he knew that marriage would do nothing to quench it. He would take Thetis to his bed but her disdain would corrupt any pleasure he might have felt with her. A nymph could love a mortal (Aphrodite ran through a brief mental list of nymphs who had done so: Merope, Callirhoe, Oenone . . .) but not Thetis, who showed nothing but contempt for this Greek.

For Athene, arriving late behind Aphrodite, weddings were always a source of irritation. The grey-eyed goddess was not as tall as Hera, but she usually wore a helmet tilted back on her head to give her the height she did not possess. Athene loathed standing close to Aphrodite, who made her feel like she was nothing but elbows and knees. Aphrodite's hair flowed into perfect locks which stroked her back, her peplos clung to her body as though it were wet. Athene looked down to see her own dress – hanging shapelessly from shoulder to ankle – and wondered how Aphrodite could look so different in what was essentially the same garment. Aphrodite always seemed strangely, desirably liquid: her eyes were the dark blue-green of the sea, her skin smelled faintly of salt. She curved beneath her dress like a dolphin or a seal, arcing through the surface of water. Athene wondered how it was possible to despise someone and desire them at the same time. She longed both to edge away from the goddess who caused her such discomfort, and to be enveloped by her. She gripped her spear more tightly, reminding everyone that her passion was for the cerebral and the martial. Men and women alike prayed to her for her skills and her wisdom. They did not pray to her with their yearnings for love or children or better health. They prayed to her for advice in their wars, for her strategy, for her deftness. So she carried her spear and wore her helmet, the better to convey that she had no interest in the things which enchanted most women. Like weddings. And she dismissed the thought of the Ithacan – a clever young man with a complex destiny ahead of him – who roused in her the feelings which other women spoke of when their menfolk were absent. Odysseus had eyes only for his new bride, his Penelope, at the moment. But Athene was clever in more than just matters of war, and she knew he would roam one day. All she had to do was make sure that she was in the appropriate place at the appropriate time. In, if required, the appropriate disguise.

The three goddesses had resigned themselves to a day of boredom and irritation: every Olympian was present for the wedding, they could not slip away. But as her fellow nymphs swarmed around Thetis, and Peleus looked at the thronging immortals wondering just how far out of his depth he was, each goddess quietly cursed the marriage. The distaste was largely mutual: for her part, Thetis would have preferred none of them be present. She would have preferred not to be marrying Peleus at all, but he had struck some bargain with Zeus, and the sea-nymph knew better than to issue a flat refusal in this situation. She would take advantage of Zeus' guilt (for surely the god must feel something like remorse, pairing her with this clod of a man) in the future, when she needed something. She would not forget.

But if she had to marry today, she could have done without the glowering face of Hera, who would look so much better if she would simply erase the perpetual expression of disapproval from her face. She could have been perfectly happy if Athene – accompanied everywhere by some squawking owl, as though she lived in some oversized nest – had chosen to absent herself. And no woman, immortal or not, wanted the sulking, pouting Aphrodite at her wedding. Every eye – even that of Thetis' groom – was drawn in her direction. Thetis had arrived in her most beautiful sea-green peplos, and her husband-to-be had scarcely noticed, so busy had he been gazing at the foam-born goddess. Thetis longed for the three of them to disappear into the sea, but her wishes held no weight today.

She turned her back on them all, determined to ignore them. She looked across the sandy shores of the low island of Aegina, where Zeus had decreed the wedding should be held. She saw all the gods and nymphs flocking together and felt a brief surge of anger that so many had come to witness her humiliation. She wished she could have her revenge upon them all.

But revenge, when it came, came from another quarter altogether, and it rolled out onto the ground, gleaming and golden.

*

Aphrodite did not notice, when it first touched her foot. She was used to people, animals and gods finding reasons to touch her, however spurious: even the trees would sometimes drop their branches to try and snag themselves in her hair. It was sometime later – when a cup-bearer hastened towards her to offer her ambrosia, before offering it to the bride, the groom, or any of the other gods – that she stepped forward to take the cup, and saw the bright sheen of metal, pushed by her sandal as it rolled away again.

Her mind was already on gold, because of Thetis' earrings. Even Aphrodite knew that it would be unfortunate behaviour to approach the groom at his own wedding and ask if she could have the earrings he was about to give to his bride. She had considered it, nonetheless. They were so lovely: a two-headed snake forming a perfect hoop around a pair of seated golden monkeys. Strings of dark carnelian beads surrounded the circle, each one finished with a tiny golden bird. How beautiful they would look, nestled beneath her own ears. They would be lost in Thetis' dark, seaweed locks. It was really absurd that they should belong to her and not to Aphrodite.

She was about to reach down and pick up the golden sphere, but Athene, always so sharp-eyed and grabby, snatched it first. Aphrodite had practically kicked it into her heel when she took the nectar cup.

'That's mine,' Aphrodite said.

Athene looked from left to right in mock-innocence. 'I don't think so,' she replied. 'It just rolled into my foot, so I think that makes it mine.'

'Give it to me,' said Aphrodite. Her mouth was set into a petulant line, but both goddesses knew that this was her starting point. In a moment, she could turn on the full force of her persuasion and Athene would have to hand over the ball, no matter how much she tried to resist.

No one could keep something from Aphrodite if she wanted it. No one except Hera.

'What are you two arguing about?' she hissed.

'Athene has stolen my toy,' Aphrodite said. 'And I demand its return.'

'It isn't hers,' said Athene. 'It's mine. Someone threw it at my feet.'

'No one did anything of the kind. I dropped it and it rolled down the sand to you. That doesn't make it yours.' Aphrodite turned to Hera. 'It doesn't make it hers,' she said.

'Let me see.' Hera reached for the ball and smirked as Athene's hand closed over it reflexively. 'I said to let me see it.' Hera grabbed Athene's fist with both hands, and prised the sphere from it. Athene tried to stop her, but as she was simultaneously trying to hold her spear, she could not.

'It's my ball,' she said again. The other gods were beginning to notice that something was going on. Never averse to a good fight, they began to gather around.

'It's not a ball,' Hera replied. 'Look.' She held up a perfect golden apple. It was almost spherical, but widened towards the top, beneath a tiny golden stalk. An indentation at the bottom allowed it to fit neatly between finger and thumb.

'It's still mine,' Athene said.

'Something's written on it,' said Hera, as she turned the apple in her hand. '*Te kalliste.*'

'I told you it was mine,' Aphrodite shrugged. 'Who else could it possibly mean?'

There was a momentary pause. 'Perhaps it's mine,' Hera said. 'Did either of you consider that?'

'Give it back,' said Athene. 'Papa!'

The gods looked around and eventually behind them to see the tall, bearded figure of Zeus, walking quickly out of earshot.

'We can all see you sneaking off,' Hera snapped. Zeus paused. A sigh shuddered through him. Somewhere thunder grumbled in a cloudless sky and men ran to his temples to placate him. He turned back to face his wife.

'Did you have a question for me?' he asked. 'Or were you sorting things out among yourselves?'

Golden-haired Apollo nudged his sister Artemis in the ribs. These goddesses were incapable of agreeing on anything and it provided them with endless enjoyment.

'This apple has the words "For the most beautiful" inscribed upon it,' Hera explained. 'There is some debate over whom it might belong to.'

'There really isn't,' said Aphrodite.

'There is,' Athene said.

'There is only one answer to the conundrum.' Hera spoke over them both. 'Someone must decide which of us should have it.' She looked out over the sea of gods before her.

Those who had pushed their way to the front of the crowd found themselves suddenly and bitterly regretful. They fixed their eyes on the ground, as though each grain of sand must be counted. 'And that should really be you, husband,' Hera continued.

Zeus looked at his wife, her expression one of irritated entitlement, and his daughter, a mask of plaintive injury. His other daughter was as perfect as always, but only a fool would think that she expected him to choose either of the other two. Or that she would forgive him if he did.

'It cannot be me,' he said. 'How could I choose between my wife and my daughters? No husband or father could do such a thing.'

'Then give me my ball,' said Aphrodite, her tiny shell-like teeth gritted.

'It's an apple,' Athene said. 'And it's mine.'

'How presumptuous you both are,' Hera said. 'I'm holding it.'

'Because you snatched it away from me!' Athene cried.

There was a shimmering and the goddesses felt the sands shift beneath them. Had Poseidon, the Earth-Shaker, joined the debate? The gods were no longer crowded around them. Rather, they saw they were surrounded by bright cloud, and then felt new, rockier ground beneath their feet. The cloud thinned, and they found themselves on a hillside, dark green pines all around and above them.

'Where are we?' asked Aphrodite.

'Mount Ida, I think,' replied Athene, as she looked around her and noticed the towers of a citadel across the plains beneath the mountain. 'Isn't that Troy?'

Hera shrugged. Who cared about Troy?

*

The young man appeared in front of them as though they had dreamed him into existence. Locks of black hair framed his forehead and his pointed cap sat slightly to one side, giving him a disreputable air.

'Who are you?' demanded Hera.

'Paris, son of Priam,' the man replied. His tone almost

hid the confusion he felt in an environment both familiar and alien. Moments earlier he had been tending his herd in the meadows which skirted the bottom of Mount Ida. Now, unaccountably, he was in a dark glade which he had never noticed before. And from the view, he was near the top of the mountain, except that the air was too warm for that to be true. And now three women – slightly too big, and glowing faintly golden, as though lit from within – were staring at him. He knew they must be goddesses.

'You are to be our judge,' said Aphrodite. She had no doubt that a mortal man would think her the most beautiful. And if he didn't, she would destroy him in a beat of his pitiful human heart.

'Judge? What am I to judge, madam?' said Paris.

'This apple says it is for the most beautiful,' Athene said, jabbing her finger at the apple in Hera's grasp. 'Give it to him,' she said. 'It's what Zeus has decided.'

Hera sighed and beckoned the boy towards her. 'Here,' she said, tossing the apple into his hands. 'You must decide to whom the apple rightfully belongs.'

'Me?' said Paris. For a moment, he had been wondering if his cattle were safe, unguarded on the slopes beneath him. But now if he'd heard the roar of mountain lions or the howl of wolves, he wouldn't have moved a muscle. He turned the apple round, admiring its gleaming warmth. No wonder they were arguing over such a lovely, solid trinket. He saw the letters engraved on its flesh: 'For the most beautiful'. He felt a brief spasm of sadness that the writer had used the feminine ending: '*kalliste*'. Had it read '*kallisto*', he would certainly have kept it for himself.

'Yes,' said Aphrodite, who recognized desire when she saw it. 'It is very pretty, isn't it?'

'As are you three ladies,' Paris said, with practised gallantry.

'We've heard it,' said Athene. 'Now choose.'

Paris looked from one face to the other in genuine perplexity. Aphrodite, of course, was utterly beautiful, as everyone had always told him. Her clothes seemed to strain over her breasts, clinging to her flesh in such a way that his eye was drawn down from her perfect face, no matter how much he wanted to gaze at it. He could imagine wrapping his hand in her honeyed hair, and feeling her body pressed against his own, her mouth opening beneath him, and then he could imagine nothing else. Of course he would give the apple to her. She was astonishing.

But then Hera cleared her throat, and the connection was broken. Not broken exactly, but temporarily dispelled. Hera was tall, he noticed, now she was standing between Aphrodite and Athene. Tall and elegant and somehow powerful, as though she might reach across to him and pick him up, before dashing him against a rock. The daintiness of her wrists and ankles made this seem an oddly alluring prospect. Perhaps he did not want to make her angry, he thought suddenly. And then stopped when he realized that he hadn't thought anything of the kind. The words had simply popped into his mind, as though he had heard them. Yet no one had spoken. He stared at her mouth as though the trick might reveal itself, but it did not.

And then on his left, there was the most surprising of the three. Troy had a statue of Athene in a temple on the citadel. Larger than life-size, it had a forbidding aspect, the clean, crisp face of a woman who would strangle you with her bare hands so you didn't bleed on her dress. But the goddess herself, now she was standing a few feet in front of him, was something else entirely. The forbidding expression was there alright, but the face which wore it looked so young that it shifted from something awe-inspiring to something charming. She was like the tomboy sister of a friend, who you grew up treating as just another boy, and then one day noticed she was turning into an intensely desirable woman who knew she was too good for you. In that moment, Paris thought he would give a great deal to become good enough for her.

Aphrodite stamped a small foot. 'She said you have to choose, and you do,' she said. The words seemed to slither across the ground between them and wrap themselves around him like snakes. 'Who does the apple belong to?'

'I don't know,' Paris said. 'You can criticize me for indecision, but the truth is, you are the three most beautiful creatures I have ever seen. There is so much distance between you and any mortal woman that I can barely perceive it. It is like asking an ant in his underground nest to tell you which mountain is tallest. I cannot.'

'You need more time,' Athene said. She was determined that he shouldn't see how delighted she was that the apple wasn't already in her sister's hot little hands. 'Can we help you with your decision?'

There was a brief pause.

'I can help,' said Aphrodite, and she wriggled until the brooches which held her dress in place at the shoulders worked themselves loose. The dress slid down to reveal her naked form and Paris looked as if he might choke on his own tongue.

'Oh really?' said Athene. 'We're doing this?' She reached up and unfastened the brooches on her own dress, standing tall and willowy, nude but for her helmet and her spear. Hera said nothing, but she too was suddenly naked.

'I can't . . .' Paris faltered.

'Can't talk?' Aphrodite asked.

'Can't breathe,' he replied. He grappled with the ties on his Phrygian cap, and worked them loose, casting it onto the dry ground. His hair was plastered to his head.

'Has this helped you to make your decision?' Hera asked him. He had not noticed before how deep and throaty her voice was.

'It honestly hasn't,' he said. 'Almost the reverse, actually.'

'Zeus brought you here to decide,' she said. 'You must choose.'

'I need a moment,' Paris replied. 'Is there a spring nearby? I could do with some water.'

'You can have something to drink when you've made your choice,' Hera said, so kindly that the threat was almost entirely concealed. She took a step towards him, and it took all his power not to step back. 'Let me make things easier for you.' If Paris had been able to focus on anything but her glowing face, a hand's width away from his own, he might have seen Athene and Aphrodite rolling their eyes in sisterly annoyance. 'The apple is for the goddess who is the most beautiful, as you see.' Paris had almost forgotten he was holding the apple, though now its weight seemed to pulse with an inner heat. 'But beauty in a goddess is different from beauty in a mortal woman. It's not just about appearance, it's about ability. I am, as you can see, very beautiful.'

Paris nodded weakly. He thought for a moment of saying something about how surprising it was that Zeus had ever strayed from Hera, given her extraordinary radiance, let alone that he did it over and over again. But something in her glittering eyes told him that this might not be received as the compliment it was intended to be.

'I am not only beautiful,' she continued. 'I am also extremely powerful. I am the wife and sister of Zeus, I dwell by his side at the top of Mount Olympus. My favour builds kingdoms, my disfavour crushes them. You must choose me.' Paris felt his hair shudder upright, as though he could feel her non-existent breath on the skin of his neck. 'Choose me, and I will give you dominion over any kingdom you desire. Any of them. Do you understand? You can have Troy, if you want it, or Sparta, Mycenae or Crete. Anywhere you like. The city will bow before you and call you king.'

She stepped back and Paris swallowed.

'Are we really going to . . . ?' Athene glared at Hera. 'Fine.' She stepped forward into the gap which Hera had left. Paris could feel sweat beading on his temples and in the small of his back. 'You don't need me to tell you that you should give the apple to me,' she said. Her grey-green eyes were so different from Hera's, Paris thought. Hera's eyes were so dark, so brown, that a man could lose himself in them, like a cave. But Athene gazed at him with a frank intelligence, which made him feel suddenly her equal, hubristic as he knew the thought to be. 'Hera offered you a city of your own,' she said. He did not speak, but she heard him just the same. 'A kingdom? She really does want that apple you're holding. You're probably wondering what I can offer which would rival that, aren't you?' Again he didn't reply, but she did not even pause. 'You're thinking that a kingdom might be more of a burden than a gift if an enemy decides to make it his own.' Paris had in fact been thinking about her naked breasts, which were practically touching his skin because she was standing so close to him, but he forbore to correct her. 'And you're right,' she said. 'A kingdom is nothing unless it is secure. And a king must be able to fight his enemies and win. That's what I can give you, Paris. I can give you wisdom, strategy, tactics. I can give you the power to defend what is yours from any man who would take it from you. What could matter more? Give the apple to me, and I will be your defender, your adviser, your warrior.'

'Is that your owl?' he asked, as the tawny bird flapped across the clearing and settled on a rotten tree trunk to his right.

'You cannot have my owl!' she said, and thought for a moment. 'I will get you another owl, if you want one.'

'Thank you,' he replied. 'It's a tempting offer.'

Athene nodded and stepped back beside Hera. The owl flew over to her, and perched on her outstretched arm. Athene stroked the feathers on the back of its head, and it pecked gently at her hand.

Even though he was watching her, could not help but stare at her, Paris did not see Aphrodite move. She was suddenly behind him, in front of him, all around him. Her hand stroked his arm, a glancing touch, and he felt like his legs might give way beneath him. He had never wanted something so much in his life as to simply fall to his knees before her and worship her. Her hair – like sun on sand – was wrapped around him, and he tasted salt on his lips.

'You know the apple is mine,' she said. 'Give it to me and I will give you the most beautiful woman in the world.'

'You?' he asked, his voice cracking on the word.

'Not me,' she replied. 'I would destroy you, Paris. You are mortal.' Paris wondered if destruction would be such a terrible way to die. 'I will give you the closest thing to me. Her name is Helen of Sparta.' He had a sudden image of a woman of extravagant beauty – flaming yellow hair, white skin, a swan-like neck – and then it was gone. Aphrodite shimmered away, like spume on the surface of the sea.

Paris looked down at the solid golden apple nestled between his fingers and thumb. He looked back up at the three goddesses who stood before him, and he knew it had only one rightful owner.

*

As the goddesses returned to Mount Olympus, Athene swore she would never speak to either of them again. Especially not Aphrodite, who radiated smugness as she cradled the apple in her spiteful little hand.

'You didn't tell him Helen already has a husband,' Hera murmured. She preferred to take her revenge at a leisurely pace, so refusing to speak to her tormentor would serve little purpose.

'It didn't seem important,' Aphrodite replied. 'Besides, how much can it matter? Paris already has a wife.'

18

Penelope

My dearest husband,

I was warned once that you were trouble. My mother used to say it was stitched into your very name, that you would never be separated from it. I hushed her, and told her that you were too clever for trouble to entangle you. You'd outsmart it, I said. And if that didn't work, you'd outrun it. I suppose I should have known that the trouble would find you at sea, where cleverness and speed offer little advantage.

A year since Troy fell, and still you are not home. A year. Can Troy be so much further now than it was when you sailed there ten years ago? Where have you been, Odysseus? The stories I hear are not encouraging. If I tell you what the bards have been singing about you, you'll laugh. At least, I hope you will.

They say you set sail from Troy and after a couple of piratical diversions, you found yourself marooned on an island of one-eyed sheep-tending giants. Cyclopes, they call them, these men each with one eye and many sheep. Have you ever heard of anything so ridiculous? They say you found yourself trapped within the cave-dwelling of a vicious Cyclops; he had every intention of killing and eating you. I think he planned to kill you first, anyway.

As the bards sing it, the spirits of your men – who were trapped with you – swiftly turned to despair. But, as always, you came up with a plan. I wonder if they change the story when they sing in other men's houses? Certainly, in the halls of Ithaca, you are always the quickest, the cleverest, the most inventive. They say you gave the Cyclops a full wineskin and bade him drink. If this is to be my last meal, you said, let me share my hospitality with you, just the same. You gave a skin full of undiluted wine to a giant who usually drinks sheep's milk. No wonder he got so drunk so fast. What's your name, traveller, he asked, his words slurring into one another. 'I'd like to know who I'll be eating.'

'They call me No One,' you replied, not wanting to let him have the glory of boasting about killing you. He was drunk, and perhaps also stupid, so it seemed to him to be a real name.

But anyone could have thought to give him strong drink. The brilliant brutality of your plan came after that. And the bards really enjoy this part, Odysseus: they sing this story over and over again. Because once the wine was flowing through the Cyclops like blood, your men wanted to kill him as he slept. They had not thought, as you had, that they would then be stuck in a cave with a dead giant. You needed the Cyclops awake and unhurt, so he could roll the boulder – which he used as a door – back from the opening of the cave. You and your men could not have done it, together or alone. They didn't believe you so you proved it to them. Three warriors, heaving against a rock with all their might, and it did not move a finger's width. No man could escape. Only then did they appreciate the complexity of the problem.

Did I say unhurt? Of course you did not want the Cyclops to be unhurt. But you needed him to be the right kind of hurt.

You saw he used a large stick to help him negotiate his way around the rocky terrain, as he was looking after his sheep. When he came into his cave at the end of each day, he rolled the boulder across the doorway so the sheep were penned inside, safe from wolves and other predators while he slept. But even a giant needed two hands to do that. So he would herd the sheep inside, then prop the stick next to the doorway, leaving his hands free to move the rock.

You took the stick and held it in the embers of the fire, turning it all the while. The men were moaning and complaining that their fate was so cruel, to survive ten years of war and then die on the way home, food for a giant. But you ignored them, turning the stick, which was as tall as you, while it blackened into a point. Even then, the men did not understand what you were planning, and you had to tell them twice to step back and hide among the giant's woolly herd. I knew, even before the bard sang this for the first time, what you were about to do. Your ruthlessness is one of the first things I loved about you, Odysseus. It still is.

You drove the sharpened stick into his eye socket, and twisted as it popped and fizzed. The way the bards sing it, his scream was enough to waken the war dead. You stepped back to join your men, nestled among the sheep, holding them firmly by their soft necks, so they could not run away. The Cyclops pulled the stake from his wet, black socket and screamed again, louder than before. He made such an awful sound that the other giants came running. They were solitary people, I'm told, living in their separate caves with their separate flocks. But none of them had ever heard such a noise before, and they could not ignore it. What's happening, they cried at the boulder's outside face. Moving it aside would be – for them – an intrusion too great. They stood in silence, listening. I'm hurt, screamed the Cyclops.

You or I would have asked the same question, Odysseus. How are you hurt? Or I might ask, how can I help? But the Cyclopes have a different custom and they asked the question which mattered most to them: who is hurting you? The injured Cyclops knew the answer, and he bellowed it out from the depths of his ravaged throat. No One has hurt me, he cried. No One has put out my eye.

The other giants looked from one to another and shrugged. They are not, as a race, given to curiosity. The tone of the Cyclops' voice seemed filled with pain, but all had heard the same thing. No one was hurting him.

Irritated at the disturbance, they slunk back to their caves and gave the troublemaker no more thought. But even though you had already achieved so much, and even though your false name had proved a far more successful stratagem than you had imagined it could, you were still thinking. That's my man.

The bards pause here for refreshments. They like to build the tension, of course, by leaving you trapped in the cave, a prisoner. They know they will earn themselves an extra goblet of wine for that. Only then do they continue: you knew when morning had come, because there was a hole in the roof of the Cyclops' cave, too small for a man to get through, and too high for a man to reach. But it let the sun in and the smoke out, and so you knew that it was dawn. So did the sheep, and they began to bleat in the thin grey light. The Cyclops knew he must allow the sheep out to graze, but he was determined that you should not escape him. So he rolled the boulder only halfway across, and sat beside it.

One of your men made a whimpering sound, lost amid the noise of the sheep. He still thought the giant would have the best of you, Odysseus. But you knew what to do. You lashed three of the sheep together, and showed your men how to hang on to the woolly bellies and hold tight. You aimed a kick at the sheep and they ran towards the door. As you began to attach the second man to another trio, the Cyclops dropped his giant hand and felt three fluffy backs and heads – no trace of a man – and sat back so they could leave. When it came to your turn – last to go as always – there was only one huge ram left. Luckily you are not a tall man. You clung to his underside and sneaked out past the Cyclops to your freedom.

You escaped unharmed, which is more than could be said for the monster which had detained you. But oh, Odysseus, trouble clung to you like fleece to those sheep. As you sailed away, you could not resist shouting back at the island, and telling the maimed giant that you, Odysseus, had bettered him. You could not help boasting of your victory. And if you had known that the blinded creature was the son of Poseidon, who would call down his father's curse upon you, I'm not sure you would have done anything differently. You never have been able to resist gloating.

The bards sing that Poseidon did curse you, Odysseus, and swore it would take you ten years to reach Ithaca once again. He swore that your men would be punished along with you, and that you would return home without them. Without any of your crew. Will they abandon you, Odysseus, or will they die trying to reach home? The two prospects are equally gloomy for those of us who wait for you all on Ithaca. I would never wish you to be anything other than what you are, husband. But I wish I'd been able to cover your mouth before you told the Cyclops your name.

Your loving wife,
Penelope

19

The Trojan Women

'What is it?' Andromache was the one who asked Cassandra what had provoked her howls. Her mother and sister had long since stopped expecting answers for Cassandra's sudden and extravagant fits of hysteria. One moment she might be sitting quietly, for all the world like a normal girl. And then the shuddering and the chewing of words would come from nowhere, and no sense could be made.

'It's him, it's him, it's him,' Cassandra screamed. Sensing that her mother was about to slap her across the back of the head, she tried to quieten her voice, but horror fought against decorum. 'My brother,' she said. 'My brother, my little brother, my youngest brother, the saved one is dead, he is dead, he is dead, he is dead.'

At these words, Hecabe stiffened. 'Be silent, or I will cut out your tongue myself. No one must know about your brother, about his escape. No one. Do you hear me? His life depends on you keeping your mouth shut.'

Cassandra shook her head, tiny movements like a tic. 'Too late, too late, too late to save him,' she said. 'Too late to save Polydorus from the Greeks. They already know who he is and that he is and where he is because he is already here and they have him.'

Polyxena reached a soft hand over to her mother's arm and squeezed it. 'She will wear herself out, Mother. You know she will. She'll be quiet before they are within earshot.'

She jerked her head at the Greek soldiers, carrying their heavy burden along the shoreline.

'Doesn't matter, doesn't matter.' Cassandra's voice was quietening to a whisper.

'Polydorus is not here,' Hecabe hissed at Polyxena. Her youngest son had been closest to Polyxena, of all his siblings, yet they had concealed his exit from Troy even from her until after he was gone. 'He is safe. We sent him away months ago to keep him safe.'

'I know, Mother. Do not concern yourself with Cassandra's words. You know they're nonsense. They always are.'

Andromache said nothing, but placed her hand between Cassandra's shoulder-blades and patted her gently. Coaxing Cassandra from her worst excesses was like consoling an anxious mule. 'Shh,' she said. 'Shh.'

Cassandra reverted to mouthing the words without sound. And by the time the Greeks arrived at the women's camp, such as it was, she was barely moving her mouth at all. Tears flowed freely down her face, mingling with the mucus which streamed from her nose.

The Greek soldiers exchanged some words with one another, and they put their litter down on the sand. It looked like a pile of rags, but the two men straightened up with obvious relief. The nearest man rubbed his knuckles into the small of his back while the other spoke to Hecabe.

'You're the wife of Priam?'

'The widow of Priam.'

'If you prefer, lady.' The soldier grinned. There was nothing more amusing to a conquering army than an uppity slave who fancied her former status would carry any weight in her new life. Especially when the slave was a self-satisfied old hag like this.

'Do you know who this is?' he said. He kicked the wrappings at his feet, but nothing moved. The cloths were too damp to unfurl. He swore and bent down again, catching the edge of a piece of fabric and throwing it aside.

No one would have recognized him from his face. It was bloated and blackened from the water, and the rocks. Part of his left cheek was torn away and there were purple welts around his neck. It was the embroidery on his tunic which forced a low, guttural cry from Hecabe's throat. She remembered seeing him wear it for the first time, catching his reflection in the polished edge of a goblet and laughing to see his face distorted in its curve. She remembered her slave woman making the tiny stitches along the neckline of the red cloth. And even though that tunic had lost some of its colour in the salt water – bleached to a fleshy shade that turned her stomach – she knew it.

Polyxena ran to her brother's side and threw herself upon him. 'No,' she cried. 'No, no, no.'

'So you know him,' the Greek soldier smirked, but his compatriot clicked his tongue in disapproval.

'Leave the body here,' said the older man. 'Leave them with their grief.'

'Odysseus said to bring anything we found to the camp,' the first man replied, losing some of his glee.

'We'll tell him what we found. Let her mourn her child, man. You would want the same for your own mother.'

Sullenly, the younger man nodded, and they headed off to the Greek camp.

'My brother,' said Polyxena. 'My beautiful brother.' She drew her nails across her face, leaving four bright furrows on each cheek. Andromache took Polyxena's place beside Hecabe, holding the old woman tightly, as the sobs wracked her brittle frame. She wanted to tear her hair, but she had not yet the strength to do so.

And somehow they all forgot that Cassandra had told them this was coming and they persuaded themselves that she had claimed something completely different. Something which had been proven false, as always.

20

Oenone

Oenone did not fit any more. She hadn't for some time. She knew where she used to belong, and that was in the mountains, running along beside the springs, resting under the shady trees, playing the pipes to rival the birds in their song. When her life had been that of an ordinary mountain nymph, she had known how to live. And then she met Paris, and everything changed.

At first, it changed for the better. But then, at first, she didn't know Paris was Paris. Expelled from Troy as a baby because a prophecy said he would bring about its downfall, he should not have lived past his first day. Neither of his parents had the heart to keep him, but neither had the stomach to kill him. Priam and Hecabe gave the baby to a herdsman to take out onto the mountainside. But the herdsman could not bring himself to do what was asked of him. It was one thing to place an infant on an abandoned patch of ground, another to raise his staff high into the air and bring it smashing down on the child's head. So he did not kill the baby, but secretly kept him and brought him up as a goatherd. What harm could a child do to a city? No one would ever find out the truth.

So when Oenone first saw Paris on the lower reaches of the mountain, a lightly muscled, delicate youth, surrounded by goats, she thought he was the son of a herdsman. But he was so handsome, so pretty even, that she followed him for days, unseen. Oenone could hide herself among the saplings if Paris ever glanced her way. And why would he? She moved across the earth more quietly than any of his scampering goats. He played the pipes too, holding them up to his chubby lips while he sat and watched the animals graze. By the time she presented herself to him, she was already half in love.

On their wedding day, he told her that the herdsman, Agelaus, had adopted him, and that he came from the palace of Troy. But, gifted in the twin arts of prophecy and medicine, she had known him to be the son of Priam and Hecabe from the first time they spoke. She felt a strange buzzing in her head when she thought about their future together, but she disregarded it. How could she not, when she was already expecting their son?

They lived in perfect happiness until the goddesses came demanding Paris' judgement. Oenone never revised this belief, although she knew others would find it hard to credit. Paris did not leave her, he was taken from her. That first time, at least, he was taken. He told her guilelessly what had happened that day: he had been grazing his flock in the foothills before finding himself shrouded in mist. And then he was in the middle of a high mountain glade, standing before three goddesses, each insisting that he choose her and award her some bauble over which they were squabbling. Oenone did not need to hear their names to guess who it had been.

She was not entirely clear on the criteria he had employed to make his decision, nor could she be sure how the argument was resolved. She knew only one thing: he returned home late, long after it was dark, because he had to clamber down the mountainside and retrieve his goats. He was uncharacteristically distracted and short-tempered that night. The next morning, he bade her farewell and said he must go to Troy and confront his parents. He had never mentioned meeting them before, never suggested he might harbour a desire for life within the city walls. Oenone knew there was no point in trying to stop him, and anyway, she thought he would return in a day or two, his questions answered.

Only once he had left did her thoughts become unmuddled. Paris would not return tomorrow, or the next day, she saw. He was heading to Troy to be acknowledged as its prince. And then – she rubbed at her temples thinking she must have this wrong – he would sail away to Greece. To Greece! What on earth for? For what reason could a happy man leave his wife and son to sail across open seas? He had no quest to fulfil, no god had set him a task to perform, she was quite sure of it. For all her gifts of prophecy, she could not see what Paris was up to. Her visions of the future were usually so detailed, but where Paris was concerned, there was now a clouding of her sight. She even asked her father, Cebren the river god, what might be happening, but he knew no more than she did.

So when Paris returned to Troy, she still expected him to return to the mountain. To return to her. It was from another nymph, all cruel smiles, that she learned the truth.

Paris, her husband, was living in the city with a new wife, a Greek. Oenone watched her boy, their boy, teeter across the baked earth and wondered how a man could care so little for his son. And how a man she knew so intimately could prove so false? Everything she had believed she knew had been lost in a small chaos.

Oenone knew that war would follow the woman. Even from the peaks of Mount Ida, she could sense the clash of metal and the stench of blood to come. So when the tall ships sailed into the bay, she was not surprised. She kept her boy safe in their mountain hideaway: what had seemed so romantic for her and Paris had become expedient, with Greek soldiers roaming the lower reaches of the mountains to pick off cattle and goats for their feasting. They never discovered her sanctuary, put off by the fast-flowing River Cebren nearby. Oenone had been abandoned by her husband, but her father still watched out for her.

*

After ten long years, Oenone had almost forgotten Paris, his sweet smile and low-lidded eyes. He seemed more like a dream than a man, and only her son – now a slender youth with hazel eyes and nut-brown skin – was proof that Paris had existed at all.

The war had raged across the Troad peninsula, first one way and then the next. Sometimes she and her boy would sit on tufts of grass and watch the chariots pour out of the Greek camp towards the Trojan defenders. They were too high up to see the faces of individual warriors, so she never knew for sure that Paris was still alive.

Except of course he was, because otherwise the Greek, Helen (it had been years before Oenone used her name, even inside her own mind) would have been returned to her husband and the war would be over. Only the obstinacy of Paris could draw out a conflict for so long.

But eventually, even a mountain nymph could see the war was lost, and won. The Trojan warriors had been so reduced in number. So too had the Greeks, but they had begun the war with many more men. When Hector fell, Oenone felt her heart wrench, as though he were her husband, her son. She had never met Paris' brother, never seen his face, but she still watched his final, lethal combat with the Greek champion, knowing it was him. Everyone spoke of Hector, bulwark of the Trojans. The Greeks respected him, the Trojans depended upon him. He was, in every way, the opposite of his younger brother. No one felt anything but disdain for a man who had endangered his city for his bed. It was one of the few things on which allies and enemies were united.

She watched a vainglorious figure preening on the battle-field – was it Achilles? She thought she had seen him die at Hector's hands a few days earlier, but now realized she must have been watching another man wearing Achilles' armour. This warrior was so fast, so slick, so cruel, it must be Achilles. She saw him cut Hector down, and then tie the corpse to the back of his chariot before parading it around the city walls, and knew she would never see such viciousness again. She tried to hide her tears from her son – to whom the whole war, battled on the plains so far beneath them, had the quality of a game – because she could not have explained to him that she was weeping for a man she did not know, because she somehow still knew he didn't deserve to die.

*

Her gifts of prophecy again proved defective when it came to her husband, and the first she knew of Paris' injury was when he staggered through the copse outside her hut and collapsed to the ground with a cry.

'Oenone,' he called. 'I beg you.'

Oenone's first response to the sound of her name was to assume she had imagined it. No one had called her by name in ten years. Her son called her 'Mama', when he was not lost on the mountains with his beloved herd. Cebren the river god called her 'Daughter'. The other nymphs used to call her by name, but she had forsaken their company years earlier, unable to bear the shame of having been shunned by her mortal husband. So she thought she must have put her name into the beak of a calling bird, as she had done many times after Paris left. But then again it came.

'Oenone, please. Please help me.'

This time, there was no mistake. She knew she had heard her name, and she knew whose voice had spoken it. She hurried towards the sound and saw something she had dreamed of a thousand times, first in fear and then in anger. When their love was new, she had loathed Paris to be away from her for long. She worried he would be gored by a mountain boar, or taken by wolves. Over and over again, she saw him lying before her, mortally wounded, and she knew it would take all her healing powers to keep him from the greedy maw of Hades. In the dark hours of the night, she told herself that this was the price to be paid for loving a mortal: the ever-present risk of death. Once he had left and she realized – too late for her dignity – that he was never coming back, she imagined the scene differently. Paris would crawl across the browned pine needles that carpeted her home, pleading for help. Her response varied: sometimes she would magnanimously allow him to beg her pardon and save his life; other times she would watch, unmoved, as his last breath caught in his perfidious throat.

Now the dream was in front of her. Paris' oiled hair still stuck to his forehead, bristling with sweat. His beautiful face was etched with lines of pain, and his colour – once the same lovely nut-brown as her son – was pallid and greyish. He had fallen forward, his head landing on his arms. His left leg sagged awkwardly, and she saw dark blood seeping through the cloth he had used to bind his wound. His breathing was ragged, and it took a powerful effort for him to summon up the strength to speak.

'Oenone, I am dying. Without you I will die.'

She looked at the man who lay at her feet, and wondered how she had ever loved him. He was so frail. So human. There was something displeasing about mortals, which gods never spoke about, because they all knew it to be true. They had a strange smell – faint, when they were young, ripening to a stench as they grew old – but always present. It was the odour of death. Even the healthy ones, the uninjured, even children had it, this invisible, indelible mark. And now Paris reeked of it.

'Please,' he said.

'How did you get here?' she asked.

'I walked until I could only crawl,' he said. 'And then I crawled.'

'My father let you across.'

'Yes. He said you might refuse to see me.'

She nodded.

'But I begged him and he slowed the waters so I could reach you.'

'You came in vain,' she said. She had not known this would be her reply until she heard the words. A spasm of pain crossed his face.

'You could heal me,' he said. 'If you chose.'

'And what if I do not choose?' she asked. 'What if I prefer not to staunch your bleeding and tend your wounds? What if I choose to keep my healing herbs for my son, for his goats, for someone who has not betrayed me? What then?'

'Oenone, don't say this. Don't be so angry. It has been more than ten years since I left . . .' His breath ran out and he coughed, then cried out from the fresh pain.

'More than ten years since you left me widowed,' she said. 'You abandoned me and our son, the son I bore you. You cared nothing for us. Now you crawl back to life, and I am a widow no longer? Did it occur to you once – once – on your journey up here to ask yourself if I might have grown accustomed to my widowhood? If I might first have learned to live with it, and then grown to prefer it? Did you think for a moment of what I might want, how I might feel?'

'No,' he said, and a mortal woman would have struggled to hear the sound. 'I am dying, Oenone. I thought only of that.'

'And that is why I will not heal you,' she said. 'You thought only of yourself. Even now, when you should be prostrate before me—'

'I am prostrate before you.' A faint smile ghosted across his cracked lips. That was the man she had loved.

'But not for me,' she said. 'For yourself. I cannot heal you, Paris. And you must leave the mountain, or you will pollute it with your death.'

She turned and walked away. And much later, as she went to welcome her boy back from the pastures, she saw there was now no trace of Paris, not even a drop of blood on the pine needles. And though she was sure that this time the conversation had been real, she nonetheless found herself thinking it must have been another of her dreams.

21

Calliope

You know, I like her. Oenone, I mean. I know the poet grows weary of these women who appear and disappear from his story, but even he is starting to grasp that the whole war can be explained this way. And would he really have overlooked Laodamia, as so many poets have before him? A woman who lost so much so young deserves something, even if it's just to have her story told. Doesn't she?

There are so many ways of telling a war: the entire conflict can be encapsulated in just one incident. One man's anger at the behaviour of another, say. A whole war – all ten years of it – might be distilled into that. But this is the women's war, just as much as it is the men's, and the poet will look upon their pain – the pain of the women who have always been relegated to the edges of the story, victims of men, survivors of men, slaves of men – and he will tell it, or he will tell nothing at all. They have waited long enough for their turn.

And for what reason? Too many men telling the stories of men to each other. Do they see themselves reflected in the glory of Achilles? Do their ageing bodies feel strong when they describe his youth? Is the fat belly of a feasted poet reminiscent of the hard muscles of Hector? The idea is absurd. And yet, there must be some reason why they tell and retell tales of men.

If he complains to me again, I will ask him this: is Oenone less of a hero than Menelaus? He loses his wife so he stirs up an army to bring her back to him, costing countless lives and creating countless widows, orphans and slaves. Oenone loses her husband and she raises their son. Which of those is the more heroic act?

22

The Trojan Women

Helen was first to see the men approaching from the Greek camp. Hecabe had spent the night grieving for her son. Polyxena, Andromache and all the Trojan women had joined her in her lamentations, although it was hard to say whether Cassandra had accompanied them or whether she had just been weeping of her own accord. Helen approached the women who despised her and told them the news.

'The Greeks are coming.'

Hecabe raised her ravaged face, thick purple lines showing the place where she had raked her fingernails across her skin. 'What do they want?' she wept. 'Are they planning to stop me from burying my son? Is that what comes next? Will they add one more impiety to so many others?'

'Perhaps,' Helen replied.

'Don't antagonize her,' Polyxena said. 'Please. Haven't you done enough?'

'I'm not trying to antagonize her,' Helen said. 'I'm doing her the courtesy of telling her the truth. Perhaps they have come to take Polydorus away. Perhaps they have come to take me away. Or you. Or any of us.'

'How can you be so guiltless when all of this is your fault?' Polyxena asked. 'How?'

'It isn't her fault,' said her mother, her voice ragged from the long night. 'It is mine.'

'Yours?' said Polyxena, and Andromache saw that she and Helen shared a brief expression of perplexity. 'How can it be your fault?'

'We were told when he was born that he would be Troy's downfall,' cried Hecabe. 'The prophecy was clear: we were to kill Paris or he would live to kill us all.'

There was silence. 'Why didn't you . . . ?' Polyxena could not finish. Even as they were inhaling the smoke from their ruined city, she could not say it. Why hadn't they killed the brother she did not even know she had until he walked into the city as a grown man and demanded his birthright?

'Why didn't we heed the advice of the gods?' Hecabe said. 'You are not yet married.'

At this Cassandra let out a low howl, but no one paid her any heed. Hecabe continued: 'You cannot know what it is like to look at your own newborn child and be told that he will be the downfall of your city. He was so . . .' She hesitated, unable to find a word which was not painfully bathetic. 'Small. He was so small, and his eyes were immense, and he was perfect. And we could not – I could not – suffocate him, as we had been told to do. He was too small. When you have your own child you will understand.'

'So what did you do with him?' Helen asked. She never spoke of Hermione, the girl she had left behind in Sparta. Helen could not even say for sure that her daughter was still alive. She did not mention it, because she knew she would be harangued by Hecabe or Polyxena for having the audacity to claim she missed a daughter she had willingly abandoned. But you could abandon someone and still miss them.

'We gave him to Agelaus, my husband's herdsman,' Hecabe said. 'We told him to expose the child outside the walls of Troy. On the mountain somewhere.'

'You sent Paris to die?' Polyxena asked.

'To save you all,' Hecabe replied. 'To save all our other children, even the ones not yet born. The terrible destiny belonged to Paris and Paris alone. If he died, the rest of you would live. The city would stand. Priam and I both agreed it was a price worth paying. We just couldn't bear to watch him die.' Polyxena stared at her. She had always known her mother could be ruthless, but this was something different, a strange combination of sentiment and brutality. As Hecabe spoke, Polyxena found herself struggling to see her mother's usual expression or hear her reassuring, irritable voice.

'But the herdsman ignored your husband's command,' Helen said. 'That is not your fault.'

Hecabe usually refused to look at Helen, depriving herself of the sight. But now she stared up into Helen's perfect eyes.

'It is,' she murmured. 'I knew the herdsman would betray us. I knew he was weak, I knew he would take the boy and keep him as his own. He was always soft-hearted. He couldn't even kill a wolf-cub if he found one away from its mother. Imagine that! A herdsman who can't kill a wolf. I knew he would be too feeble to kill a child. But I said nothing.'

'Did Priam also know the herdsman had this weakness?' Helen asked. Hecabe nodded. 'So, again, it is not your fault. Or at least not your fault alone,' Helen said. 'Priam made the same decision, and Paris was his son, Troy his kingdom. You were his partner in all things, but you were not his ruler. The larger share of the blame lies in Priam's hands.'

'In Priam's grave,' Hecabe said. 'But among the living, I carry the guilt. And now Paris has cost me my youngest, blameless son. One last grief to reproach me for my self-ishness and my folly.'

'Polydorus would not reproach you.' Andromache spoke quietly but still everyone turned to hear her. 'He was a kind boy, open-hearted and sometimes foolish, but not reproachful or cruel.'

Hecabe felt her eyes prickling, but she did not intend to cry again. 'He was a kind boy.' She nodded.

'He would not be angry with you, Mother,' Polyxena agreed. 'Let us seek the Greeks' permission to bury him.'

'And what if they refuse?' Hecabe asked. Her anguish was already shading into a quiet fury.

'We shall throw dust over him now,' Andromache said. 'He will enter the gates of Hades, and he will dwell on the island of the blessed. The formal burial will come later, or it will not. But by then he will already be where he belongs.'

The women carried out their duty in silence. They washed Polydorus clean of his blood and of the sand and weeds which clung to him, and they cast handfuls of dust over his body and murmured prayers to Hades, and Persephone, and also to Hermes, who would accompany him to the Underworld and show him the way. The Greek soldiers were almost upon them, but Polydorus was safely out of their reach.

23

Penelope

My dear husband,

Another year gone, and still you are no closer to home.
Or maybe you are. I heard a tale from one old man, some
wandering bard in search of his supper, that you had
earned the favour of Aeolus, god of the winds. And that
thanks to him, you had sailed to within sight of Ithaca,
our rocky outpost. Then your sailors did something foolish
– disregarded some simple instruction – and the winds
turned against you once again and blew you all the way
back to the island of the wind-god. Even Aeolus will not
aid the same weary traveller twice. He knows, as we all
do, that such misfortune must be the result of divine
disfavour. And who is he to argue with another god on
behalf of some mortal?

I've no doubt that you believe Poseidon is simply toying
with you for a while, forcing you to sail now this way,
now that. But what if he is not, Odysseus? What if this
is your punishment for the blinding of his son, the Cyclops?
To a god, a human life is nothing more than the blink of
an eye. He could keep you from home for one year or ten.
To him, they would feel no different.

I worry about you, of course. The story of Aeolus and the favouring winds he tried to offer you is a frustrating one. To think you might have been only a short distance away from me, and I didn't know it. I can almost taste the disappointment, sour on the back of my tongue. But compared with the other stories which have reached us here, it is a positively encouraging tale. If I believed even a tenth of what I had heard about your tortuous journey home, I would be certain that by now you were dead. Perhaps you are dead. I feel I may as well be scratching my message into the sand as the tide comes in, for all the certainty I have that you will one day know what I wanted to say to you.

I hope you have not lost every ship but your own, as the old bard claimed in his song. Be assured that I did not give him a comfortable bed to sleep in that night. He dined on hard bread and slept on hard stone. The next evening, he sang a sweet sequel to his tale, where you were safely beached on a shore somewhere. It was obvious that he had composed these new verses to appease me. It did not work.

I have already forgotten the name of your safe haven that he sang about on that second night. A strange word, but it will come to me. On the first night, he had you under attack by more giants. First the Cyclops, he sang, and then – after your audacious escape – the Laestrygonians. We had not heard of these giants before, but the poet assured us they were a gargantuan race of cannibals. I asked him how they differed from the Cyclopes, since Polyphemus (the name of the one you blinded, Odysseus, since you didn't trouble to ask) had also been determined to eat you and your men. The bard had no answer apart from some half-hearted half-line about the number of eyes they have. No wonder I find it hard to believe much of what these poets sing.

Because really, how many cannibalistic giants can one Greek plausibly meet as he sails the open seas? Even I, expert in your ability to create trouble, think one set is probably sufficient for your story. But then, if you did not meet with the Laestrygonians, if you are not deprived of most of your companions, if you have not lost every ship but your own, then what is the answer to the question that is on my lips from the moment I wake every morning: where are you?

The bards all sing of the bravery of heroes and the greatness of your deeds: it is one of the few elements of your story on which they all agree. But no one sings of the courage required by those of us who were left behind. It must be easy to forget how long you have been gone, as you bound from one misfortune to another. Always having to make impossible choices, always seizing opportunities and taking risks. That passes the time, I would imagine. Whereas sitting in our home without you, watching Telemachus grow from a baby into a child, and now a handsome youth, wondering if he will ever see his father again? That also takes a hero's disposition. Waiting is the cruellest thing I have ever endured. Like bereavement, but with no certainty. I'm sure if you knew the pain it has caused me, you would weep. You always were prone to sentiment.

Ah, the name of the safe haven has returned to me. Aeaea. I wonder where it is, or if it exists at all. The bard must have run out of man-eating giants to set upon you, so he created an even stranger story about what happened to you when you landed on Aeaea. After the Laestrygonians had hurled boulders at you, drowning most of your men, you and your crew sailed as far and fast as you could, then disembarked on the first island you saw. To have lost all those ships, Odysseus. All those men. I cling to the hope that the bard sings your story wrongly. Or how will you tell all those fathers and mothers, all those wives and sisters, that their menfolk survived Agamemnon's war, but not Odysseus' voyage home? How will I look them in the face, after visiting such horror upon them?

So if that is true, and so many of your companions are dead, I can well believe what the bard said happened next. That you instructed your men to wait by the ship while you went to explore the island. You would not have put the last of your comrades in danger after what you had all suffered. You would have undertaken the risk yourself. That is the man you are. So you set off with your spear (always so proud of your sharp eyes and keen aim) to try and find food. You explored the lush greenery, remarking to yourself that you had never seen such fertile soil so close to the ocean before. Almost as though the island were enchanted. And even as you said that last word, a shudder passed through you, and you hoped it was just the cool sea breeze. You had climbed the steep dunes from the water's edge and soon saw that you had moored your ship on the high side of the island, which turned out to be thick with tall pines. Ahead of you, you saw that the land rolled gently downwards. You had to look twice, to be sure, but you made certain of it: there was smoke rising somewhere ahead of you, among the trees. Your pulse quickened when you thought of those other two perilous islands where you had recently hoped to find succour. You did not want to take the risk of exploring the centre of this island yet, not if you could avoid it.

And – because you are my clever, wily and, above all, lucky husband – you could. Because at that very moment, a huge stag stepped out of the undergrowth ahead of you. You were barely into the woods, and here was your prize offering himself to you, with his high, reaching antlers and his proud neck. You had not seen it yet, but your sharp ears could hear it: you were right on top of the spring where he came in the heat of the day to drink.

I could see it as the bard sang. I could see every moment. You did not pause. You reached for your bronze-tipped spear, and let fly. Your blade pierced the beast's neck, and it sank to its knees by the water. You hurried down the rock-strewn ground, which cut away beneath you, and when you arrived to claim your prize, you saw your eyes had deceived you. The stag was far bigger than it had appeared from above. You could barely lift such a creature, but you would not abandon your kill. You wrenched your spear free and the beast gasped its last breath.

Then you hacked at the vines which grew along the ground, and used them to tie the stag's feet together. You could not carry it on one shoulder, but had to sling it across your neck so you could stand under its weight. You used your spear as a walking stick, to help you keep your balance as you staggered back to the curved prow of your ship.

You and your men feasted that night on roast venison

and sweet wine, and then you slept on the shore and imagined what you might find further inland. The next morning, you decided you needed more men to cover more ground. But you preferred a more cautious investigation than you had employed with the Cyclopes and the Laestrygonians. Your men were understandably wary after two such terrifying experiences, and they readily agreed to split up. The bard was quite specific: you took one team, your friend Eurylochus led the other. Twenty-two comrades each. You and Eurylochus set off in opposite directions, agreeing to meet back at the ship before sundown.

Your party had an uneventful day: though no deer presented themselves to you this time, you caught some rabbits, which pleased the men. You returned to your ship as the light was fading and the sun was riding his chariot past the distant ocean. There, you waited for the second team of men to come back, but they did not. Only Eurylochus eventually appeared. And the story he told was scarcely believable.

He wept as he told you his men had set their course for the centre of the island, where the trees thinned away. They approached a clearing and were startled to see high stone walls. Several men wanted to turn back. This building was more than tall enough to contain a giant or two. They argued quietly among themselves about staying or fleeing, before discovering that they were surrounded.

Mountain lions had emerged from the woods and as the men turned around, backing away, they found that a pack of wolves had crept up behind them. But although the men were afraid, they soon noticed that the animals were behaving oddly. The lions flicked their tails, as though begging to be scratched, and the wolves nuzzled at the men's hands, like loyal hounds. Your men did not know, of course, that these animals were not animals at all, but men. And they did not wag their tails in affection, but in desperation, because they had lost the power of speech.

Then the gates of the palace flew open, and there stood a nymph, whose beauty (as the bard sings it) was all-surpassing. Her hair was twisted into intricate plaits and she sang a low song that made your men ache for home. For Ithaca.

Of course they followed her inside, and of course they sat down at her table. It sounds foolish, doesn't it? They were so trusting, these men of war. But I know that they had endured ten long years of sleeping on the ground, eating charred meat from their fires. Then another year at sea, buffeted from one disaster to the next. So is it any wonder that when a beautiful woman bade them sit on carved wooden chairs, they were caught off-guard? The dignity was as tempting as the food. They wanted to feel like men again, having lived for so long like animals.

She gave them cheese and barley and honey, and they washed it down with wine. She had laced all of it with her drugs, of course, but they could not taste it, unaccustomed as they had grown to the delightful sweetness of honey. Only Eurylochus had held back, had waited outside the palace doors, watching through the crack between door and wall, suspicious but unable to say why. His men stuffed their mouths with as much as they could.

It takes a certain kind of cruelty, Odysseus, to look upon desperate men and see only swine. But that is what Circe saw, and that is what she did to your men. Eurylochus watched in horror as his companions finished eating, and seemed to shrink. He rubbed his eyes, hoping to see the men as they usually were. But he was not mistaken. First their arms shortened, and then their legs, and then they tipped forward onto all fours. Their faces were suddenly bristling with blonde hairs. Their teeth sprouted from either side of their jaws, and their noses turned up into snouts. Circe took her staff and smacked the nearest man into his companion. She drove them out into her pigsty, where they clustered together. The men had lost their human shape, but inside their piggish forms, they retained their minds and memories. They squealed in horror at what had become of them, imprisoned together with a trough of acorns as their only nourishment.

Eurylochus raced away from the palace, running through the woods without caution, desperate to reach you and tell of the dreadful things he had witnessed. When he found you, he begged you to leave your transformed comrades behind, to set sail with him and the men in your crew who still walked on two legs. But you decided to take matters into your own hands. You had lost too many men already to sacrifice twenty more.

You set off alone into the woods. So impetuous, Odysseus, which is not like you at all: you have always preferred to make meticulous plans. Perhaps you have changed, in the time we have been apart. Or perhaps you were, as the bard suggested, inspired by some god. As he tells it, you followed the route your comrades had taken, up the steep hill and down through the woodland towards the smoke you had seen the day before. A tall young man, handsome and proud of it, stepped out from behind a tree, and you shouted in alarm. He grabbed your arm.

'The thing the gods like about you, Odysseus – well, most of the gods – is how determined you are. Even when the odds are against you. What chance do you have – one man, alone – against an enchantress like Circe?'

'I must rescue my men,' you replied. 'Let me past.'

The young man held your arm a little tighter. 'Your pigs, the last I heard. But if you accept my help, you will set sail with them again as men.'

'Who are you?' you said. You have never liked surprises.

The young man laughed and said, 'I bring you a message from the gods. Does that not tell you the answer to your question?'

'You're Hermes.'

This moment rings truer than almost anything else the bards have sung, Odysseus. Who but you would assume that the gods had nothing better to do than assist you with whatever impossible scheme you had embroiled your-self in? And who but you would be right?

'At your service,' he laughed, and gave a little mock-ing bow. 'Now listen to me, Odysseus. Your life depends upon it.'

He gave you a small black-rooted white flower, and told you to eat. The plant, which he called moly, would protect you from Circe's concoctions and allow you to keep your human form. But that was only the beginning of his advice. After feeding you her poisoned food, Circe would try to strike you with her staff, and drive you into her pigsty, as she had done with your men. At that moment – and not before – Hermes told you to rush at her with sword drawn.

Then, he said, she would try to seduce you, but you should force her to swear a binding oath by every god that she would leave you unharmed and release your men from their swinish prisons. Only then, Hermes said, should you agree to share her bed. You nodded, and repeated the instructions, expecting him to congratulate you on your excellent memory. But he had already disappeared, as gods are wont to do.

You swallowed the flower and followed his advice: entered the palace, ate the food, rushed at the witch with your sword drawn, forced her to swear not to harm you, and to release your men.

And it is at this point, Odysseus, that I am not quite clear what happened next. Obviously you would not have spent, as the bards have it, a year in her halls, living as her husband, for the excellent reason that you are my husband, and such behaviour would be beneath you. A long, long way beneath you.

And yet here we are, another year passed, no sign of you and your men.

Your wife,

Penelope

24

The Trojan Women

The women watched the Greeks approaching, led by a stocky, thick-chested man, scarred and tired beneath his soft grey eyes.

'Madam,' he said to Hecabe, bowing with an ironic smile, so it was impossible to judge whether he was being courteous or not. 'You must be the queen of the late city of Troy.'

'Is that what you're calling it now?' Hecabe asked. She did not return the bow, but stayed standing in front of the body of her son, determined to hide her fatigue.

'Your city is dead, madam. You see its smoking remains.' He waved his right hand in the direction of Troy, as though he were revealing an honoured guest from behind a curtain.

'I see them.' She stared at him, but he did not stare back. Rather his eyes scanned the faces of all the women in front of him. There was nothing avaricious in his expression; it was not the face of a man picking out his slaves.

'Let us dispense with pleasantries,' he said. 'I am Odysseus, you are Hecabe.'

The women said nothing. This, then, was the man who had destroyed their city. Odysseus of the many wiles, plots, plans and schemes. This was the man who had thought to build the wooden horse. This was the man who had persuaded Sinon, his great friend, to wait behind as bait for the kind-hearted people of Troy, and trick them into thinking Odysseus wanted to make a human sacrifice of him. This was the man who had brought the war to such a sudden and disastrous end. What could they now say to him?

Not that Odysseus seemed to expect a response. He spoke quickly, the harsh Greek sounds softening on his lips.

'And this was one of your sons, yes?' He gestured at the body which lay next to his men's booted feet.

'My youngest,' Hecabe said. 'Polydorus.'

'You sent him away?' he asked. 'When you feared Troy would fall?'

'You would have done the same,' she snapped.

'I would.' He nodded. 'I would have sent my boy as far away as I could get him, if my home were besieged. Had I been in Priam's place, I would have sent all my children away. Let other men's sons fight a war I didn't start and couldn't win. His city was always going to be taken, it was only a question of how many of his subjects it took when it fell. And I only have one son, madam, and I haven't seen him in ten long years.'

'Then you have one son more than I,' Hecabe said. 'Polydorus was my youngest, the last surviving boy.' Cassandra was muttering about something but Hecabe continued without heed. 'And now even he is dead. How dare you compare your loss to mine? You miss your son? You could have sailed home whenever you chose. No one was keeping you here.'

'Ah, but they were. When a man makes a vow that he

will fight to bring back another's wife if she strays.' He tilted his head towards Helen, his eyebrows raised. She gazed at him in mute annoyance, before turning away to watch the tide as it retreated once again. Odysseus smiled and turned back to Hecabe. 'He must keep that vow, or the gods will punish him. I can't deny that there were times when I wondered if one woman could be worth so much trouble, so many lives.'

'I thought the same myself,' Hecabe said. 'Many times.'

Odysseus shook his head slowly. 'But now I look at her, perhaps I understand why men go to war over her, and fall silent when her name is spoken.'

'You have not fallen silent,' Hecabe remarked.

'Ah, but I was here for the treasure, madam, that your king kept in his citadel. That, and avoiding the ill will of the gods. Beautiful women I can take or leave.' He paused. 'Sometimes both.'

'Your wife must be a patient woman.'

'You have no idea,' he replied. 'Do you need my men to help you bury your son?'

There was silence. It was Polyxena who answered. 'We can manage it ourselves. But thank you.'

'You should bury him over there.' Odysseus pointed at a cave behind a pile of large rocks. 'The water doesn't reach that far. He'll be safe there.'

'Thank you.' Hecabe nodded at her captor as though he were her steward. 'We shall do that today.'

'I came to ask you a question,' Odysseus said. 'As well as to offer you my men's assistance.'

'What is that?'

'Do you have any other sons, madam?'

'I had many other sons,' she replied. 'But you Greeks have killed them all, one after another, like a pack of wolves.'

'We thought so, too,' Odysseus said. 'But then this one washed up on the shore, and we realized we had not.'

'You think I might have sent more sons away for safe-keeping.'

'Not so safe, perhaps.'

'I have only daughters now,' Hecabe said. 'All my boys are gone. Do you hear me? All of them.'

'You lost a war, madam.'

'You could have ransomed my sons. You chose to kill them.'

'With what could you have paid the ransom?' He laughed, his head tilting back towards the sky. 'All your treasure belongs to us now.'

'Is this an example of the great heroism of the Greeks?' Hecabe asked. 'Gloating over an old woman whose sons have all been slaughtered?'

'Is this the honesty of the Trojans?' he replied. 'The queen of a hostile city presenting herself as nothing more than a poor old woman?'

Hecabe stared at the space between his eyes, so she did not have to meet his gaze.

'Madam, you know why I must ask you this,' he added.

Andromache had been trying to place the emotion which touched his eyes as he spoke – her Greek was not good enough to follow all that was being said, so she concentrated on his mannerisms. It was not anger, not sorrow, not triumphalism, for all that Hecabe perceived it. Finally she placed it. Delight. This Greek warrior was enjoying his argument with her queen.

'Of course I know,' Hecabe said.

'If you have a living son, he may try to take his vengeance upon the Greeks, in years to come.'

'I said I know. You need not fear the blade of a ghost, Odysseus. As I told you, my sons are all dead.'

'What happened to this one? You called him Polydorus?'

'Priam and I were deceived. We sent him to an old friend, and that friend has revealed himself to be the most treacherous of men.'

'A traitor to his friends,' Odysseus said. 'Is there a worse thing for a man to be?'

'Our fear,' she continued, 'was that he would sell Polydorus to you Greeks. But he did not.'

Odysseus shook his head. 'Madam, I can promise you that. We probably would have bribed him to betray you, if we'd known. But I did not know you had another son until he washed up with the tide.'

'You had guessed there might be one.'

'I had.'

'Even before Polydorus was returned to us by the ocean?' He nodded. 'Because you would have done the same as Priam, though you would have chosen your friends more carefully.'

'He is the light of my heart, madam. Even though I have not seen that light for ten years, and he was scarcely more than a baby when I left Ithaca. Still, I did not know where you would have sent your son. So many of your allies . . .' His words tailed off.

'Have betrayed us already, yes. Or died, fighting your armies.'

'I didn't know who was left for you to trust.'

'Polymestor,' she said.

'The king of Thrace?' Odysseus could not quell the note of astonishment. 'You trusted your son to a Greek?'

'As you have already noted,' she said, 'our options were somewhat curtailed.'

'And he proved unworthy of your trust.'

'As you see.' She gestured at Polydorus, her hand letting slip a little of the dust they had used to sanctify him, which had caught under her fingernails.

'Did you send him with a lot of gold?' The smile played around Odysseus' eyes again, but Hecabe was still gazing at her son.

'With too much,' she said.

'It was an easy mistake,' he replied. 'If you had sent less, Polymestor might have refused to take him in at all. You cannot blame yourself.'

'Perhaps not. But there is no one else to blame.'

'How about the man who killed him?' Odysseus asked.

'Of course. But how can I be revenged upon him?' she asked. 'My city has fallen, as you have been quick to remind me. I am queen no more.'

'Let me think about it,' he said.

'I hear you're good at that,' she said.

'I am.'

25

Eris

Eris – goddess of strife – hated to be alone, but that was
how she spent most of her time: in the dark recesses of
her cave dwelling, halfway up Mount Olympus, home of
the gods. Even her brother, Ares, the god of war, preferred
to avoid her nowadays. She remembered how they had
once been inseparable: just children, squabbling over a
toy, pulling at each other's hair to settle the dispute. How
she missed him, now he was absent from Olympus. Where
had he disappeared to this time? She was always forgetful,
but she tried to think, although the black snakes she wore
twisted around each wrist were distracting. Thrace? Was
he sulking on Thrace? But why? She pushed the scaling
creature back down to her left wrist. Because of Aphrodite.
That was it.

Ares (she thought of him spitefully even as she missed
him) was always involved with someone or other, but the
affair with Aphrodite had been more consuming than
most. Eris couldn't remember who had told Aphrodite's
husband about it. Had it been Helios? Had he seen them
sneaking around together while Hephaestus was away?
The sun-god saw everything, after all, if it happened

during the hours when his light illuminated the world. But he couldn't be looking everywhere at once, could he? Or his horses would drive the chariot off course. So had someone mentioned it to Helios, encouraging him to point his gaze in the right direction? But who would that have been? Eris had the faintest recollection of the last time she had spoken to the sun-god, but although she sensed it was quite recent, she couldn't remember when it had been, or what they had discussed.

Still, someone had told Helios, and he had told Hephaestus that Ares and Aphrodite were carrying on together. But of course they were. How could Hephaestus, bent and lame as he was, ever have expected Aphrodite to be faithful to him? No one was shallower than Aphrodite, Eris remarked to herself: she had the depth of a puddle formed in a brief rain shower. She would never have been able to resist Ares, so tall, so handsome, so beautifully turned out in his smart, plumed helmet. What was Hephaestus to her? He would forgive her eventually, however she behaved. Everyone always did. As she thought about Aphrodite, Eris felt a familiar stabbing pain in her torso. She looked down, expecting to see one of the snakes removing its ill-tempered fangs from her flesh, but they were both twisting around her forearms where they belonged. She must have imagined the injury.

But on this occasion, Hephaestus had not been ready to forgive his wife straightaway. Not when he discovered she had been seducing Ares in their marital home, their marital bed. Told by Helios of the infidelity, he determined to catch her in the act. He went to his smithy and forged golden bonds so fine that they were like a spider's silk.

He hid them in the bedroom, tying them around the posts of the bed, beneath it, and even above it, though none of the gods could say how the little blacksmith had reached the ceiling to attach them there. Someone must have given him assistance, but who? Not Helios, who was busy with his chariot all day. Eris had a hazy memory of seeing the bedroom herself, but she couldn't imagine why she would have been there, or if Hephaestus had been present. Still, someone must have helped him, someone who could reach up high. She admired her own long arms as a snake curled behind her wrist.

She felt a sudden itch in her left shoulder-blade and reached round with a clawed nail to scratch the base of her wing. She pushed the nail between the shafts of her black feathers and sighed with relief. She flexed her shoulders and felt the wings flap out behind her as she tried to remember what had happened next. Ares and Aphrodite had been unable to resist one another, of course. Him so handsome, her so beautiful, no one was surprised. But still, when the shouts rose from Hephaestus' house – his of anger, hers of panic – all the gods clamoured to see what had happened. Ares looked perhaps a little less handsome, tied up in golden threads, unable to move. Every flail of his limbs bound him tighter to another god's bed. Meanwhile Aphrodite, quick to recognize her husband's handiwork, lay still: she knew there was no point struggling. Her perfect mouth was turned down into a furious pout, as the other gods crowded round, laughing at their folly and Hephaestus' neat little trap. But Hephaestus, his darkening face contorted with fury, did not laugh. Nor did the errant couple, even when Athene – so skilled at weaving that she could immediately pick out the quickest way to unravel the binding threads – released them both. Instead, Ares disappeared to no one knew where. And Aphrodite withdrew to Paphos, where her priests would salve her wounded pride. Laughter-loving Aphrodite, the bards called her. Proof if any were needed, Eris thought, that they had never met her.

If Eris had been another god, she might have enjoyed the moment of camaraderie which came from watching the downfall of two such stuck-up creatures. The gods might all have nudged one another, and toasted Hephaestus for his ingenuity, and praised Athene for her uncharacteristic mercy, and a delightful tableau might have unfolded in which Eris played a central role. But – for reasons which were never quite clear to her – this did not happen when she was present. Instead, Hephaestus began shouting at Athene for interfering. Artemis began cursing Aphrodite for her vulgarity, and Hera began shrieking at Zeus, because Helios was crossing the sky above, and that was all the reason she ever needed. Apollo snarled at Eris that it was all her fault, though she couldn't imagine why, and the peaceful moment splintered into collective ill-temper. Eris had withdrawn to her cave as she often did, since no one wanted her presence. But after a while spent sitting balefully in the dark (she was not good at measuring time), she had grown bored.

Eris watched a dark feather spiral dolefully from her wing to the ground, and decided she would go to find someone to talk to. Even Athene would be better than nothing. Well, almost better than nothing. Eris could not think who she would most like to see, because the truth was that all the gods irked her in some way or other. But still, she had wearied of her own company, and she would rather be irritated than alone. So she flapped her ungainly way up to the top of the mountain, to the grand palace which Zeus called home.

There was something wrong, but Eris could not immediately identify what it was. It took her a moment to realize it was the sound of birds singing, and only birds. No one was talking at all. She padded through the halls of the gods, but she could see no one and once she was well inside the building even the birdsong retreated and all she could hear was the sound of her own clawed feet scratching the marble floor. Where was everyone? She unfurled her wings and flew through doorways and across corridors, eventually perching up in the rafters. The halls were empty.

She felt a momentary stab of fear, wondering if something terrible had happened which she had somehow missed: another war against the giants, perhaps? But even when she was squatting in her cave (she preferred the calming dankness to the honeysuckle stench in the halls of Zeus and Hera), she would have heard the giants if they had come climbing up the mountain to fight. The one thing you could say about giants was that they were rarely subtle and never quiet. So the gods had all left Mount Olympus of their own accord. Together. Without her. She felt the snake on her left wrist coil itself around her hand and slither between her fingers. And then she remembered someone saying something about a wedding. Who had it been? Hera? Yes, that was it. Eris had been sitting out of everyone's way, in the rafters as she was now, in the bedroom of Hera and Zeus. Hera had called it spying, but that was because she was a vicious-minded shrew, as Zeus had just told her, and everyone knew it. Besides, Eris had hardly been spying, she had simply been resting her wings.

But when Hera saw the feathers floating down towards her, landing on the edge of her ornately carved couch, first she cursed the crows whose black plumage she thought was defiling her chamber, and then – when she realized her mistake – she cursed Eris. Rounded on her, in fact, and threw her out of the halls altogether. Eris had skulked back to her cave, swearing vengeance. But now she could not even find Hera. Because – the snake's darting tongue touched her third finger – because they had all gone to a wedding. That was it. Every single god had been invited to a wedding except Eris. Every one of them. Even Athene.

Eris felt a jolt of rage consume her. Whose wedding was it? Who dared overlook her, Eris, queen of strife and discord? Who had been so discourteous, so hurtful, so cruel as to not invite her to their wedding? She patted the snake's head idly and the name came to her. Thetis, that was who. The jumped-up little sea-nymph with her greenish hair and watery eyes was getting married, though you would have to be blind to think it was what the damp little thing wanted. How dare a sea-nymph – Eris grew taller with each moment of increasing wrath – a sea-nymph think to exclude her from a divine banquet? How dare—

Her thoughts broke off, as her head clattered into the ceiling. No, it was not Thetis who would have decided who to invite and who to refuse. Thetis didn't want to attend the wedding herself, she was hardly likely to be making lists of desirable attendees. No. Someone else had decided which gods should be present, and they had invited everyone but her. Eris felt a sudden prickling behind her eyes, though she could not identify the cause.

But if she did not know who had scorned her, she knew one thing at least. This was an affront. She had overlooked her eviction from Hera's bedroom. She had moved past the moment when the gods turned on her and each other as they mocked Ares and Aphrodite. But this, this was an insult too far. Eris was not stupid, she knew that chaos followed her black wings. But that was no excuse. And this time, she would have her revenge.

She stalked through the halls knocking over anything which looked precious or loved: perfume bottles and jars of oil smashed, dented shields bounced on the stone floor, a string of beads split and spread to every corner of the room. She did not know exactly where the gods were but she could see a glow coming from some island below Olympus and she was certain that all, or at least most of them, were there. Laughing at her, having their fun at her expense. What else would anyone do at a wedding?

She would fly down there and sow the discord that made her feared. She would stir god against god and man against man. By the end of this day—

Her thoughts were interrupted once again, just as she was about to take to the air. She fluttered back down to the ground, her eyes caught by the sight of it winking in the morning light. Bright and dull at the same time, warm and cool, hard and round. She grabbed at it. Was this for her, this golden ball? She turned it round in her claws. No, not a ball, an apple. Whoever had left it here obviously didn't want it, or they would not have abandoned it. And, looking closer, it had an inscription on it. 'The apple of Eris, most beautiful of the gods,' she imagined it might say. Perhaps this was the apology for her cruel mistreatment. It did not make up for the unkindness, but it was, she supposed, a start. It might have been nicer if someone had thought to bring it down to her cave, but no one ever visited her.

She couldn't quite read the words, which curled into one another, so she rubbed her feathers against the golden surface and angled it towards the light. No, it didn't say it was hers. But that didn't mean she couldn't have it. It was in her clawed hand now; she already had it. She looked again, tilting it, trying to read the squashed script. She traced the words with her finger: '*Te kalliste.*'

For the most beautiful?

Eris smiled. She would take the apple. But she would not keep it.

26

The Trojan Women

The women buried him under sand and rocks. At first, Hecabe wanted to refuse the burial spot Odysseus had pointed out to her because she resented the way he had known so confidently and immediately where Polydorus should lie. But she could not propose an alternative and in the end, the women lifted her lifeless son and carried him slowly up the shore. Cassandra took his head, since she seemed the least disturbed by his ruined face. The rest of them gathered round his limbs and trunk. So when Odysseus returned to their makeshift camp, as the sun was climbing to his highest point overhead, the task was completed.

'Two things,' he said to Hecabe. 'When the Ithacans set sail from here tomorrow, you will accompany me.'

'Why would I accompany you?' Hecabe asked.

'Because you lost the war.' He shrugged. 'I don't wish to keep reminding you, madam, but you make it difficult to avoid. You are slaves now.' He threw his arms out wide, encompassing them all. 'Our slaves. This group will be disbanded, divided among the Greeks before the end of today. And you, madam, you will come with me.'

Hecabe's face contorted into a sneer. 'You have drawn the shortest straw, then? An old woman is not what you must have wished for.'

Odysseus smiled. 'I had the first pick of you.' He paused. 'Well, not quite the first, but Agamemnon – who has precedence, of course – was unconcerned when I told him I would prefer to take you. He may change his mind when the distribution takes place later on, but I like my chances.'

She stared. 'You know Agamemnon will choose one of my daughters.'

'Yes. He is a proud man, and only a princess could appeal to that pride. Having the queen of fabled Troy in his retinue would be,' Odysseus scratched his bearded chin, 'appropriate for his status, but not for his tastes. Unless she was a very young queen.'

'You say proud, but you mean vain.'

Odysseus smiled again, and spoke quietly in the Trojan dialect. 'Not all these soldiers are mine, madam.'

She nodded, unsurprised to discover Troy's wiliest enemy had knowledge of its tongue. 'I understand. But for you, then, is an ageing widow appropriate to your status?'

'It is, madam. And I think it is appropriate to yours, too.'

'I have no status. As you have been so quick to remind me, I am a slave now.'

'Old habits,' he said. He turned to the rock which Helen sat upon, her long hair flowing down along her straight back. 'Menelaus asked me to bring you back to him, lady. Would you gather your belongings?'

Helen shrugged her magnificent shoulders. 'Anything I

own belongs to the Trojans, or it has remained in Sparta these past ten years,' she said. 'I have nothing but what I am wearing.'

'Really?' he asked. 'You wove no tapestries while you waited for your husband to bring you home? I thought you would have created something quite ornate in all these years.'

'My weaving was nothing compared to that of these women,' she said, turning her gaze from the sea to look him full in the face. She saw him take a shallow breath. 'I have other skills.'

'So I see.'

'You can't begin to imagine,' she said. She looked at the men who accompanied him. 'Menelaus has hardly sent the cream of his men to escort me back to the camp,' she murmured.

'Errant wives don't warrant a processional guard,' Odysseus said.

'And yet, when he sees me, he will fall prostrate before me.' She gave no sign of having heard Odysseus speak. She nodded. 'I'm ready, you may take me to my husband.'

'Thank you, highness.' Odysseus bowed low before her, but his smirk gave him away. She took slow, sinuous steps towards the Spartan guards who owed their lives and their allegiance to Menelaus, who had fought to the death for her, and who despised her even as they could not take their eyes from her. As she passed Odysseus she paused, reached over, and placed her fingertips on his beard: an act of supplication. But not in Helen's hands. She did not fall to her knees or bow her head. She simply stared into his grey-green eyes as he flushed a deep, dark red. 'You would give your life for me in a heartbeat,' she said. 'You cannot disguise it any more than other men can. So don't mock me, Odysseus. Or I may decide that you will regret it.'

Hecabe, her women, the Greek warriors, all saw the same thing: a daughter of Zeus turning her full and terrifying attention towards a mortal.

'I understand,' Odysseus said. His voice barely quavered, but the smile was gone. She gave the smallest of nods and let go of his jaw. She walked past him to the Spartans, who fell in behind her, like youths in a religious procession following the statue of Aphrodite as it was carried to its shrine.

Hecabe was tempted to gloat over his humiliation, but she did not. There was something about Helen – a simmering menace – which made even the queen of Troy think twice.

'He's welcome to her,' Odysseus said, once the Spartan party was out of earshot.

'What is he like?' Hecabe asked. 'Menelaus? Is he a match for her?'

Odysseus' eyebrows gave the answer his tongue could not.

'You will accompany me in the morning,' he said. 'I will give you the rest of today to spend with your daughters. Although the other Greeks may not be so considerate. Do you understand?'

'Why are you taking me? Tell the truth.'

'I thought you'd enjoy the voyage home.'

'Your home is not mine.'

'Our ships will sail north before they head west,' he said.

She tried to conceal the hope dancing in her eyes. 'Where will you put down first?'

'Thrace,' he replied. 'I've sent a messenger to tell the king – Polymestor, I heard he was called – that I would very much like to meet him on the Chersonese shore.'

27

Calliope

I know what the poet would like to be doing now. He'd
like to follow Helen back to the camp like a faithful dog.
He'd like to describe the scene where Menelaus falls at
her feet and thanks all the Olympian gods for her safe
return. He'd like to sing of her beauty and her grace, and
the way every man bows to her every whim. Well, he
cannot.

I have had enough of Helen. Enough of her beauty,
enough of her power, enough of her. I despise the way
they all melt at the merest mention of her. She is only a
woman. And no one's looks last forever, even daughters
of Zeus.

I shall teach him a lesson. Let him follow the future of
another woman, another queen. Let him see what Cassandra
sees: her mother's future. That will show him to be careful
what he prays for. Not every story leaves the teller
unharmed.

28

Hecabe

Cassandra saw the future as though it were the past. It was not for her as it was for the priests who read signs in the flight of birds or the entrails of beasts. From their murky pronouncements, you would believe the future was always swathed in cloud and fog, tiny strands of isolated brightness in the dark. But for Cassandra, it was as clear as a recent memory. And so when she heard Odysseus say he would take her mother to Thrace, she knew what was to come, because for her it had all the clarity of something she had already seen happen.

She felt a wave of revulsion rip through her and the familiar sour taste rising in her throat. She did not dare vomit, as Hecabe would punish her for the mess, her mouth curling in disgust as she slapped her daughter across the cheek. Cassandra felt a flicker of heat from the tiny white scars on her brow bone, from the time her mother had hit her while wearing her full ceremonial jewellery. That gold was gone now, of course, stowed in the strongboxes of the Greeks. Cassandra swallowed two, three times in rapid succession, took a deep breath and tried to focus on the faint taste of salt in the air. Salt had always quelled the worst of her sickness.

But how could salt take away the sound of those eyeballs popping, the sight of black jelly pouring down a weather-beaten face? Her breathing became uneven. She pushed the vision away, but every time she blinked, it was all she could see: ruined sockets and thick dark blood. She tried to come back to the present, turn away from the future and be where she was. Sometimes she could walk herself back, step by step from tomorrow to today, and the taking of each small step reduced her potent desire to scream.

But this time she found that she could not travel backwards, only forward to disaster, over and over again. She watched her mother leave her – was she, Cassandra, the last one to leave the shores of Troy? She wanted to look around and check: where was Andromache, where was her sister, Polyxena? But she could only watch what played out in front of her: the following morning. It must be the following morning, mustn't it? Because Odysseus had said to her mother that she would be leaving with him then. And her mother's expression, as the Greek hero held out his arm to help her onto his ship, was almost triumphant. She still carried herself like a queen, even if the queen wore a soot-stained chiton, torn in two places at the hem.

Hecabe was preparing herself for the meeting with Polymestor, Cassandra could see. She took some brief solace when she saw that her mother was not alone. Odysseus had taken a small group of Hecabe's serving-women along with her, so although she did not have her family, she had the women whose company she had often preferred.

Cassandra wondered if Odysseus had been forced to barter with his fellow Greeks to take a whole gaggle of women, or whether no one had cared where the old ones went. As she walked on Trojan ground for the last time, her mother made no effort to hold Cassandra, or kiss her goodbye. But Cassandra saw something in her eyes which was not familiar. The exasperation which usually marked Hecabe was gone. She did not kiss her daughter, it was true. But she did not kiss her because she feared the humiliation of breaking down in tears.

The scene dissolved and reformed as Odysseus' ship landed high on the sands of the Chersonese coast. Cassandra knew it was Thrace – a place she had never seen – as well as if she had grown up there. Her visions were never wrong, never lacking in detail, even if she could not always understand them. In the short time it took for Odysseus' men to disembark and put up a few small tents, two messengers dressed in ornamental garb appeared from somewhere further inland. They bowed before Odysseus, almost on their knees to ensure his favour for their king. Odysseus might be the guest in Thrace, but no one was under the illusion that his host – the king, Polymestor – was anything other than desperate for his approval. The messengers paid no heed to the old women, a little cluster of slaves. Why would they? Cassandra felt the sour pressure in her throat once more and she pressed her tongue against the roof of her mouth. Not now, not now, not now. She tried to focus on the sand beneath her mother's sandaled feet: full of round grey pebbles and bright white shells which she would have liked to pick up so she could run her thumbnail across their neat ridges.

She felt another rush of memory, like a blow to her stomach. But this was a true memory, even if it was not hers. It was not the future she could sense now, this was the past. Her mother was right near the spot where Polydorus' body had been rowed out of the bay, into the open sea, before being dumped overboard with a few hand-fuls of stones stuffed into his tunic to weigh him down. Hecabe's feet would stand in the footsteps of the men who had pushed the small boat out into the water. She would be so close to Polydorus but yet too late. Cassandra's visions were always too late, even when they should not have been. She had long since learned that no one heard the truth from her, that even if they listened, they did not hear.

The men who had committed this impiety against her poor brother, Cassandra saw, had not realized that he would tip in the water, the stones dropping from his clothes before he was an arm's length under the surface. He should have sunk to the seabed, been eaten by fish, watched in silence by the sea-nymphs. But they had not weighted him down properly. No wonder he had washed up a day later on the sands near Troy.

She saw that his face had been battered long before he met the rocks on the Trojan shoreline. Her beautiful brother had been beaten before he was killed by the treach-erous Greek king, who had thought no one would ever find out. Cassandra tried to cling to this – the unspeakable man's vicious motivation – as she watched Odysseus talking to his slaves, telling them to invite their king to come and visit his tall ships, and be made welcome by the conquering heroes of Troy. She watched the messengers scurry away, taking word to Polymestor. She saw her mother's lips disappear into a thin line. She saw it all.

Again the scene disappeared and this time it reappeared as Polymestor strode down the grass-tufted sand. He was dressed in all his finery: a heavily embroidered robe, gold chains around his throat, gold rings on his fat fingers. His thinning black hair was oiled in the Trojan style, and Cassandra saw a spasm of distaste pass over Odysseus' face before he accepted the man's two great hands in greeting. Cassandra could smell the suffocating sweetness of cinnamon and myrtle with which the man had scented his hair oil.

'Odysseus,' he said, smiling broadly. 'This is an honour.'

'Yes, so your slaves led me to believe,' Odysseus replied. 'You have been anxious for news from Troy, it seems.'

'Of course, of course,' said Polymestor. 'We have sacrificed many heads of cattle in the hope of winning the gods' favour towards the Greeks.'

'Generous of you,' Odysseus said. 'You didn't want to join the war effort yourself?'

If Polymestor heard the faint edge in Odysseus' voice, he did not allow it to show. 'My Thracian kingdom is the bulwark of Greece,' he replied. 'I knew I must be sure to keep our dominance secure in case you needed our aid. I sent messengers to Agamemnon, my lord. He has always known we were ready to assist. He had only to send word.'

'Agamemnon never spoke to me of these messages,' Odysseus said.

'He is such a private man,' Polymestor agreed.

'That hasn't been my experience at all. But no doubt you know him better than I do.'

Cassandra saw Odysseus' men, going about their

business. Building a small camp they knew they would never use. No wonder they had found the Trojans so easy to trick, she thought. Duplicity was second nature to the Greeks, to these Ithacans. They went about it as naturally as cleaning weapons or fetching water.

'I know him only by his great reputation,' Polymestor said. 'I suppose there is a temptation to fill in the gaps in one's knowledge by imagining what sort of man behaves in such a way.'

'In what sort of way?' Odysseus asked.

'Refusing all offers of help so generously. Never wanting to impose on another man's good nature.'

'Ah, I thought you were being modest, but I see you have spoken nothing less than the truth.'

'I'm not sure I understand.' The black pupils of Polymestor's eyes were the only thing that conveyed his unease.

'You really don't know him,' Odysseus replied. He laughed, and clapped the Thracian king on the shoulder. And Polymestor broke out into a great bark of laughter himself, relieved to find he had not spoken amiss.

'I bring more than just my own men to your fine shores today,' Odysseus continued.

'Oh?'

'Yes, I have brought an old friend to see you. We could not resist the chance for you to be reacquainted.'

'Who can you mean?' Polymestor asked. He turned this way and that, trying to pick out the unexpected visitor from the motley mass of sailors.

'Ah, you will not find your friend out here on the shore,' Odysseus said. 'She awaits you in that tent.' He pointed to the grey cloth which had been stretched over a few poles to create a makeshift shelter.

'She?' Polymestor asked, his expression acquiring a lascivious tinge.

'Hecabe, queen of Troy,' Odysseus said. His eyes were fixed firmly on the Greek king, who looked only slightly disconcerted.

'It was not a crime to have friends in my own region.' Polymestor's tone was quiet and measured.

'Of course not. Hecabe said you had been a friend to her husband long before the war broke out.'

Relief suffused the Thracian king's face. 'That's true,' he said. 'It is just as she told you. We were trading partners and more, bound by ancient ties of guest-friendship.'

'As I hope you and I will be,' Odysseus said, patting him on the back once more. 'Before the sun sets on our ships today.'

Polymestor nodded in delight. 'We shall be, Odysseus. We shall be firm friends.'

'One more thing,' Odysseus said. 'Hecabe has confessed something to me, on the voyage from Troy.'

'What is that?'

'She sent away her young son to your safe-keeping.'

Cassandra watched as Polymestor wrestled against his nature, to talk when he was nervous.

'I . . .' He paused and looked out across the bay. Even for those bound by the vows of guest-friendship, harbouring a young man from an enemy city might be a step too close to treachery for the Greeks.

'Ah, I see I've made you uncomfortable,' Odysseus said. One more pat on the shoulder and the Thracian king would be nursing bruises. 'I understand that you gave the young man shelter. It was your obligation to Priam.'

'You do understand,' Polymestor said. 'I did not choose for the boy to be sent here, but once he arrived . . .'

'What could you do?' Odysseus asked.

'What could I do?' he echoed.

'You could give the boy every comfort and bring him up as your own,' Odysseus said.

'Yes,' Polymestor agreed. 'I did just as you say.'

'You have sons of your own?'

'I do. Two boys. Younger than Priam's son,' he said. 'They are just eight and ten years old. And already the older one stands so high.' He placed his hand at the height of his heart. 'The younger one is shorter by barely three fingers' width.'

'Ah, send one of your men to bring them here,' Odysseus said. 'I have left my own son at home. I would be happy to see your two fine boys.'

'Of course.' Polymestor beckoned one of his servants, and muttered instructions. The slave nodded and hurried away.

'You might bring Polydorus as well,' Odysseus called after him. The slave froze and turned, gazing wordlessly at his king.

'What?' Polymestor's smile no longer hid anything.

'That is his name, is it not? Polydorus? Ah, I can see from your confusion that I've made a mistake. What is Priam's boy called?'

The smell of fear was unmistakeable now.

'No, you are quite right, quite right,' Polymestor said. 'But I cannot send for him.'

'Why ever not? His mother is here. It is his last chance to see her before she sails off to Ithaca with me. Surely you would not deprive the boy of such a meeting?'

'I would not, of course I would not.' Polymestor thought quickly. 'But he is away, hunting in the mountains.'

'The mountains?'

'Yes, further inland. Several days' ride. He likes nothing more than a hunt.'

'So odd. First I misremember his name, and then I imagine he has no taste for riding a horse. I was sure Hecabe said—'

'No, no, quite right,' Polymestor replied. 'He did not have a taste for hunting when he arrived here. But he has grown to enjoy it greatly.'

'Ah, yes. Making up for the years spent penned behind the high walls of Troy, no doubt.'

'Exactly,' Polymestor said. Cassandra could see the sweat soaking through his thick embroidered robe. The sour stench battled with the sweet cinnamon perfume and Cassandra felt as though her throat was closing up.

'So his mother will not get her hoped-for reunion after all,' Odysseus said.

'I fear she will not.'

'But perhaps it will be worth it, to know he is living such a healthy outdoor life.'

'I hope so.'

Again the scene slid away. Cassandra blinked and saw the boys running behind the slave, running towards their father. The younger one pointed at the high mast of Odysseus' ship. He had never seen a vessel so tall and could not stop yammering to his brother, who adopted the expression of a man who has seen every type of ship before. They reached their father, and were suddenly shy in front of all the strangers.

'Papa, are these the heroes of Troy?' the older one asked. His expectations had not been met by this ragtag crew.

'They are,' Polymestor replied, lifting the boy up to his waist and then scooping up the other one in his right arm. 'What do you think Odysseus? Fine heroes of the future, yes?'

'You echo Hecabe's words about her own son. I shall keep old friends apart no longer.' He nodded to one of his sailors, who opened the flap of the tent and brought the women outside.

'My dear friend.' Polymestor turned to Hecabe, dropping his boys gently to the ground and opening his arms. 'I would not have recognized you.' He strode forward to greet her, his boys alongside him. All these unknown men on their shore had made them nervous, and they wished to be close to their father.

'I have grown old in the years since you were last in Troy,' Hecabe agreed.

'No, madam, I did not mean—'

'You did, and I have no vanity left. It died in the war, like my husband and my sons,' she said. 'If you could have seen me even a year ago, you would have known me straightaway. It is grief which has left its mark on me, not time.'

'Your losses have been great,' Polymestor said.

'They have been intolerable,' she replied.

'It must have seemed so.'

'It was so. It is so. I have long since been unable to bear the burdens which the gods have placed upon me,' she said. 'One loss after another. Just in the past year: Hector, then Priam, then Paris, then . . .'

'The gods have treated you most harshly,' he said. 'I will make offerings and beg them for mercy on your behalf.'

'Will you?'

'Of course. Madam, no one could see you and not wish to alleviate your suffering. Why, even Odysseus, a long-held enemy of your city and the house of Priam, has brought you here to receive comfort from your old friend.'

Hecabe shook her head slowly. Her maidservants gathered about her, clustering around Polymestor. 'How can you speak to me after what you have done?' she asked.

'Madam?'

'Don't lie to me, Polymestor. It is beneath me to listen to the words of a murderous, avaricious traitor like you. Did you not have gold enough? Was this territory too small for you? Was your palace too cheaply made? Your shrines too shabby?'

'I don't —'

'Priam sent you a vast sum to look after our boy. Don't try to deny it and don't try to trick me, you old fraud. I placed the gold in his pack myself. And if that was not enough for you,' she spat the words out, saliva landing on his embroidery, 'I would have given you the same sum again to keep my boy safe. You had only to send word that he was worth so little to you. His worth was beyond gold to me. The Greeks have all the treasure of Troy now anyway. What difference would it have made to me if the gold had come to a Thracian instead of a Spartan, an Argive, an Ithacan?'

'He is safe! What lies have you been told?' Polymestor cried.

But Hecabe had no desire to talk further. There was a glint of metal, reflecting the rays of the sun, though he must have closed his eyes to spare himself the sight of it. In a flash, Hecabe had dragged her small, sharp blade across the neck of Polymestor's older boy. The blood spurted out indecently as two of her womenfolk did the same thing to the younger child.

'I buried him with my own hands, Polymestor,' she screamed. 'How dare you lie to me?'

'What have you . . .' The Thracian king roared in horror, but there was more carnage to come. As his boys spilled their dark life blood out onto the sand, Hecabe and her women turned their short knives on him. They did not aim for his throat or his heart. As he tried to gather his sons in his arms, desperately willing life back into them, the women instead plunged their blades into his eyes. His cries of horror mingled with howls of pain, and the blood pouring from his blackened sockets pooled with the blood of his children. His slaves did not attempt to help him, seeing themselves outnumbered by Odysseus' battle-hardened crew.

'You wiped out my line,' Hecabe whispered. 'Now I have wiped out yours. And I leave you alive to remember that had you not been a traitor, a murderer, a breaker of vows and deceiver of friends, your sons would still be delighting you into your old age. You would have seen them grow up as you grew old. Now you know that the last thing you will ever see was their death. I hope the gold was worth it.'

She stood back from the butchery and nodded to Odysseus. 'Thank you.'

Odysseus and his men began to load themselves back onto their ships, ignoring Polymestor – hunched over the bodies of his sons – nearby. The king's roars subsided into sobs and then into helpless mewling. Odysseus stared at him in contempt. Every one of his men had been elbow-deep in the blood of his comrades more than once in the past ten years of fighting. They had little sympathy for a traitor who took payment from the Trojans and would have brought up a boy from the royal household, who might have grown up determined to avenge his father, his brothers, his city. The Greeks could not afford to leave the Thracian king unpunished for his two-faced dealings. Polymestor had followed his instincts, which were to maximize profit wherever he saw the opportunity, irrespective of the cost to others. That could not be allowed to stand. His punishment would remind any other Greeks who thought to betray their word that such behaviour was not tolerated, at least not by Odysseus.

As the last of his men boarded, he called Hecabe and her women to accompany him. Polymestor, hearing the name of his enemy, let go of his dead sons and turned towards the sound of the waves.

'You will die before you ever reach Ithaca,' he shouted. 'You will drown in the seas and no one will mourn you and no one will mark your grave.'

Hecabe stopped beside the ruined king. 'I have been

dead since I buried Polydorus,' she said. 'It makes no difference where I fall.'

*

Cassandra took in jagged breaths, desperate to remain calm. She closed her eyes and then opened them again in the present, to see her mother, her sister, her sister-in-law, all sitting beside her on the rocks, just as they had been before she followed her mother to Thrace. But then the scene began to play out from the beginning once more. It was no less horrifying to see it again. More so, in fact, now she had seen so much of what was to come. But still, one detail was missing, right at the beginning when Hecabe first stepped onto Odysseus' ship. She, Cassandra, was standing there on the sands of Troy, watching her mother leave. She could sense that Andromache had already gone. She could see other women – cousins and neighbours – heading off with different warriors to disparate kingdoms. She had accounted for all of them. All except one. Where was Polyxena?

The answer came to her in a rush. And this time she could do nothing to prevent the sickness overwhelming her.

29

Penelope

My husband Odysseus,

I now know you are in the land of the dead. When the bard first sang of your voyage to the Underworld, I confess I wept. After so many years, I believed I had no more tears left to shed, but I was mistaken. I had made a simple error when I heard his song, of course: I had assumed that only the dead can enter the kingdom of Hades. It doesn't seem so outlandish to think that, does it? I mean, who else has ever courted the favour of the dread Persephone, without having died first? Orpheus, I suppose. But he had the strongest possible reason for his katabasis: he took on Cerberus, the three-headed hound, to try and earn the restoration of his beloved Eurydice, cut down by the sharp tooth of a serpent on their wedding night. An exceptional and heart-breaking circumstance, as I'm sure you would agree. And, try as I might, I cannot see why you would essay the same perilous journey to consult a dead seer. Would a live one not have sufficed?

They say that Circe, your witch friend, told you the consultation was necessary. I suppose I should be grateful that she only persuaded you to sail to the end of the world to do her bidding. Some women really will do anything to avoid returning a husband to his wife. But honestly, Odysseus, did you believe this journey was necessary? You were already so far from home (I am not entirely sure where Aeaea, Circe's island, is situated, but probably not as close to the edge of the earth as I would hope)? And then to sail to the river that circles the world in perpetual darkness? I think it is fair to consider this one of your more unusual choices.

But I am thinking like a stranger, like one of the bards who sings your story. You have not sailed to the place of perpetual night in spite of the danger, have you? You have done so because of it. I know you, Odysseus. There is little you would enjoy more than the chance to boast that you had taken your ship to the end of the world and back again. What a fantastic story, people would say. And you would demur, no, anyone would have done the same thing in your position. Except, somehow, no one else is ever in your position, are they?

The other Greeks have all returned, to warm (some less warm) homecomings. But you followed the advice of Circe, an enchantress you knew you could not trust, and found yourself in the darkest region, pouring sacrificial blood into a trench to lure the spirits up from Erebus. The shades of the dead dwell there, always hungering for blood. And you came along to feed them in the hopes of speaking to the dead seer, to Tiresias. But it was one of your men whose ghost appeared first. Elpenor, who died on Aeaea. He had drunk too much wine, climbed onto the roof of Circe's palace, and thence fallen to his death. It is not the pitiful stupidity of his death which moves the listener, when the bard sings this section (in case you were wondering). It is the triviality of it, of him, a fallen comrade whom none of you even noticed was gone. Imagine that: fighting beside the same band of Ithacans for ten years; sailing home alongside them. And not one of them misses you when you fall. I'm sure you were simply distracted, organizing the provisions for your difficult voyage ahead. But not to have even noticed a man's broken body on the ground? Let us hope you never have to muster another force, Odysseus. Your reputation may leave you short of volunteers.

Elpenor made you promise to go back to Aeaea and bury his body with due ceremony and – though I'm sure you were desperate to avoid returning to Circe's island – you, of course, agreed. Always so considerate. And what are a few more weeks at sea after all this time, you probably thought. You might as well take the scenic route.

You poured a little more blood into the ditch and waited for your prophet. But it was not him who appeared next. Ah, even as I am angry with you, my heart aches to think of you there alone, catching sight of the shade of Anticleia. What a way for a man to find out that his mother has died while he has been away. Still, you held your nerve and forbade her spirit to drink until the seer had given you the benefit of his wisdom. She bared her teeth at you, but she obeyed, and you waited.

And when Tiresias finally arrived, drawn by the stench of animal blood, what did he tell you? What I have already told you, with none of the inconvenience of a trip to hell and back. You have offended Poseidon by blinding his son. Your journey home is more difficult and more treacherous than that of any other Greek, because you have earned the enmity of a god. And what else did he tell you? Oh yes. That your homecoming would be painful. That you would be welcomed by a palace full of suitors who had been living in your home, determined to woo your wife.

That is a prophecy for me, too, then. Although I knew men would start gathering as news from Troy dried up. It is one thing to wait for a conquering hero to return, another to wait for a man lost at sea for – do you even know how long you have been gone? We are in the third year now since the war ended. But fear not, Odysseus, I will hold off these suitors who would marry your widow (as they consider me) for as long as I can, of course.

Then Tiresias fluttered away into the blackness, and your mother Anticleia finally approached you and drank the blood which feeds the dead, feeds what is left of their senses. Her horror when she recognized you must have been quite terrible to witness. For on her deathbed she had been hoping you would return before too many more moons. She died from a broken heart, Odysseus, waiting for her son to come home.

In that moment, I felt truly sorry for you, Odysseus. But when the bard sang this next part, it was all I could do not to have him thrown over Ithaca's rocky outcrops and left to drown in the darkening sea. First you asked your mother how she had died. Then you asked after the health of your father. Then your son. Then your honour. Then your throne. And then, when you had asked about everything else except the dog, you remembered to ask after your wife.

Once you had finished speaking to your mother, you stayed among the dead for a little while longer. When else would you get the opportunity to see so many great figures from the past? You saw Alcmena, Epicaste, Leda, Phaedra, Ariadne. Even dead women can't seem to leave you alone. But I could listen to no more by then, I am afraid, and retired to my bed. To our bed. Perhaps you remember it.

The dog is fine, by the way. Getting older, but aren't we all?

Penelope

30

The Trojan Women

The shadows of the Greeks were stretched long and thin. A man with greying sandy hair led three of his men towards the women. His mouth was set in a sullen line. He had not wanted this task, whatever it was.

'Which is the girl? The daughter of Priam?' he asked bluntly. Cassandra was mewling like the gulls swooping overhead to catch the last of the day's fish as they glittered in the late afternoon sun. She was still watching her mother's fate play out behind her eyelids, though she could tell no one what she saw. The man looked from one face to another: every one of them soot-stained, tear-stained, dishevelled. He had never seen such an unappealing selection in his life, and no quantity of renown – the queen of the horse-taming Trojans, for example – could make up for the lack of quality. What did it matter what status someone had held in a city which had fallen?

Hecabe spoke first. 'You don't look very happy, my lord, for a man who has his wife back.' The man's sparse brows drew together. 'You are Menelaus, are you not?' she asked.

He nodded. 'My wife faces a death sentence when we return to Sparta. Adultery is a crime in Greece.'

'It's a crime here, too,' Polyxena said. 'You'll remember, Paris fought you in single combat because he was the guilty party.'

Menelaus reddened as he remembered the unfortunate duel. He still could not understand how he hadn't won. The effeminate Trojan prince must have had the help of a god on that day. Or a goddess, more likely.

'You harboured the two of them for ten years,' he snarled. 'Ten years. And look what it has cost you, your immorality.' He gestured at the broken walls of Troy. 'This is no more than you deserve.'

'Thank you for your kind words,' Hecabe said. 'If it is any consolation, I would happily have sliced your wife's throat for you at any time. I have rarely wanted to do something more. But my husband the king was a kindly man, and your wife has – as you know – an appealing manner.'

Menelaus scratched his puffy, flattened nose. 'She has that.'

'You won't put her to death,' Hecabe said. 'She will have charmed you back into her bed before you return to Sparta. She will have done it by tomorrow.'

'You pride yourself on your wisdom, I see.'

'Some things don't require wisdom. Just eyes.'

'Perhaps I will let her live,' he said. 'Do you think the Greeks would thank me for it?'

Hecabe shrugged. 'Would you rather have the approval of your men outside your bright sunlit palace, or the approval of your wife, in the dark inner chambers?'

He ignored the question. 'I came for your daughter.'

'The Greeks have voted you a princess, from the royal house of Troy, in addition to the restoration of your wife? What loyalty.'

'The Greeks did no such thing,' he said. 'Your daughter – do you have more than one?'

'I had more,' Hecabe said. 'Now I have two.' She pointed at Cassandra, and reached a protective arm towards Polyxena.

Menelaus appraised them both. Polyxena turned her eyes modestly towards the ground. Cassandra looked straight at him, unseeing. 'Does she always make that noise?' he asked.

'She always makes some noise,' Hecabe said. 'People say she was cursed as a girl. Certainly, she was a delightful child. Sweet-natured, obliging, quiet. But she began this tiresome display a year or two ago, and now she only stops to sleep.'

'She's beautiful, in spite of . . .' Menelaus gestured at Cassandra's drool-stained chin. 'Someone will be happy to find ways of keeping her quiet.'

Hecabe said nothing.

'I'll take the other one, then,' he said. 'Come.' He jerked his hand and the men stepped forward, ready to take Polyxena.

'If she is not for you, then why have you come to collect her?' Hecabe asked. She would not demean herself by begging to be allowed a few more moments with her beloved girl. But she could not bear to see her go.

Menelaus shook his head. 'Drew the short straw,' he said. 'Come on, girl.'

Polyxena kissed her mother, and Andromache, and tried to embrace Cassandra. But her sister clutched at her arms and began to scream. The soldiers wrenched her free so they could march her away as their captive.

31

Polyxena

When she had murmured her prayers growing up, Polyxena had never wished for bravery. There would have been no point. Her city was under siege; she had only hazy childhood memories of it being any other way. So courage was not something special, to be wished for; it was something commonplace, required of everyone. She had always known fear for those she loved: her brothers as they strode out of the city gates in the mornings, her sisters, when the city's food supplies ran short. Her mother, as her shoulders began to hunch, like a crone. Her father, as he stood on the high walls, watching his sons fight off the men determined to take his city by force. Each dead man was a source of personal grief and civic fear: a husband, a son, a father lost and one fewer defender left to fight the next day.

But feeling fear was not the same as lacking courage. Anyone could be brave if he felt no fear. The Trojans murmured that this was true of Achilles, this was why he was so lethal. He rode into battle on his chariot, with no care whether he lived or died. None at all. He cared only for the safety of his friend, for Patroclus. If the Trojans

236

kept clear of him, Achilles would scythe through their ranks seemingly at random. It was many months, perhaps years, before the Trojans realized the better way to fight was to send a small group of men after Patroclus, which would draw Achilles to his side. The men died, of course, every time. They drew lots to decide who would take on this unwinnable fight to protect their comrades.

Polyxena had seen these men, as they bade their wives farewell, and cherished their last few moments with their sons. They had an air of calm about them, as everyone around them rushed to fasten their armour and make their weapons ready. They knew they would die and so the time for fear was past. All that was left was the chance to die courageously, to remove Achilles from the battlefield for long enough to allow their fellow warriors the opportunity to push forward elsewhere, to drive the Greeks back towards their ships. At the time, Polyxena had thought these men to be out of their minds with grief or sorrow. How else were they so unconcerned about dying? Now, she wished she had their certainty. She would have given a great deal to know the fate she was being taken to meet.

The Greeks spoke quickly in their own tongue and she did not understand the thick accent or the dialect. They were not as lascivious as she had been led to believe. One of them grabbed at her, under the guise of helping to steady her on the uneven ground. But Menelaus shouted something and the man removed his hands, his face reminiscent of a dog caught stealing milk from a jug.

Above all, she hoped that Menelaus had not lied to her mother and that he wasn't taking her for himself. No fate could be worse than being enslaved by him, leaving her homeland to become the handmaiden of Helen, the cause of all their grief. Well, perhaps not the whole cause. Polyxena knew her mother had always let Paris off too lightly. Her brother Hector had made no such mistake. He had been quick to censure Paris, and Polyxena had known he was right. But still, she did not wish it to be Helen who ordered her to fetch water or grind meal. Even if they made her a maidservant, she was sickened by the thought of plaiting the hair of her former sister-in-law, or helping her to dress each morning, or looking the other way when her secret lovers arrived (Polyxena had no doubt that Helen's character would be unchanged when she returned to Sparta).

She felt a sudden rush of anger flow through her, at Paris, at Priam, at Hector, at all of them. At all the men who should have protected her and who had instead left her. And her anger was tinged with the jealousy that they had died and she would be enslaved. Men would have vied with one another to win her in marriage, and now she would be impregnated by her owner, or another slave, and there would be nothing she could do to prevent it. Her offspring should have been royalty but would now be the lowest of the low: born into servitude. The shame of all this was hers alone to bear.

She knew that her mother, her sister, Andromache and the other Trojan women would share her fate, but none of them would be present to console her and nor would she be able to offer them words of comfort. The cruelty of it was typical of the Greeks. If the war had been reversed, and the Trojans had sailed across the ocean to besiege a Hellene city, her relatives would have behaved to the Greeks much as the Greeks had behaved in Troy. They, too, would have killed the men and enslaved the women and children. That was what it meant to win a war, after all. But, although those women and children would have suffered the loss of their freedom, they would have remained together. A consolation for one another. Whereas the Greeks stemmed from so many different cities and islands that they were separating every Trojan woman from the tatters of her surviving family. She called down a quiet curse and turned to Menelaus who trudged along in silence, dragging one leg a little in the shifting sand.

'To which of the Greeks are you taking me?' she asked. Her Greek was stilted, formal. Menelaus said nothing and for a moment she thought he had not heard her or that she had failed to make herself understood.

'I asked you where you were taking me,' she repeated.

'I do not owe answers to a slave,' he replied. She felt the colour in her cheeks but she kept her temper.

'I did not think you were too much of a coward to tell a powerless slave what her future holds,' she said. 'My brother Hector spoke well of you, he said you were a brave man.'

She did not smile when she saw him straighten his back and carry his head a little higher. As if Hector would have said anything of the kind. Everyone – Greek and Trojan – knew that Menelaus was a boor; a man who could not put down a wine jar until it was emptied of every last drop. Who drank his wine till too late every night with too little water, and who wondered aloud why his wife had left him while his companions hid the answer behind their hands. His brother Agamemnon was less pitiable but more petulant, so the Trojans had said. Neither of them was a good king by Trojan standards but the Greeks were less demanding, she supposed.

'I am no coward,' he replied. 'I drew the shortest straw and I have done my duty, as it was decreed by the council of Greeks when we gathered last night. I have collected you from your family and I will deliver you to Neoptolemus.'

Polyxena suppressed a shudder. The Trojans had feared Achilles as the great warrior he was: quicker and more lethal than a mountain lion. But his vicious nature was also like that of the lion. There was no grudge against the Trojans, or any of the other victims he cut down like so many stalks of wheat, at least not until Hector had killed Patroclus. They were simply his prey and he slaughtered them because that was what he was born to do. The same could not be said for his son.

Neoptolemus was feared by Trojan and Greek alike: unpredictable and sulky, burdened by the knowledge that he could never be as great a man as his father. It was Neoptolemus who had cut down Polyxena's father, Priam, as he clung to the altar in the temple of Zeus. What kind of man had so little fear of the king of the gods that he would violate his sanctuary? Her only certainty was that Neoptolemus would be cut down in turn for his blasphemous crimes. Thetis herself would not be able to save her grandson from the wrath of Zeus when it came.

'You are right to fear him,' Menelaus said, though she had not spoken. 'But Neoptolemus will not keep you for long. You are to be a gift for his father.'

'His father is dead,' she said. And then she understood what was to become of her.

She gave silent thanks to Artemis. She had said to herself many times that she would rather die than live as a slave. And her prayer would be granted. She added to it, hoping her mother would not find out that her youngest daughter – the last one in her right mind – would shortly share the same fate as her youngest son. One sacrificed for a Greek's lust for money; the other for a Greek's desire for blood.

Although perhaps she misjudged her mother. Hecabe was a proud woman who resented the yoke of slavery on her own account, quite aside from her children. Perhaps she would be happier knowing Polyxena was dead rather than enslaved, relieved if the shame could be contained to herself and would not cascade down through the generations of the children of Priam. And surely her mother would grieve less if she knew her daughter had gone willingly to her death. Polyxena kept walking ahead of the soldiers, beside Menelaus. They would not be able to call her a coward.

*

There were fewer soldiers present than she had anticipated. In her imagination she had built up a huge dais, a gaggle of priests in full ceremonial garb, a vast array of Greeks looking on, all willing the sacrifice to be completed quickly so they could eat and drink and prepare to set sail tomorrow. But when she arrived at the Myrmidon camp, it was a more threadbare gathering than she had expected. She saw a few small tents, patched up, salt-encrusted. Was this where Briseis had slept, she wondered. The woman who had held the whole Greek force back when Achilles had refused to fight until she was returned. Was she still here, now Achilles was dead? Had she been inherited by his son or gifted to one of his lieutenants? Polyxena was surprised by her own curiosity. It was odd to care about another's fate when her own was coming to such an abrupt finish. Yet she found she cared about this woman she had never met. She found herself staring from face to face, hoping to pick out the features of a woman who could alter the direction of a war. But none of the women she saw – camp-followers and slaves – had such a face. She felt unreasonably disappointed. And then she realized that had their places been reversed, she could not have stood by to see a girl sacrificed like a heifer. She, too, would have hidden herself away.

Menelaus shouted something she could not understand and a young man stepped out of his tent into the harsh afternoon light. He frowned at the glare and this added to his already peevish demeanour. Polyxena had heard that Achilles was beautiful: golden hair and long, golden limbs. But this man had a mess of auburn locks that sat girlishly around his soft face. His chin was weak and his blue eyes were too pale and too small. He might have been beautiful even so – his skin was like ivory – but for his cruel expression. His mouth was a petulant stub, and his brow already bore the traces of frequent disapproval. Polyxena saw immediately why he was so ruthless: even as he stood in front of his own tent surrounded by his own men, he gave the impression of a boy wearing his father's clothes. But this boy was the man who had slaughtered her father as he knelt in the shrine of Zeus.

'Is that her?' Neoptolemus asked.

'Who else?' Menelaus replied. His dislike of the boy was quite audible to Polyxena, but if Neoptolemus noticed it, he said nothing.

'I thought she would be more impressive. She is meant to be a gift to my father, who gave his life to fight in your war.'

'She is a princess of Troy,' Menelaus said. 'They're all covered in soot and salt: we burned their city and left them on the shore.'

'Wash yourself,' Neoptolemus said without looking at her. 'Take her and find her something to wear that isn't in rags.' Two mousy women stepped away from their soldiers and approached her slowly. She nodded to them – she would not scream or resist – and followed them into a nearby tent.

Polyxena waited while they heated water in a large open cauldron. She took a cloth from the smaller of the two women and tried to thank her. But wherever she had been captured they did not speak the same dialect as the Trojans. Polyxena could only nod and shake her head to be understood. She soaked the rag in warm water and drew it over her skin. She wiped away the greasy soot with relief. It took her longer than any bath she had ever taken. The women waited patiently, but still they both cast anxious eyes at the opening of the tent, waiting for a sudden explosion of rage from Neoptolemus. As the glances became more frequent, Polyxena hurried herself, rinsing the blackening cloth more quickly.

Eventually she stood clean and one of the women offered her a small bottle of oil. She took it gratefully and worked a thin layer into her skin. Then the taller woman opened a chest and unfolded a white dress, embroidered in red and gold. It was so incongruous that Polyxena almost laughed, like seeing a perfect flower amid a sea of mud. She reached her arms upwards, and the women helped her into the ceremonial gown. The last time she would ever put on a new garment, and she had women to help her, just like in Troy. She gave thanks once again to Artemis for saving her from the indignity of servitude. Better to die than live as these women, frightened by every gust of wind.

She gestured to the women to help her unbind her hair. Neither woman offered her a comb, so she pulled her fingers through it. It would flow across her shoulders and down her back. Her dark hair against the white dress would be striking. She had no jewellery to wear, but the embroidery would serve as decoration enough. She took the narrow leather thong which she had tied into her hair that last morning in Troy, and set it aside. She untied her sandals and placed them beside it. She had no further use for these last things which connected her to her old life. It was fitting that she leave them here.

She nodded to the women that she was ready and they scurried to open the flap of the tent. They stood back, holding the thick patched cloth to one side so it didn't touch her dress. She stepped into the bright light, but it brought no tears to her eyes. One soldier noticed her and murmured something to his comrade, who turned and spoke to another Myrmidon. As she watched, they formed a line. The one closest to her beckoned her and she took an uncertain step towards him. He nodded, making a reassuring clicking sound with his tongue, as though she were an animal. As she reached him, he stepped away from her, nodding all the while so she would follow him as he went. She could not look away from his dark eyes, and the sounds of the camp, the sight of the other soldiers gazing at her, even the sour smell of them, all seemed to recede from her. She focused on nothing but his ox-eyes.

Gradually, he came to a halt and held up his hand so that she would stop too. The men behind her had broken their ranks and formed a tight semicircle. But she did not notice, any more than she saw the rest of the Myrmidons complete the circle ahead of her. She saw nothing but the man's eyes and when he gave her one last gentle nod and stepped aside, she saw nothing but red hair and a glinting blade.

32

Themis

The judgement of Paris – as the gods had come to call it, because it placed all the blame so neatly on one mortal man for whom only Aphrodite had the slightest tolerance – had provided a rich vein of enjoyment. Old grudges could now be settled in a spectacular setting: a war at Troy. The gods picked their favourites among the warriors who were massing to fight on the Trojan plains. Some made their choices because of a particular relationship: Thetis supported her boy, Achilles; Aphrodite favoured her half-Trojan son, Aeneas. Athene had a long-held weakness for Odysseus: she always did like a man who was clever. Other gods had a more general animus or favour: Hera would never forgive Troy for spawning Paris; Apollo tended to favour the city, but sometimes changed sides depending on who had irritated him most recently.

They were relishing the prospect of a drawn-out conflict so much that it never occurred to any of them – even Athene – to ask where the golden apple which began everything had come from. It was obvious to all that Eris was responsible for producing it at Thetis' wedding – the goddess of strife could not help herself, any more than Ares could stop fighting or Apollo could miss his mark. But Eris was no craftswoman, she could not have made such a trinket herself. No one even thought to ask her how she had come by the apple, with its inner radiance and its beautiful inscription. It was certainly not man-made: everyone knew the Greeks could only scratch ugly, linear words onto their artefacts. The writing on the apple was fluid and sinuous, almost demanding to be traced over with reverent fingers.

The only god who could have made such an object was Hephaestus, and he swore he had done no such thing. He disputed it hotly when Aphrodite was gloating over her bauble and demanding to know why her husband (who had no beauty, save in what he could create in his forge) had not simply given it to her when he had finished making it. He was more troubled about the apple's origin than anyone: was there another god who could craft such wonders? And if there was such a god, what did that mean for Hephaestus, whose skill was his only claim to status among the Olympians? Without his ability to melt and hammer the most finely wrought bronze objects, which of the other gods would value him at all? Certainly not his wife, who had already shown her preference for the superior beauty of the thuggish bully, Ares. And where had the apple been made? It was inconceivable that it could have been produced anywhere but in his divine forge. So someone must have sneaked in when he was absent. His suspicion fell on several gods in turn, but he had no proof. And in fact, the guilty party was one he had never even considered.

The Olympian gods had a tendency to treat the previous generation as rather lofty and uninvolved. The early gods were so unspecific. At least with Aphrodite, or Ares, or even Zeus, a god knew what he was getting. They had particular areas of interest – love, war, perjury, or whatever – and they stuck with them. The gods did not always have much respect for one another, but if one had a matter to discuss, whether it was an extramarital affair or a martial engagement, a god would be in no doubt over whom to approach. But the early gods were not like that at all. What could a god find to talk about with the three Seasons, say? The weather?

So it was not surprising that Hephaestus gave no thought to Themis. Themis, the deity responsible for the divine order of things, attended the odd banquet or wedding but she never involved herself in petty squabbles with Hera, or the day-to-day annoyances of the other gods. This was all the more curious when one considered that Themis had been married to Zeus before his Olympian wife took on the frustrating role herself. But where Hera was all slights and jealousies, Themis was unconcerned. Perhaps they had no place in the divine order of things. And where did the older gods call home? Hephaestus could not even have said when he last set eyes upon Themis. He had only ever dwelt – feeling like an outsider, even so – on the heights of Olympus. Where else might a god live?

He would have been startled if he could have looked back to see Themis a few days before Thetis and Peleus were due to be married. She was sitting on a large, shallow tripod, as though it were an ornately carved chair. The tripod was placed in a temple, its three sturdy feet next to a slender column, which supported the finely decorated frieze that ran around the edge of the roof. The pattern was regular – alternating stripes of red and white – exactly as Themis liked things to be. And the tripod was perfectly symmetrical, its legs evenly spaced around the shallow bowl on which Themis liked to perch. Her long feet, with the slender toes which Zeus had so admired once upon a time (and would admire again now, if his eyes were not perpetually in thrall to the foot not-yet-seen), swung free, as she crossed and uncrossed her ankles. Even so, she had noticed Zeus noticing them when he approached her to ask for her advice. Advice, for the king of the gods himself! Themis would have been flattered, had she not considered flattery a disruptive emotion. She preferred to think of herself as unruffled. But she swung her feet a little higher, just the same.

Themis was pleased (not delighted, it would have been too much) with her new gown, which had a regular, repeating pattern of antelopes upon it. One row marched from right to left, and the row beneath marched in the opposite direction. Nothing unbalanced about that: each antelope's head dipped towards his front hooves, each set of antelope horns pointed neatly upright. Her black hair formed perfect, repeating circles from the midpoint of her brow down to each ear. And she smiled at the unchanging, bearded face of her once-husband.

'You need my help,' she said. Themis preferred statements to questions.

'There are too many mortals.' Zeus nodded. 'Far, far too many.'

'Gaia has told you she suffers,' Themis said. 'Their weight is too great for her to hold.'

'So she said. We must take many thousands of them.'

'Plague,' she suggested, but the king of the gods shook his head.

'Too inexact. Sometimes it just picks off the old, who would be dead soon anyway.'

'Flood,' she said.

'Too indiscriminate. It'll take out the livestock as well.'

'Always so mindful of your sacrifices,' she laughed. He licked his lips at the thought of calf fat sizzling in flames.

'Volcano.' She followed his thoughts towards fire.

'Too local.'

'Earthquake.'

'Too low a death toll.'

'Large earthquake.'

'Poseidon is too prone to partiality. You know how he is. He will obliterate Athene's or Apollo's favourites and keep his own intact. It will cause more trouble than it's worth.'

Their eyes met. 'War, then.'

He nodded. 'It must be a war. Does it matter where, do you think?'

She stretched her legs up until they were parallel with the floor, gazing at her own feet. 'I don't suppose so. It depends if you prefer the idea of civil war or . . .' She searched for the right term, and eventually shrugged when she couldn't find it. 'Or ordinary war.'

'Not a civil war, I don't think.' Zeus stroked his beard.

'East against west is a good one,' she said.

'Tried and tested,' he agreed.

'Troy would work.'

He nodded. 'How do we get the Greeks to invade Troy?'

'Isn't your daughter married to a Greek king?'

Zeus took on a hunted expression.

'Helen,' she clarified. She should have remembered that Zeus had only the haziest notion of the number of sons and daughters he had sired over the years, let alone what had become of them all.

'Oh, Helen.' The king of the gods allowed himself a moment of wistfulness. Helen's mother really had been the most beautiful woman. Worth becoming a swan for. 'Yes, she's married to some redheaded fool.'

'Send a Trojan prince to steal her away,' said Themis.

Zeus barked with glee. 'Good idea!' Then he frowned. 'For that we would need the help of Aphrodite.'

Themis did not let her irritation show. She barely acknowledged it to herself. But really, Zeus had been rather quicker than this once, she was sure. 'Bribe her,' she said. 'That always works.'

Zeus nodded again. 'Yes, a bribe. What does she like?'

'Baubles and trinkets and the desperate prayers of mortals,' Themis replied.

'Do you have anything which might do?' he asked. 'It's just, I don't get much time alone on Olympus . . .'

Themis thought for a moment. 'I know exactly what to give her,' she said. 'I found it the other day when I was looking for something else at the back of my temple. I think if she comes across it in the right way, you won't need to ask her for her help.'

Zeus was confused. 'Then how will she help me?'

'She will begin the conflict of her own accord,' Themis replied. 'She won't even realize she is doing your bidding.'

'So I won't owe her a favour?' This was better than he had hoped.

Themis shook her head. 'No,' she said. 'You'll owe me one.'

33

Penelope

Odysseus,

It seems almost superfluous to mention that my patience is stretched like the thinnest thread, held above a fluttering candle. It can only be a short time before the flame burns through and my anger snaps in two. Because now another full year has passed since you left the island of Aeaea (and the sorceress who had entertained you so lavishly) for your completely unnecessary trip to Hades. One more year after the twelve which have already passed since you first left Ithaca. It probably doesn't seem like much to you. What's one more year, I'm sure you would say. Look at the adventures I have to tell you about: that's worth a year of my time, surely. A year of your time, perhaps. But I grow no younger, Odysseus, and your palace grows no safer.

You left the Underworld, I hear, and sailed straight back to Circe – her loyal hound. Of course, all admired your sense of duty, sailing across a whole ocean to bury your late comrade, Elpenor. You remember him, Odysseus, the one who got drunk and fell from Circe's roof. The one you didn't notice was missing. The one none of you noticed was missing. That one. Still, he was obviously more important to you than your wife and – do you know, I was about to say 'infant son'? But Telemachus is an infant no longer. He hasn't been for quite a while.

I mention this, because it seems to me that somewhere along the way, you have lost the ability to measure time. Perhaps you have sailed so far that the days run backwards instead of forward? Perhaps you are in some god-inspired place where time does not pass at all. How else to explain, Odysseus, the impossible number of days you have been away?

To my enduring surprise, you left Circe's island again quite quickly. Well, I suppose you'd seen it all before, hadn't you? And why would you remain when you could instead sail past the Sirens? Always one for an adventure, of course. An adventure which brings you no closer to Ithaca. But you could never resist a challenge, and this one was special. No man has heard the song of the Sirens and lived to tell of it. So of course you had to. You obeyed Circe's instructions (good dog) and sliced a chunk of beeswax into small pieces. You kneaded each piece until it was soft and you gave them to your men with orders to stuff their ears tight. Their lives depended upon it.

But there was no beeswax for you, was there? Not for brave Odysseus, who had to seize the opportunity to become that man, the only man ever to hear the Sirens' song and survive. You had ordered your men to lash you to the ship's mast and bind you there. You warned them that you would struggle and beg to be freed, but that they must ignore you and keep rowing. And – good men that they are, or were – they did.

So you and you alone heard the Sirens raise their deadly

song. The version I hear (from a bard whose singing is also pretty deadly in my opinion) is that the Sirens begged you to sail closer to hear their song. Begged you, as a Greek of great renown.

They say the Sirens know the way to a man's heart, and that is how they wreck his ship so unerringly. Well, they certainly knew the way to yours. Did they sing of your beautiful homeland, your growing boy, your devoted wife? All these things would have broken any other man, any other hero. But when the Sirens saw it was you, they changed their tune: 'Come closer, Odysseus, a Greek of great renown.' You are wedded to fame, more than you were ever wedded to me. And certainly, your relationship with your own glory has been unceasing. Laodamia, who died for love of her Protesilaus (you probably don't remember him, Odysseus, but he was the first of the Greeks to die at Troy, all those years ago), could not have been more devoted to the object of her affections than you are to yours. In a way, it's really quite moving.

What do the Sirens look like, Odysseus? The way the song goes, they are the size of mortal women, but with bodies of birds: clawed talons, plumed wings and long feathery tails. But they have the heads of women. And their voices, could you describe them? The bard says they make the most beautiful sound anyone has ever heard – man or beast. He says to imagine the most perfect woman's voice, mingled with the sound of the nightingale. Ithaca is craggy and perhaps you know where the beautiful-voiced birds might nest, but I know only the squawking of seabirds, which is hardly the same. But still, it plays on my mind: what does the most beautiful song a man has ever heard sound like? Perhaps one day, if you ever come home, you will tell me.

After that cluster of cannibals you met on the start of your voyage, Odysseus – the blinded Cyclops, the Laestrygonians who ate your crew or smashed their ships with rocks – you now seem to have entered the sea-monster section of your journey. Who knew there could be so many kinds? First, you survived your brush with a musical death. And then you had to sail past Scylla and Charybdis. The former is a man-eating monster, the latter is a ship-eating whirlpool: have I got that right?

This route was Circe's idea, I believe. I find myself wondering if you might have annoyed her in some way. Hard to imagine how, of course. But she does seem to have advised you to take the most perilous journey any man could hope to sail. And though the continuing wrath of Poseidon is clearly your doing, the sea-monsters are a nice touch of hers. She would rather you drown, I think, than sail home to your wife and son.

Because otherwise she would have sent you a different way. You see, there are two routes, as the bard sings it, between Aeaea and Ithaca. Two routes, Odysseus, neither of which you have managed to traverse successfully. One takes you through the Wandering Rocks, a narrow passage between two steep cliffs, against which huge waves smash and break. Had you trusted your helmsman to hold his course and steer down the middle of these rocks, you might well have been home by now. They say Jason sailed safely through these straits with the help of Hera. Perhaps she might have extended her help to you, too.

But instead, Circe sent you through a different strait,

between a second set of terrible cliffs. Two vast peaks nestling beneath an angry sky. The tallest rock is so high that its crest is invisible, always covered in cloud. It is so smooth that no one could climb it: no footholds or handholds mark its gleaming stone. There is an opening in the rock, however, which Circe told you no mortal man can make out from the deck of his ship beneath (I can almost see your expression as she told you this. No other mortal man, maybe. But you are not like other men. Is this what swung your decision to try this route? The chance to reveal yourself, once again, as better than any other Greek? It seems all too likely). And in that dank cave dwells Scylla, a terrifying monster with twelve legs and six heads. Each head has three rows of teeth and each tooth is lethally sharp. No passing ship is safe from her, for each of her six heads will suddenly appear from her cave as a ship goes by. Each head will open its gaping maw. And each mouth will seize a sailor between its vicious jaws. And six men will be lost.

So the temptation must be to avoid this higher rock and sail closer to the lower of the two peaks, which lies opposite. You could shoot an arrow from one to the other, Odysseus, so narrow is the space between these two rocks. This second rock is not so steep, and on its peak grows a huge fig tree. Imagine that, a fig tree growing on a bare rock in the middle of the sea. How strange it must look. And beneath the fig tree, at the base of the rock, is Charybdis. And where Scylla eats men, Charybdis eats ships. A monstrous whirlpool that drinks down the ocean water three times a day, and then spits it back up. The water may survive this hideous journey, but your vessel – churned into splinters – would not.

I know you, Odysseus. There is no chance that you were told of these twin perils and did not try to concoct a plan which would allow you to pass between the whirlpool and the monster, unscathed. Could you not have steered clear of Charybdis, but approached Scylla with sword drawn, ready to chop off her voracious heads? Circe would have told you, I think, that Scylla does not have the frailty of a mortal neck, or six. Try to fight her, Circe would have said, and you simply give her enough time to swallow the men she has taken, and make a second attack. Your only choice was between losing six men or twelve. Losing no men was not an option.

So because of Circe, or perhaps in spite of her, you took the route past Scylla and Charybdis, the smooth, high rock on your right, the fig-tree on your left. You skirted Scylla's rock and lost six men. You looked back to hear them screaming your name, dangling from her multiple jaws like so many fish on hooks. You will have found this especially painful, I think, more so than the cannibals and the crews they drowned, more than the Cyclops and its vicious unseeing eye. You never have liked to see a man deprived of the chance to defend himself. It offends your sense of justice.

And at the same time, you heard the deafening roar of seawater foaming into the whirlpool of Charybdis, but even then you did not lose heart. Your ship was just far enough over to come through safely, although you had been close enough to see the black sand and bedrock, when she had swallowed all the water from above her.

Terrifying though this journey was, you made it through the straits to the safety of Thrinacia, a lovely, verdant island sacred to Helios. It scarcely needs saying – does it? – that Circe had given you one more instruction. If you chose to land at Thrinacia, you had to be sure not to harm any of the cattle there, because they belong to Hyperion, the father of Helios, and he takes a dim view of losing even one of them to a ragtag bunch of sailors. The safer course would have been to sail right past, but how could you tell your men – exhausted and frightened by the voyage through the straits and the loss of six of their remaining comrades – that they should sail past an island which contained nothing more lethal than cows and sheep?

Even the bard does not pretend that you didn't warn your men, Odysseus. He has line after line about how you repeated the warnings given to you twice over, once by Circe and once by Tiresias in the Underworld. But your men were no longer willing to obey your instructions on this matter. You had led them through so much danger, and they had lost so many friends. No wonder they over-ruled you and made for the shores of Thrinacia, just for one night. Just to allow themselves time to recover from their trauma and rest a while on dry land. Even then you did not let them go blindly to their deaths. You made them swear an oath that they would leave Hyperion's creatures alone. And they obeyed you gladly. What was one night without meat? They would soon be sailing home to Ithaca.

Sometimes it's hard not to think that you have offended more gods than you have impressed. Because what else could explain the cruel south wind, which blew for a whole month – a month without cease! – and kept you on Thrinacia for all that time. Greek sailors are so rarely lucky with the wind, almost as if the gods themselves want to keep you out of the water. Don't you think? And while the rations which Circe had given you were plentiful, they were not infinite. And after so many days without fresh supplies, your men grew hungry and restless. They waited – having learned this sort of trick from you, I imagine – until you were asleep. And then they killed the pick of Hyperion's cattle and sacrificed them to the gods, before eating the remaining meat. How could the gods take offence at that, they said. A sacrifice could not be an act of impiety, could it? Besides, they would build a temple to Hyperion when they returned to Ithaca, and he would forgive them a cow or two. The gods would rather have stone monuments than mere cattle. But the father of the sun needs no new temple. He can see every temple to every god, every single day. What he needed was for his herds to remain unharmed, as they had always been. He complained bitterly to Zeus, and to all the gods, and they agreed that an outrage had been committed. Once the winds changed and you set sail, the gods took their vengeance upon you. The one ship of your fleet which had remained intact through all your tribulations was the price for your men's hunger and their theft. You were driven all the way back to the rocks of Scylla and Charybdis. Your men – every last one but you, as the man sings it – were drowned. I hope the meat was worth it.

You survived death because you leapt from your splintering ship and clung on to the fig tree above Charybdis. You hung there until she spewed her water back up, and then you let go. You landed in the water, and were washed ashore days later on Ogygia. This seems so extravagantly unlikely that I almost believe it.

The first time I heard the bard reach this part of the story, I thought he would sing that you built a new ship and began to sail home. This should be where the story ends, shouldn't it? But that is not what he sang next. I demanded to know why. Do you not know where Ogygia is, he asked, his blind eyes moistening. I did not know. Why would any Ithacan have heard of such a place? It took you nine days to drift there, if the poet tells it rightly.

So after all the danger you endured, after all the risks you took, I have it on good authority from the poet that you have never been further away from me than you are at this moment. That's right, Odysseus: you are further from home now than you were when you were at Troy, or on Aeaea. You are further than you were when you were trapped inside the cave of Polyphemus and you are further than when the Laestrygonians pelted you with rocks and smashed your ships. You are further from home than when you were clinging to a fig tree for the thinnest chance of life. You are further from me now than when you were in the land of the dead.

Your wife/widow,
Penelope

34

The Trojan Women

None of the women had been able to settle since Polyxena had been led away. They knew they would all be taken, picked off one by one. But once Polyxena had gone, it was hard to think about anything but who would be removed next. None of them guessed correctly except Cassandra, who knew. Because when the herald finally came, he did not come for a woman.

The women would have recognized him even if he hadn't been carrying his staff with its twin ovals at the top, the lower one quartered by a cross. His robe was gathered at the neck with a large gold brooch, and his black boots were decorated with fine rows of metal studs. He winced as he put his weight on the left foot, as though a sharp stone had worked its way through the bands of leather and wedged itself beneath his heel.

Every truce, every shift in the ten-year war, had been heralded by Talthybius. The Trojans had seen him many times walking across the plains outside their city to consult with their own heralds, or with Hector. He carried himself across the sand with the pomposity of a man who has been sacrosanct for years: no one was permitted to harm a herald. And yet he moved slowly. It was not just Cassandra who could see he was reluctant to perform the task he had been allotted.

When he finally reached the women, Hecabe stared at him. Sweat poured down his face beneath his ornate cap, its brim pushed back so his black hair sprouted out from beneath it.

'You should remove your thick cloak,' she said. 'It is not as cold as all that.'

Talthybius nodded, acknowledging in his mind the warnings he had received from Menelaus and Odysseus about the sharp tongue of the Trojan queen.

'I have no time for your words, old woman,' he said. 'I am here for the son of Hector.'

The scream which rose up did not come from Cassandra. She had watched this happen so many times before that she felt almost dizzy with the repetition. But for Andromache, the widow of Hector, it was new. And so it was her voice which keened so piteously. It was all the more distressing for her family, because she was always so quiet. Softly spoken before the birth of her son, Astyanax, she had acquired a low, soothing tone when he was born. Her son – unused to hearing his mother in such distress – began to howl.

'No,' said Hecabe. 'You cannot mean this. He is a baby.' Her voice cracked in two, like a dropped pot.

'I have my orders,' Talthybius said. 'Give me the boy.'

Andromache wrapped her arms tighter around the bundled child she had kept safe through a war and a city on fire. His face was growing purple with the effort of screaming.

'Please,' she wept. 'Please.' She fell to her knees before the herald, but she did not let go of her son.

Talthybius' supercilious eyebrows dropped a little at the sight of this hopeless woman lying at his feet. He bent down on his haunches, resting his elbows on his bare brown knees. 'You know why the Greeks have decided this must be so,' he said. He reached out and touched her hair with his fingertips. His voice was quieter now, speaking to Andromache alone. 'Hector was an outstanding warrior, the great defender of Troy. His son would grow up to be a warrior too.'

'No.' Andromache shook her head. 'He will not. He will never carry a sword or spear, I swear it on my life. He will become a priest or a farmhand. He will not learn to fight. The future you fear will not come to pass.'

The herald continued as though she had not spoken. 'He will grow up to hear his father's name spoken with admiration, how brave he was, how audacious.'

'I will never mention his father.' Andromache's voice was rising into a scream. The child paused for breath before he too renewed his wailing. 'Never. The name of Hector has passed my lips for the final time if you will only spare my baby. Please. He will never know whose son he is. He will never remember Troy. We will never speak of it. I swear it on the shade of my dead mother.'

'But other people will mention him,' Talthybius replied. 'Hector cannot be excised from the story of the Trojan War. The bards sing his name already. Your name is mentioned in the same songs. You son will grow up wishing to avenge his father. He will have the murder of Greeks in his heart.'

'I will change my name,' she cried. 'I will leave

Andromache here in Troy and become someone else in Greece. Who cares what a slave is called?'

'Your master will care,' the herald said. 'Your name makes you a trophy. Another name would carry less weight.'

Andromache's eyes were darting around as she looked for some sort of escape.

'Then I will tell him that Hector deserved to die.' she said. 'I will tell him that the bards sing it wrong. I will bring him up to believe his father was a coward and he deserved the death he received at Achilles' hands.'

Hecabe opened her mouth to rebut this lie, but her voice had not yet returned. She looked around for Polyxena, to remonstrate with Andromache, or plead with the herald, or control Cassandra, who was beginning to rock to and fro on the sand. But Polyxena was gone, and there was nothing anyone could do.

'No,' Talthybius said. 'You will not have to lie about your husband, madam.' He stood up again, rubbing his fists against his aching thighs. He looked behind him to the Greek soldiers who accompanied him. 'Take the child.'

'No,' Andromache screamed. 'Let me come with him. Don't take him from me.'

The herald turned back to her, his expression unreadable. 'You know he will die?' he asked.

'If I cannot save him, I ask only to die alongside him.'

Talthybius sighed. 'You do not own your life to give it up,' he said. His soldiers wrenched the baby from Andromache's arms. Astyanax was silenced by the shock of it. The herald continued: 'You belong to Neoptolemus now. I cannot stand by while his property is destroyed. He would blame me, and his temper is remarkable.'

There was a moment of silence before the baby began to wail again.

'Please,' said Andromache, sensing the men's discomfort. None of them knew what to do with a crying child. 'Let me come with you.'

'You would not wish to see it,' Talthybius said. She fell prostrate at his feet, her hands gripping his metal-studded boots. If the herald could not leave, her son could live a few moments more.

'Where are you taking him?' Hecabe had found her voice at last. The herald turned to look at her. The sharp-tongued old witch had lost some of her vinegar now, he thought.

'He will be thrown from the city walls,' he said. 'He will die where he was born.'

'No, no.' Andromache made one last plea, flinging her arms around the herald's legs, almost taking him off his feet. 'If I cannot die with him—' she said. Cassandra gave a low moan. This part always made her sick. 'If I cannot die with him,' she continued, 'at least let me be the one to kill him. Don't throw him from the walls. Please. Don't let his body fall onto the rocks below. He is a baby. Please. I will smother him. He will not grow up to avenge his father. He will die in his mother's arms. What could be wrong with that? Your Greeks will allow it. Won't they?'

'We will return his body to you,' the herald said to Hecabe. 'You can bury him beside your son.'

35

Calliope

So he does have children, my poet. Or he once had them. Tears flow from his blind eyes. He can't look at me, can't bear what he's just composed. I want to reach down and stroke his hair, and tell him everything will be alright. But it wouldn't be true. Who could say that, about a war?

He was expecting something else from me, I suppose. I depend on war for my very existence. But depending on it means I need to understand it. And if he wishes to write about it, so must the poet. He is learning that in any war, the victors may be destroyed as completely as the vanquished. They still have their lives, but they have given up everything else in order to keep them. They sacrifice what they do not realize they have until they have lost it. And so the man who can win the war can only rarely survive the peace.

The poet may not want to learn this, but he must.

36

Cassandra

Cassandra had to admit it: Apollo's punishment of her was an example of almost perfect cruelty. She had longed to have the gift of prophecy. Longed for it. She spent so many hours in the temple with her brother, Helenus. Each of them a sea of dark locks and a pair of dark eyes, but only one of them beautiful enough to catch the interest of the god himself. She loved Helenus but, like many twins, she felt she needed something which he didn't have, so she could be sure of where he ended and she began. He had always told her that her beauty was distinction enough. But she wanted something more, something that would not fade over time.

When Apollo revealed himself to her, it was in the cool hour of the night. She and Helenus sometimes slept in the temple, if their devotions had kept them there late: he on the left side of the door, she on the right. They wedged soft cushions beneath their heads and she would wriggle under an unfinished robe and use it as a blanket. It was not impious to take the god's clothing if the embroidery had not been finished yet and it had not been dedicated to him. So when the god appeared, he was kneeling behind her head, his tongue licking her earlobe to wake her. She woke with a start, thinking it was a viper whispering in her ear. She sat up and turned, expecting to see it slithering away across the cool white stone. But instead she was faced with the radiant glow of a god, slightly larger than a mortal man, and possessed of a strange inner light. He demanded her and she refused. He asked a second time, and now she was fully awake she refused again, unless he gave her something in return.

'What do you want?'

'To see the future,' she said.

'Some people think of that as a curse,' he replied. His golden hair, which flowed back from his forehead in luscious waves, was oppressively bright. He was beautiful but somehow cold, for all the warm light that he exuded. She found herself squinting to keep her eyes from watering. 'But if that is what you want, you shall have it.'

She expected him to do something, to touch his gold hand to her brow. But he lay motionless beside her as the visions filled her mind. Everything that had been was somehow less real to her than everything which was to come.

'Now give me what is due,' he said, reaching his hand out to touch her skin, which looked almost blue in comparison with his radiance. The vision of what was about to happen was potent. She feared what the god was about to become, so much so that she pulled her hands across her body and her knees up to her chest.

'No,' she said. 'No.'

Apollo's beauty was transformed in the time it took to blink. The ever-young, ever-glowing Archer was suddenly a vicious, vengeful man, his open hand contracting into a fist.

'You dare to refuse me?' he asked. 'You dare to refuse your god after making a bargain with him?'

She screwed her eyes shut and tried to block out his rising voice by balling her hands into her ears. Where was Helenus? Why was he not awake? Apollo lunged at her, like a snake moving towards its prey. She felt the sudden curdling of his saliva in her mouth, and then he was gone.

No one had ever spat on her before, and she scraped her fingers along her tongue in disgust. But the damage was done. Her gift for prophecy was flawless and perpetual. Her gift for persuasion – for the words formed by her defiled tongue to be believed – was gone. And she knew it, long before she spoke another word. She could already see herself being disbelieved by everyone she loved, even Helenus. She could see her warnings falling on ears which refused to hear. She could see the frustration bubbling from her lips as no one listened to her. And she realized that in one gesture, Apollo had cursed her to a lifetime of solitude and what would appear to be madness. Her one consolation – and it was like a tiny pinprick in the blackness – was that she would not be mad. But she would always know what was coming. And all of it terrified her.

Over time, Cassandra had learned to cope with the horror of what had befallen her. At first, the sheer weight of tragedy – of every sickness, every death, of every person she knew and every person she met – overwhelmed her. She found herself screaming warnings at anyone she saw, trying to ward off disaster. The harder she tried, the deafer they became. Time and again she watched the shock on people's faces, when precisely what she had predicted – and they had ignored – came true. Sometimes she imagined she saw a flicker of recognition in their eyes, as if part of their minds knew that she had given them a warning. But the flicker soon died, and in its wake it left only an intensified hatred of the babbling priestess, which all attributed to her gibbering lunacy. She became unable to cope with meeting anyone outside her close family and servants, because it required her to see a whole new set of tragedies, in addition to the stillborn children, sickening spouses and crippled parents which already filled her mind. So when they locked her in a thick-walled room in the citadel, with only one slave (whose child would die from an untreated injury, and who would eventually string herself up by the cord which bound her tunic at the waist), it came as a relief.

The room was dark, with small high windows, and it reminded her of the temple. Helenus came to visit her sometimes, and her grief at what he would do was tempered by the knowledge that he would survive the war, albeit held in captivity by the Greeks. But she also knew that her mother would die believing all her sons had been killed because she could not believe Cassandra. And how was it possible that her beloved twin would betray Troy to the hated Odysseus? That he would take the gift of prophecy which he had acquired – to a lesser extent than his sister, but with the advantage of being heard – and use it to betray their city? And all because he was not given the hand of Helen after Paris had died, though he must surely have known that Helen of Troy would become Helen of

Sparta once more. Cassandra could almost smell the rocky terrain of the Peloponnese on her: Helen would never remain in Troy once the war was over.

Cassandra did not have to try to forgive her brother, because she had already seen the resentment twist him out of shape, long before it happened. He could no more help the jealousy than a bird could help its wings. She maintained her brother's innocence, even as she foresaw his guilt. She held to it still, even on the day that Troy fell, and she found herself clinging to the feet of Athene's statue as a Greek warrior wrenched her away from her sanctuary by her hair, before raping her on the floor of the temple.

A year after Apollo had cursed her, she had grown gaunt from the sickness which so frequently accompanied her visions. She was never sure if the nausea was an element of the vision itself, or a consequence of the horrific things she saw. She found it hard to eat, harder not to vomit when the power of prophecy was at its strongest. But gradually, she learned that she could control some of the effects of the visions, if she could only focus her mind on the part of someone's future that preceded or came after the worst thing that would happen to them (which was what she saw first, and with most clarity).

And sometimes, of course, the visions were a comfort. So even as Troy fell, even as she fled to the temple of Athene, she knew her cries for sanctuary would be ignored and she was not shocked. Even as the Greek warrior Ajax tore out her hair to drag her away from the goddess's statue, even as he chipped one stone foot as he wrenched at her desperate fingers, even as he drove himself into her, even as she cried out in blood and pain, she knew her rape would be avenged. She saw the hated Odysseus appeal to the Greeks for Ajax to be punished for violating the temple and image of Athene, and she saw the Greeks ignore him. But she also knew that Athene would have her revenge: the goddess would forgive no Greek for this outrage, save Odysseus. It did not bring back Cassandra's ripped-out hair or her ripped-out virginity, but it was a solace, nonetheless.

And after living for so long with the terrible foreknowledge of the sack of Troy, with the slaughter of brothers, of father, of sister and nephew, she was perhaps as relieved as the Greeks to see it fall. The anticipation of disaster was more agonizing than the disaster itself and at least as the fires raged, the dread was over. Partially over.

When the screams of Andromache, as her son was taken from her, pierced Cassandra's perforated heart, she tried to focus her mind on her sister-in-law in one year, in two years, in five years, in ten. But the technique which had worked in the past was not working now. She could see nothing but devastation wherever she looked: the multiple griefs of Andromache and Hecabe were too much for her to overcome. As always, when faced with an assault on her senses, her mind returned to its greatest horror. She tried to breathe slowly, knowing that it sometimes quelled the panic. But she could not. For her, there would be nothing after her worst thing. The worst thing that was coming for her would cost her her life and the lives of—

She lost her capacity to breathe for a moment, and passed into unconsciousness.

*

Sleep gave Cassandra no respite. The visions came to her as dreams, just as vividly as they did when she was awake. She had always known that it would be Agamemnon who claimed her, though she had never known why – she could see the future only of those to whom she was in physical proximity, so only her own role had been clear to her until the Argive soldiers dragged her from her rock and took her to their king.

Cassandra was the last of the house of Priam to leave the Troad peninsula. Neither Hecabe nor Andromache remained to bid her farewell. Hecabe had already sailed with Odysseus, to be revenged upon Polymestor. And Andromache had been taken by Neoptolemus. But she could not distract herself with thoughts of Andromache, however much she tried. She would come back to her sister-in-law during the voyage to Greece. She would be unable to do anything else.

When she first saw Agamemnon, she felt a shock of recognition. This pudgy, greying man with thick oil in his fading hair and a roll of fat clearly visible at his waist had haunted her. He was identical to her vision, right down to the ugly twist of his lip when he looked upon her and found her wanting.

'This is a princess of Troy?' he asked his men. 'She's in rags.'

'They were all in rags, king,' said one of his men. The tone of weary patience was so familiar to Cassandra that she almost felt it was one of her brothers speaking. She had to remind herself the man was a stranger, whose voice she had heard a thousand times. 'This is the priestess, daughter of Priam and Hecabe.'

Agamemnon nodded, his eyes now focused on her. 'She has a sort of beauty perhaps,' he said. 'More so than the one who went with Neoptolemus?'

The weary Argive did not allow his face to betray his irritation. 'I believe so, king, yes. And the woman who went with Neoptolemus was only the daughter-in-law of Priam, remember. She was not even Trojan by birth.'

'She was Hector's widow, wasn't she?' Agamemnon said. Neither Cassandra nor the tired Argive was fooled by his feigned ignorance.

'She was, king, but she was no Trojan. This one,' he jabbed his finger into Cassandra's back, 'was born into the royal household. And she was the priestess of Troy. They say she was blessed by Apollo himself.'

Agamemnon rolled his eyes, which Cassandra had never understood before. Now – standing in front of him – she could see that he had not long ago been deprived of another girl, the daughter of a priest of Apollo. That the priest and the god himself had intervened for her return. She saw the girl reflected somewhere in his eyes, hiding behind a tent, dropping leaves into his drinks. So Agamemnon had crossed Apollo too. She wondered why the Archer let them sail back to Greece instead of sharing Athene's rage and capsizing their ship. But wishing to drown was no use to Cassandra. She already knew she would reach Argive soil and she knew what awaited her there.

37

Gaia

Gaia – the Great Mother, born from Chaos, the first of the gods – stretched her aching limbs and the earth moved. The mountains shook, but so faintly that the only evidence was the quivering of leaves on branches. She heard the distant sound of men fighting men, and she knew a larger conflict was coming. Zeus had heard her pleas, had consulted with her daughter, Themis, and the decision was made. There would be an almighty war, the like of which men had never seen.

Gaia had seen a more ruinous war, but long ago. She had been witness to the Titanomachy, when the Titans waged war on the Olympian gods, and the destruction had been impossible, endless, deafening. She had never believed, as the Titans were locked away from the light, behind bronze doors which could never be broken, that she would yearn for another war. But now she yearned.

Mankind was just so impossibly heavy. There were so many of them and they showed no sign of halting their endless reproduction. Stop, she wanted to cry out, please stop. You cannot all fit on the space between the oceans, you cannot grow enough food on the land beneath the mountains. You cannot graze enough livestock on the grasses around your cities, you cannot build enough homes on the peaks of your hills. You must stop, so that I can rest beneath your ever-increasing weight. She wept fat tears as she heard the cries of newborn children. No more, she said to herself. No more.

They made offerings to her, sacrifices of meat and grain and wine. But they were still too many and she ached from carrying them. She sent her message to Zeus, son of Cronos, son of Ouranos, husband of Gaia. Zeus would not let her pain go unanswered. She had supported him too well in the past. And he knew the truth of her complaint. He knew the increasing population could not be sustained. She would not tell him how to diminish their numbers, she would leave that to him. He would speak to Themis, and the two of them would come up with a plan. The divine order of things would be restored once the mortal problem had been corrected. Gaia thought back to the last time mankind had become too heavy, and remembered that Zeus had not left her to suffer for long. The Theban Wars, when seven warriors had marched against the city of Thebes, and a civil war had spilled over into the rest of Greece, had served his purpose then. But this time the problem had grown weightier. A larger war was needed.

She felt sorrow course through her: her purpose was to nurture and provide for men. But they kept taking more from her than she had to give. She looked out across the expanse and saw trees denuded of their fruits, fields ploughed until they could give up no more crops. Why could men not just be less greedy, she wondered. Her sorrow morphed into irritation. And why could they not heed the lessons given to them by Zeus? They spent enough time in his temples, after all. Why did they not look at the wars which had ravaged Thebes, and understand that these were necessary because they would not stop consuming everything? That if they carried on as they were, the seas would be empty of fish and the land would be empty of grain?

When there were fewer men, fewer women, fewer children, she would grieve for those who had gone, but she would know it was the only answer. She was so tired, she could feel herself sinking beneath them. Forgive me, she murmured into the breeze. Forgive me, but I cannot hold you any longer.

38

Penelope

Odysseus,

    I honestly don't know where to begin. But since you are surely dead by now, I don't suppose it can matter very much. I might as well be howling these words into an abyss as trying to send them to you. Perhaps that is what I am doing. In which case, there must be an echo, because I would swear an oath that I can hear the words howling back at me sometimes.

    This just gets better and better. Ten years waging war against one city with all the forces Greece could muster alongside you. It sounds ridiculous, doesn't it? And that is the most defensible part of your absence. Ten years of war, followed by three solid years wandering about the high seas, failing to come home with one excuse after another. You met a monster. You met a witch. Cannibals broke your ships. A whirlpool ate your friends. Telemachus himself would never have come up with such excuses and he was a boy. Not any more, of course. Now he is twenty. A grown man, in need of his own wife and child. In need of his own father, too, of course. But that rarely seems to occur to you.

And now seven more years – seven! Odysseus, can you even remember what that means? Twenty-eight more seasons, seven more harvests, boys grown to men, mothers dead, fathers ailing – with no word from you. But rest assured (and I am sure you are having a very long rest), the bard has you covered. You are held captive, so he sings, on the island of Ogygia. Captive, I asked him, the first time he sang this part of your story. Who holds him captive? What cruel jailer locks my husband away from the light and deprives him of a free man's liberty? What vicious tyrant, with what forces at his command, could imprison my poor Odysseus?

To be fair to him, he did at least have the decency to look ashamed. It was no tyrant, he said. No man held you (this is starting to sound like one of your alibis, Odysseus: who has blinded the Cyclops? No one. Who holds you captive? No one). Eventually, under sustained questioning, he admitted that it is a woman who has taken you prisoner. A horrible old crone, I asked? Who lives in a tumbledown old house in the woods and has adopted you as her son to chop firewood and hunt wild boar on which she can feast? No, came his shamefaced reply. A nymph. Of course it is.

Calypso is her name, so I am told. No wonder he was trying to cover that up. She has – if the bard can be trusted on this – a delightful singing voice. Well, you always did like a tune, didn't you? Perhaps she reminds you of those bird-women you were so desperate to hear.

Her island is in the middle of nowhere, far from Ithaca and far from everywhere. She lives in a large cave, which sounds practically bestial to me, but apparently she has a hearth and burns cedar logs for the warmth and the homely scent. You used to have a home on Ithaca, of course, but perhaps our logs weren't quite up to your current standards. Her cave is surrounded by thick woodlands, apparently, which sounded so much like a euphemism when the bard first sang it that I threatened to have him flogged. He assured me he was describing nothing more vulgar than poplar and cypress trees, home to owls and hawks and other birds. I can't decide whether he is laughing at me or not. It all sounds positively idyllic – as jails go, I mean – with a vine full of ripe grapes growing around the mouth of the cave, and springs murmuring with fresh water bubbling up nearby. Meadows of parsley grow outside, dotted with violets, because I presume she likes the colour. Or perhaps she eats them. With your dalliances, Odysseus, it becomes increasingly hard to guess.

And Calypso seems to have been the perfect hostess, so long as you overlook the part where you are – and it seems almost quaint that I still remember this – my husband, and not hers. The bard describes her excellence at weaving, at her golden loom, for example, which I'm sure you appreciated as much as anyone. You probably needed a new cloak after your shipwreck, I would imagine.

I also have been weaving, in case you were interested. You're probably wondering what else I have been doing with the last twenty years: I could have woven cloaks for the whole of Ithaca in this time. And perhaps I would have, if I were not engaged in weaving an endless shroud. No, don't despair: your father has not yet journeyed to meet your mother in the Underworld. Laertes lives, though he is old, and frail, and bent almost double from the grief of waiting for his son to return.

But you have been gone so long, Odysseus, that Ithaca no longer regards you as its king. Some of the old families do, of course. They remain loyal to you, as have I. But there are many more young men, vying to take your place. If you could see them, brawling with one another like stags. I hoped that Telemachus would be strong enough to see them off, but he is a quiet, cautious young man, prone to tears. He grew up without a father, of course, and it has left him uncertain of how he should be. For many years, I was strong enough to keep them at bay, calling on your reputation. The tales which came back to us from Troy were so impressive. You were a warrior king, no one would dare disobey your wife.

But those stories have not been fresh for a long time now. When did we last hear news of you? Seven years ago, and you were facing an array of impossible, implausible obstacles, one after another. By the time the bards had done their work, none of us knew whether you lived or died. Seven years of silence means that most Ithacans are sure you have died. I find myself unable to accept that you are dead, but equally unable to believe that you are alive. Perhaps it is your shroud I'm weaving. The noblemen's sons, who were too young to sail with you all those years ago, have grown up to be spoiled, entitled men. Each is convinced he should replace you. Each knows the best route to that goal is marriage to your widow. And so, Odysseus, I find myself with a houseful of young men who are eating and drinking everything we have in our stores.

Remember the wine, and the grain, and the oil, which

we kept in casks beneath the great hall? I used to hug myself – do you remember – when we went down the cool stone steps, out of the heat and light, to the storeroom? The first time it happened, you thought I was shivering from the cold. You loosened the pins of your cloak and swung it around my shoulders. The smell of you on that soft wool made me almost cry with delight (I was pregnant, of course. I am not usually such a sentimental fool). So I clothed myself in you and breathed deeply. But the next time, and the next, you noticed that I always wrapped my arms around myself in the storeroom, whether I was cold or not. You didn't have to ask: you just knew that it came from an abiding sense of happiness. Of satisfaction that no matter what the winter brought, we were ready. We had so much, stored away from the mould and the mice, in our cool, dry storeroom.

Well, those stores are almost gone now. These boorish, cavernous men have invaded my home and demolished everything they can find within. They sleep with my serving-women, so I no longer know who to trust. And if the thought of your wife in jeopardy does not stir you to action, they also plot to kill your son. He has gone travelling in search of news about his father: to Pylos, I think, and perhaps Sparta. So he is safe for now (as safe as a man who travels away from home can ever be. I am hoping you are an exceptional case). But eventually, he will return, and they will not leave him alone for long.

Telemachus' best hope is that I marry one of these young, handsome, greedy men, and thus reduce the threat he poses to them. Is that what you would want, Odysseus, if you were alive? I cannot pretend I haven't considered it. They are so very, very young. And I am not. The thought of their hard, youthful flesh is a tempting one. It's not as if you have been faithful, after all. Your infidelities are the subject of song all over Achaea and beyond. There are children learning to play the lyre who can sing of your other women. And nymphs. And goddesses.

You have humiliated me, and I am sorely tempted to return the favour. A young man would be delicious. And grateful. But, oh, Odysseus, they are all so stupid. I cannot abide it. I would rather my clever old husband came home than set myself up with a witless young one. What would we ever talk about? Although I suppose they would not want to talk much. Young men so rarely do.

I have delayed them for three years (nothing to you, of course, but a lifetime for a woman with a house filled with unwanted guests) by telling them I cannot marry until I have woven Laertes' shroud. They believe me, of course. He is so bent and tired, they cannot imagine he will last the night. And it is such a blameless task for a woman: weaving. I have always been good at it, as you know. But the shroud is never finished. As I said, they are stupid. So it never occurred to them that I spent my day weaving the shroud, and my night unravelling it again. It would have occurred to you straightaway, if you had seen so much industry going nowhere. Perhaps it did not enter their minds that a woman would put so much time into deceiving them. It takes precisely as long to unweave as to weave, of course. The shuttle must pass across the loom in exactly the same way. So I have spent three years doing and undoing, advancing and retreating.

They would not have guessed my scheme even now,

had one of those maidservants not betrayed me to her lover. I could have strung her up. But it was too late by then, she had his protection. And I had lost mine.

The bard tells me that you gaze out over the ocean and pine to come home. That you plead with Calypso to release you. That you promise her I am less beautiful than she, especially after so many years have passed, but that I am your wife and you love me nonetheless. I can't lie, Odysseus, I would have preferred it if you had not said that. No one wishes to hear about their age and lack of beauty in a song.

So perhaps I should give up on you altogether, no matter how you long to return. Perhaps I should leave you to Calypso, who needs a husband so desperately that she stole mine and kept him for seven years. But the bard sang something else the other day. He said that Calypso offered you immortality if you would stay with her on her island of pleasure. The consort of a nymph, you would receive the gift of endless life. And, so the bard sings, you refused.

One of the suitors – drunk, of course, on my wine – slurred his disbelief. No mortal man would give up the chance of eternal life, he said. It doesn't happen in any story I've ever heard. And – drunk as he was – he was quite correct. There is no other story where a mortal man is offered the gift of immortality and turns it down. But you did.

Come home, Odysseus. I can wait no longer.
Penelope

39

Clytemnestra

Ten years was a long time to bear a grudge, but Clytemnestra never wavered. Her fury neither waxed nor waned, but burned at a constant heat. She could warm her hands on it when the nights were cold, and use it to light her way when the palace was in darkness. She would never forgive Agamemnon for murdering her eldest child, Iphigenia. Nor for the thuggish deceit of his wife and daughter with talk of a wedding. So all that was left to think about was how she would take her revenge upon him, and how she could persuade the gods to sanction her actions. She was sure Artemis would be her ally, because everything had been caused by Agamemnon's affront to the goddess all those years ago at Aulis. The slaughter of Iphigenia had been the priest's idea to win Artemis back to the Argive cause and give them a fair wind to Troy. But if the goddess had been angry with Agamemnon once, she would be angry with him again. If anyone knew that, it was his wife.

Clytemnestra did not set out to murder him at first. For a year or two, she prayed daily that he would be killed in the war, and she prayed that his death would be ignominious. That he would not die on the Trojan battlefield (which was hardly likely, given his tendency to skulk behind his men), but be stabbed in the night by someone he knew and trusted. Yet the years came and went, and still he lived.

Once five years had passed, she decided on a new strategy. Every day he was not killed was a day she spent planning how she would kill him on his return to Mycenae. Her plan was complex and she luxuriated in it. She would wake up at first light and stretch out in it, considering all its angles and corners until she was fully satisfied. She needed to be in a perpetual state of readiness, because who knew when the endless war would end? And she needed the revenge to be apt. Killing him would not be sufficient to repay him for the horror of what he had done.

The first step was to send a messenger to Aegisthus, Agamemnon's cousin and bitter enemy, inviting him to the royal house of Mycenae. It was a drawn-out process, and it was some months before he could be persuaded that it was not a trap. Her own servants were aghast that she should make any contact with the son of Thyestes. But Clytemnestra did not require their approval, or their understanding, of her actions. In fact, she was relying on the opposite.

She was resourceful and she was persistent and eventually Aegisthus arrived in Mycenae, attended by his guards. Slaves ran through the lofty halls of the palace to find their mistress and tell her that the great enemy of the royal household was outside, claiming an audience. They were startled when she rose from her seat and strode towards the palace gates to greet the man, chiding them for the abuse of guest-host friendship because they had left four armed men outside the halls instead of making them welcome.

Clytemnestra had never met Aegisthus before (the family enmity was an old one), and she was surprised to see so little resemblance between the cousins. He had the same womanish mouth as Agamemnon, a man she could no longer think of as her husband but only as her enemy. His hair sprang back from a similar point in the middle of his brow. But Aegisthus was younger, and taller, almost willowy. His expression was uncertain, as if he were nervous but trying to disguise it. She wondered if he had ever wielded a sword in battle. But she did not wonder for long.

She saw him before he saw her, noticed him staring around at the great height of the citadel, gawping at the pair of stone lions which topped the gates through which he had walked to reach her. He was not intimidated, she thought, but he was certainly impressed.

Her slaves opened the doors and she walked outside, tall and assured. She saw his expression shift. Nervous. But also stricken with unexpected desire.

'Cousin,' she said, bowing low before him. 'Please, come inside.' She appeared slightly flustered, although she was not. 'I am sorrier than I can say that my slaves have left you standing here while they went to fetch me. The discourtesy shall not go unpunished. I will have them all flogged.'

Aegisthus' face shifted again into an eager smile. 'It is no matter, madam. The wait was brief and gave us a moment to enjoy the magnificent view.' He gestured behind him to the mountains fading into a blue distance. Mycenae nestled in an unparalleled location, Clytemnestra's land stretching out on all sides around it. It would be – she had often thought – easy to defend.

'You are too kind, cousin,' she said, straightening to her full height.

'Please – don't have the slaves flogged on my account,' he said. 'It is not necessary.'

She watched him believe that he was being magnanimous, and saw the extra confidence it gave him. This was going to be very easy.

'I will do anything you say,' she replied. 'You are my honoured guest. Will you come indoors and let us offer you refreshment?'

'It would be an honour.'

'The honour is all mine,' she said. 'Would your men care to join us? Or would you prefer to dine alone?'

Aegisthus' bodyguards were too well trained to show their surprise. A married woman – a queen – offering to dine alone with a man whom she had not previously met? This was hardly customary behaviour. Still, one of them shrugged, who knew what sort of things happened in Mycenae?

'My men will dine with your servants, if that is acceptable to you,' Aegisthus said. Clytemnestra nodded and gestured to her slaves.

'Feed these men, they have had a long journey,' she said. 'Not long in distance, I know. But it has been so many years since our halves of the family were united, that it must have felt like an endless road to get to here.' She reached out to Aegisthus and took his hands in hers. 'This is our chance to make old wrongs right,' she said, and she pulled him slightly towards her, almost taking him off balance. 'Come with me. We'll begin our friendship with wine.'

And as she laced her arm through the arm of a stranger and steered him along the corridors of her palace, they both realized that the length of their stride – he in his travelling tunic, she in her long, fluid dress – was identical. She pointed out to him the beautiful tapestries – in finest, darkest purple – that hung along the walls. He could see how wealthy she was, even without having his attention drawn to the most opulent work. But as she gazed at the knots of thread which made the intricate patterns so lovely and so precise, she had the unshakeable sense that a new fabric was being woven, by her. And the knots in her tapestry, once tied, would prove impossible to undo. She gave a delighted shiver, and squeezed Aegisthus' arm more tightly.

*

Seducing him was the easiest pleasure she could remember. He was so keen to be liked and so desperate to be told what to do. She loved his young skin, his lithe limbs, his narrow waist. She loved him in the dark hours of the night, and she loved him more when the morning sun bathed his skin and turned him to gold. Sometimes she had to remind herself that she had a greater ambition in mind than an adulterous relationship with her husband's sworn enemy. But she never forgot for more than a moment, no matter how distracting he was.

His devotion, once earned, was not easily lost. He had

an almost doglike character: it was all she could do to stop him from following her around the palace. He loathed Agamemnon at least as much as she did, which meant they always found something to talk about. He also loathed any reminder that her life had existed before he entered it, despising Orestes and Electra equally. The two boys – she found it hard not to think of Aegisthus in this way – almost came to blows several times. And so she sent Orestes away to live with distant acquaintances. She wanted to keep him safe, and it was the only way she knew. She had no doubt that otherwise Aegisthus would kill him before long and Orestes had not yet proven himself to be much of a warrior. He was his father's son in this regard, she thought. She enjoyed the way her lover was quick to anger, but never with her.

Clytemnestra would have had little to complain about had she not also been the mother of daughters. The ghost of Iphigenia was never far away: she felt her daughter's breath on her neck sometimes. She had brought Iphigenia back from Aulis to Mycenae, buried her at the closest priest-sanctioned place she could (though why she should ever listen to a priest again, after what one of them had taken from her, she had no idea). She made offerings of a lock of hair every year, on the day of Iphigenia's death. But her daughter could not rest, unavenged as she was. And each year, Clytemnestra would bow before her tomb and promise that she would punish the man who had sired her and killed her. But the war dragged on and she could not make good her promise. So Iphigenia never truly left her.

She was also haunted by Electra. Daily, she wished it

had been Electra who was sacrificed by Agamemnon rather than Iphigenia. For reasons which were unclear to Clytemnestra, her surviving daughter idolized her absent father, seemingly unconcerned that he had sliced open the throat of her sister for the sake of a following wind. If it was the gods' will, she once said, when Clytemnestra asked, begged really, to know how she could have so little care for a sister. Of course, Electra had been too young to know Iphigenia. Too young to know her father either. But hating her mother as she did, and hating Aegisthus just as much as he despised her, she chose to ally herself with a murderer. This one thing she and her daughter had in common, Clytemnestra thought. Though Aegisthus was not a murderer just yet.

Clytemnestra grew increasingly sure the gods would take her side. She knew that Agamemnon had offended them during the Trojan conflict. Boorish, stupid man – of course he had. Any god would be offended that such an oaf walked in the light, let alone that he could boast himself a king. They had punished him at Aulis, rightly, for his hubris. But she had no belief that they had wanted the price to be paid by her beloved daughter. Why should they? Iphigenia was just a child.

And the murder had been – she hesitated in her mind to find the appropriate phrase – so dishonest. To kill a girl, a daughter, was bad enough. But to do so in a ritual which had made a mockery of her youth, of her maiden-hood. A false marriage! Had any mother ever suffered something more vicious or cruel? To dress the girl up, promise her a great warrior to be her husband, and then to cut her down. At the very least, she knew her husband had earned the enmity of Achilles for dragging his name into the whole disgusting affair. What Greek prince could be anything other than appalled to see his name used as a trap for a defenceless girl? Agamemnon might be so shameless that he could stoop to this, but other men had higher standards.

Clytemnestra knew who to pray to and she prayed to them all. To Artemis, against whom the original outrage had been levelled. To Hymenaeus, the god of marriage, whose institution had been so affronted by this despicable crime. Then she prayed to Night, who would conceal her plans for vengeance. Lastly she prayed to the Furies, who would accompany her as she worked their will.

And all the while, she sent scouts in every direction across the mainland to bring her news of Troy.

*

Nine years after Iphigenia had been slaughtered like an animal, Clytemnestra sent her watchmen out for the last time. Don't come back, she told each man, unless you bring me news of his return. And send a message here every ten days, so I know you are alive and watching. She knew they complained about their postings, these men sent from the fine city of Mycenae to wait on the cliff-tops and demand news of any travellers coming into any port from the east. But she did not care.

And after a year – a whole year of waiting – the message finally came back. It came in the form of fire, like her fury. Her watchmen lit beacons on the top of each mountain, one after another, and the news reached her before it reached any other Greek city.

She sent her most trusted slaves to find out more. They returned on foot, having ridden their horses to exhaustion. The Argive ships had left Troy, the slaves reported. The city was in ruins: its temples had been overturned and emptied. Its wealth had been spread among the Greeks, its towers had fallen. Its horse-taming men were killed, its women enslaved. Agamemnon – long-lost king of Mycenae – was returning home in his ship laden with treasure and concubines. She had only days to prepare a fit welcome for her husband. Clytemnestra greeted this news quietly. She was ready.

First, she explained to Aegisthus one more time why he must hide when Agamemnon returned. He must hide and perform a vital task: to keep Electra from speaking to her father, lest she give away their plan before the time was right. Aegisthus was such an impetuous boy: he would have rushed at the king with a sword as he stood on the palace steps, if she let him. He could not see, until she explained it, how this would lead to an uprising from the Mycenaeans. There was little affection for their absent king in the city, but not so little that she could afford to kill an unarmed man on his return from war. Especially if he brought wealth to spread among his people (although privately, Clytemnestra scoffed at the very idea that Agamemnon would share anything with anyone, even his wife).

'What should I do with Electra?' Aegisthus asked. 'She will not come anywhere with me if I ask her.'

Clytemnestra shrugged. 'Gag her and throw her in the storerooms if that is what it takes to keep her out of the way.' Electra had performed a sacrifice of thanksgiving when she heard her father was returning at last and the queen was not in a forgiving mood. 'Did I tell you they overturned the Trojan temples?'

Aegisthus nodded but his interest was not caught by this part of the tale. He cared far less than his lover did about the endorsement of the gods. His father had taught him when he was young that the gods' approval mattered very little compared to a man's will. But Clytemnestra relished this news above all. Of course Agamemnon's men had assaulted the temples and the priests. If the rumour she had heard was correct, they had not even respected Priam's pleas for sanctuary as he cowered at the altar of Zeus himself. She shook her head, astonished that even men who answered to Agamemnon could have such little respect for the king of the gods. And then there was the second rumour, which filled her with white rage and delight in almost equal measures: that the concubine Agamemnon was bringing home to Greece was a priestess of Apollo. The arrogance made her catch her breath. To take a priestess, whose body was sacrosanct to the Archer, and use her as his whore. Now it was not just Artemis whose support Clytemnestra could count on. Apollo would be on her side, too.

She counted the days of Agamemnon's voyage across the water and she told her watchmen to come home. She needed no further confirmation of the rumours: she would know soon enough who travelled with the once-king of Mycenae. She readied herself for his return. A small lie in place about her son, Orestes. Electra out of the way. She looked into her dark mirror and admired her strong jaw. She should try to conceal the lean, hungry expression which had come upon her over the past ten years. She wondered how those years had affected her sister, Helen. Was she still so beautiful that men wept merely to see her? She rolled her eyes in remembered irritation. She probably was.

She summoned her maidservants and had them plait her hair into neat braids. When she was with Aegisthus, she had grown into the habit of wearing it loose, to reflect his age rather than her own. But as matron-queen, welcoming her adventuring husband, she needed to present a different appearance. As she admired her own long neck (less swan-like than Helen's, no doubt, but even so) she realized that she was looking forward to the day ahead. She had planned it for so long, and now she had the twin pleasures not just of enacting her revenge after such a long delay, but also of seeing her plan come to fruition.

*

Clytemnestra sensed him before she heard the stamp of men's boots on hard rocks. She would have known – even without her watchmen and their beacons of rage – that Agamemnon was nearby. The birds still sang, the cicadas still buzzed, the breeze still moved the dry yellowing grasses around her palace. But she knew something had changed: she could feel the heat glowing inside her. She took a breath and held it, closed her eyes for a moment. She gave the word to her slaves, and they ran to do her rehearsed bidding. The tapestries came down off the walls, and were carried to the front gates of the palace. The slaves stood in fours, each holding a corner of the dark purple cloth which seemed to glisten in the unaccustomed sunlight.

The day was hot and dry, the breeze bringing none of the cool sea air up to her citadel. She could taste the dust, kicked up by the feet of soldiers who were marching from their ship to their home. The path curved up the hill from the shore, so they heard the men before they saw them. When they came around the final corner, she had her slaves perform obeisance and she herself bowed low. She held the pose for a moment before straightening her back to see her husband for the first time since their eyes met across the body of their daughter in Aulis, ten years earlier.

How small he seemed. Her memory had made him taller, she supposed. And if the years had made her leaner, they had made him greyer. And paunchy. She wondered how a man could get fat during a war. He was red-faced, sweating in his ludicrous regalia. What kind of man wore a bronze breastplate and a plumed helmet to return home? One who believed that his power was seated in his costume, she supposed. The red leather of his scabbard was very fine, studded with gold flecks. She did not recognize it, and realized this must be part of his share of the fabled wealth of Troy. To have killed her child for a decorated bit of animal skin. She could feel the contempt shaping her mouth into a sneer, and stopped herself. Now was not the time to lose control. That would come later.

The Argive men had not escaped the war without casualties. She tried to calculate how many men Agamemnon had lost: a quarter, a third? Some had died noble deaths on the battlefield, she knew. They had been interred by their comrades, their armour shared out among those to whom it could still do some good. Some had died of disease: a plague incurred by Agamemnon – of course –

297

with his refusal to respect a priest of Apollo. She had laughed when she heard about the plague, laughed until her face hurt, in bed with Aegisthus, where laughter was safe. All her husband had to do to keep Apollo's favour was not rape his priestesses or the daughters of his priests. It was laughable in the dark hours of the night, even as she sent messages of condolence by day to the Mycenaeans who wept to discover their son, their father, their brother had been culled by the Archer's arrows. Agamemnon was so magnificently self-absorbed, he could not even see that the simplest abstinence would have kept his men safe. He was like a spoiled child, grabbing at things because he wanted them, with no thought for anyone else, not even a god. The arrogance was remarkable.

Some of the men nursed injuries from the Trojan battles: missing limbs, missing eyes. Livid purple scars spilled across arms and faces; sores and ulcers wept from wounds which would not heal. Clytemnestra found herself wondering if their wives would want these damaged creatures back. Would she have welcomed home a cripple? She thought for a moment, and decided she would not. But still she was sure that she would have preferred any one of these ruined men to her own husband.

And in the very centre of the group, just behind Agamemnon, surrounded by his men, she saw the priestess. It was all she could do not to laugh. Was this his trophy from the war, while his brother took Helen, daughter of Zeus and Leda? She was barely more than a child, though she wore her priestess's robes, the fillets around her hair waving as she walked. Her mouth moved all the time, Clytemnestra noticed, as though she were muttering words without pause. She was smaller, darker than Iphigenia had been at the same sort of age. Clytemnestra had done this every time she had seen a girl in the past ten years: was she taller or shorter than Iphigenia, with more or less beautiful eyes? Did she carry herself with the same poise that Iphigenia always had? Would her skin look as radiant in a saffron gown, would her hair flow as copiously down her shoulders, would her feet move as neatly as she danced, would . . .

She drove her fingernails into her palms to break the thought. Iphigenia would not rest uneasy for much longer.

The men came to a halt before her, and she bowed again.

'Husband,' she said. 'Welcome home.'

'Clytemnestra, get up,' he said. 'You behave as though I am your barbarian king.'

Nothing else. No apology, no affection, nothing. There was – Clytemnestra was honest enough to admit to herself – nothing he could have said or done that would have saved him. But it was lazy of him not to even try. As though he wanted to be killed. Or – she considered a second possibility – the gods wanted him to be killed. That was surely it.

She stood up, and waved her hands at her slave women. 'Lay the tapestries down,' she said. 'My husband will enter his home on a stream of red, the blood of the barbarians he has crushed.'

The women surged forward, laying the glistening red tapestries on the ground.

'What are you doing, woman?' Agamemnon looked around him, to see if his men were shocked by this fawning display. Their faces remained still and it made him pause. Was it not such a peculiar thing his wife was doing? 'Only gods would walk on such brocade,' he hissed. 'Men must walk on the sandy earth.'

'You would walk on them if a god ordered it,' she said. A silent shudder seemed to pass over them all, as though Poseidon had tapped his trident on the ground, feather-light.

Agamemnon looked at his wife's impassive face to see if she intended the meaning he had just heard. He had sacrificed their daughter because Artemis ordered it. No one would ever be able to call him impious: he obeyed the gods even when they demanded terrible things of him. Even when they demanded his eldest child, he did not hesitate to do as the priests instructed. It was Zeus' will that Troy should fall, everyone knew it. And if the price was his daughter, then his only choice was to sacrifice her himself, or let someone else do it. He had done the courageous thing, but he found himself wondering if his wife realized that. Perhaps she would have preferred it if some other Argive had taken his knife to the girl.

'I would do anything the gods ordered,' he said. 'As would all wise men.'

'If the message was given to you by a priest?' she asked.

Again, he searched her face, looking for the signs of contempt around her mouth. But her eyes were fixed modestly on the ground, and he could see no trace of her feelings.

'Yes,' he answered. The priest, Calchas, had delivered the message that his daughter must be sacrificed. Agamemnon had raged at him, threatened to cut him down or at least lock him up, but Menelaus had reasoned with his brother, explained that someone must take the girl's life. He even offered to do it himself – Agamemnon still thought well of his brother for this kindness – but in the end, it had not been necessary.

'And what do you think Priam would have done in your position?' she asked.

Priam had never been in his position. The old man had lost his war, lost his city and lost his life. Dragged screaming from an altar, someone had told Agamemnon. Pitiful old creature. After all those years of war, Agamemnon thought the Trojan king would have had the courage to die like a warrior instead of crawling on the ground like an insect.

'He would have marched upon the purple weave, likening himself to the gods,' he replied.

'So he did not fear the comparison with a god, in the way that you do?' she asked.

'He was an arrogant man.'

'Kings are often arrogant men,' Clytemnestra said. 'It is what reminds the rest of us that they are kings. Walk on the tapestries, now we have laid them out for you so carefully. Reward us for our gratitude that you have returned. Do as we beg of you, so we know that you are gracious in victory, as you have never had to be in defeat.'

Agamemnon sighed and looked down at his feet. He gestured at the slave women who had placed their beautiful crimson burdens on the ground. 'Not in these old boots, at any rate,' he said. 'One of you help me to take them off. If I am to walk on the blood of my enemies, I shall do it with my feet bare, in honour of the gods.'

The women looked over to their queen, who nodded.

They rushed to the feet of their king, and unlaced his old leather boots. It was impossible to say what colour they had once been: red, brown, tan? The mud of the Trojan peninsula had soaked into them, and the sand of the Trojan shore had worn them away.

A moment later, the king stood in front of his ancestral palace, in front of his men, in front of his wife. His nut-brown legs ended with strangely pale feet, like creatures that had lived only in the dark. The king looked down and laughed at the incongruity. 'There was never a good time to take boots off in Troy,' he said, looking around at his men for agreement. They were beginning to disperse, peeling off from the edges of the group to rejoin their own families. Agamemnon gave a small nod, convincing himself that he was granting them permission to leave.

Clytemnestra opened her arms and gestured at the carpet. 'Walk, king,' she said. 'Walk on the blood of your enemies, trample them into the ground. Walk on the wealth you have won for your house. Walk on the tides of blood which sailed with you back from Troy. Walk.'

And Agamemnon crossed the crimson ground and disappeared into the palace.

*

'You too,' Clytemnestra said to the priestess. 'Come inside.' The girl did not respond. The queen turned to one of her maidservants. 'What did he say she was called?'

'He didn't say.'

Clytemnestra clicked her tongue against her teeth. 'Not the king. The messenger who told us the king was on his way.'

The maidservant thought for a moment, but could not find an answer.

'Go ahead,' Clytemnestra said. 'Heat the water for the king's bath.'

'Yes, madam.' The girl ran into the palace.

'The rest of you, take these inside and place them back where they belong,' Clytemnestra said. 'Don't forget to brush off the dust.'

The women gathered up their tapestries and shook them gently in the breeze before rolling them up and carrying them indoors.

A few people were still milling around outside the palace, but Clytemnestra ignored them. The old men of Mycenae did not know where to go now their king had returned but their sons had not. But what could she do to help them? Their loss was no greater than her own.

'You, girl.' She spoke to the priestess again. 'Come on.' Cassandra was gazing at the palace roof, an expression of utter horror on her face. Startled, Clytemnestra turned to follow her gaze, but there was nothing there. 'What can you see?' she asked. As she spoke the words, she realized that she could not remember the last time she had been curious about someone else. She had wanted to know specific information of course, not least Agamemnon's whereabouts and health. But she had no recollection of being interested in anyone else's views on anything for ten years at least. Perhaps longer.

'I can see them dancing,' Cassandra said quietly. She waited for the slap that her mother would have given her, but Clytemnestra merely looked again at the roof and then back at the priestess. She did not seem angry, only intrigued.

'Who can you see dancing?' she asked.

'Black. Three black creatures, black fire licking around them. Why isn't the roof alight? All those black flames kissing it and teasing it, why doesn't it catch fire?'

'I don't know,' the queen replied. 'Why doesn't it catch fire?'

Cassandra shook her head, chewing at her lips with tiny frantic bites. 'Don't know, don't know, don't know,' she said. 'Not real fire, it must not be real fire. Is it real? Can you see them now? Can you see the women dancing in the fire? Can you hear them screaming? Can you hear the hissing of the flames and the snakes?'

The queen thought carefully about her next question. 'Are they screaming because of the fire?'

'No, not the fire. The fire doesn't burn them. The fire is them. Do you understand? They are wreathed in fire, they bathe in fire. They do not scream for it. They scream for justice. No, not justice, that is not right. It is something like justice, but stronger. What is it?' Cassandra flicked her gaze at the queen before turning it back to the roof, which still held her attention.

'Did you say it was black fire?'

'Yes! Yes, yes, yes!' Cassandra screamed. 'Black fire. That's it. Can you see it?' Knowing this would be her last day, having known it for so long, one thing she had never expected to feel was hope. But the sudden sense that another person might be able to see what she could see made her feel it nonetheless. It had been so long since she had been able to share anything with anyone.

'No, I don't have your gift,' the queen said. 'But I know

what it is you see. Women wreathed in black fire? Those are the Furies.'

'Yes!'

'And it is not justice they scream for,' she said. 'It is vengeance.'

'That's it. They scream for vengeance, and their snakes are screaming, too. Their jaws are pulled back and their fangs are bared. You must give it to them, it is everything. They are waiting for you, they have been waiting for you.'

'They are my daughter's guardians,' Clytemnestra said. 'They have danced around these halls for ten years.'

'With a knife? Oh no. He took her with a knife. Your poor girl, your poor little girl. On her wedding day. She was so happy and then – oh. Your girl. At the altar for her wedding.'

Clytemnestra felt the tears forming. 'Yes,' she said. 'That's right. He killed my daughter. Did he tell you? The man has no shame.'

Cassandra shook her head again. 'Didn't tell, doesn't talk,' she said. 'Never talks to me except be quiet, lie still, stop crying. Nothing else.'

'So how did you know? Did the soldiers tell you?'

'She told me,' Cassandra said. 'Iphigenia. Pretty name, such a pretty name. Pretty name for a pretty girl. Your baby girl. You laboured so hard to bring her into the world. So hard. She nearly did not survive, you nearly did not survive. She was your precious, precious girl and he took her. But you will see her again, sooner than you think. She promises. Her brother and sister promise.'

The tears streamed down Clytemnestra's face. 'Of course they do. They will want to avenge their father.'

Cassandra wrenched her gaze down from the roof and focused on the woman standing before her: tall, broad-shouldered, handsome and strong. Her hair was streaked with grey, and soft lines framed her eyes and her mouth. 'You believe me?' Cassandra asked. No one had believed her for as long as she could remember. Who was this woman who was immune to Apollo's curse?

'Of course I believe you. I saw him kill her.'

'No one believes me.'

'You can see the past and the future?' Clytemnestra asked. Cassandra frowned. She had stopped noticing the difference between these two things so long ago that it seemed peculiar anyone else should. The queen seemed to hear her thoughts. 'Ah, they are the same for you. So you know what is coming, and yet you do not run away.'

'No,' Cassandra said. 'No point running from what has already happened.'

'But it hasn't already happened,' said the queen. 'If you ran away now, you might live. You are young, you have quick legs. You could run away down the hill, hide among the trees, wait for a shepherd or someone to find you and make you his bride.'

'Apollo's mind is made up,' Cassandra said. 'It ends today.'

'You will not fight the will of your god?'

Cassandra removed the priestess's headdress, which she had worn since one of the Mycenaean men had given it to her on the voyage home. He had pinned new ribbons to her hair, not realizing that Cassandra knew he had looted them from the temple of Hera in Troy. But she did not complain. She sat patiently muttering while he took the stained ribbons from her headdress and replaced them. He murmured platitudes quietly the whole time, as if he was speaking to a wild animal. 'There, there,' he said, as he stepped back to admire the garland he had rejuvenated.

Now she wrenched the pins from her hair. Clytemnestra was surprised to see that she did not wince. Cassandra dropped the headdress on the ground and placed her small left foot on top of it. Clytemnestra felt a sudden rush of memory of Iphigenia's beautiful white feet. 'You spurn the god at last?' she asked.

'He has left me,' Cassandra replied. 'He is my god no longer.' It was the only explanation for why the queen believed her when no one had for so long. Apollo's curse no longer twisted her words on their way out of her mouth. The god was absent.

'He would have protected you,' Clytemnestra said.

Cassandra laughed, a terrible scratching sound, rusty from disuse. 'He would have guided your hand,' she said. 'He may still. Take me inside. You have your altar ready.'

Clytemnestra nodded. 'All that's needed is the sacrifice,' she said.

'We'll conduct the sacrifice together.'

*

Clytemnestra had waited for so long to have her revenge that sometimes, in the darkest hours, she wondered if killing Agamemnon would be enough. Because then what would she do? She could hardly kill him twice. What if – a small voice, a daimonion, spoke in her mind – she looked down upon his corpse and felt no rush of victory? What then would be the force which impelled her forward?

But she need not have worried. Killing him was every bit as satisfying as she had hoped. Partly because he had skulked behind a war for ten years, growing older and more bitter with each passing month: while the men around him died so lightly, he had clung to life. And so she knew – knew in every part of her mind – that she was taking from him something he valued highly. Too highly.

She moved quickly through the halls, making sure everything was being done in the right order. She checked his bath was being drawn the way he preferred it: hot, scented like a temple offering. She took the priestess to the altar room inside the palace and bade her wait there. She threw incense on the fire, and the girl – mute again – knelt on the ground before the hearth and mouthed her prayers and prophecies in silence. The sweet smoke almost choked Clytemnestra, but it seemed to make the girl calmer. A priestess was used to burning incense, Clytemnestra supposed.

'I will return for you,' Clytemnestra murmured. 'You still have time to flee.'

But the girl was deaf as well as mute, and so the queen pulled the curtain across the doorway and left her in prayer.

She walked through to the bath: a huge circular indentation in the floor of the palace. The water was steaming and she paused so her eyes could adjust to the flickering torchlight and the suffocating haze. She could see Agamemnon – pudgy and shrunken – sitting in the middle of the room. She scooped up the purple robe she had woven so carefully for this moment. 'Here, husband,' she called out, and walked towards the water's edge. 'Let us envelop you in purple and take you next door. We will cover you in scented oils and scrape the last remnants of Troy from your skin.'

'You startled me, woman,' said the king, as if she hadn't noticed. 'Can the slaves not bring the oil in here?'

'We have a couch laid out for you,' Clytemnestra said. 'With wine and honey waiting in your cup.'

The king rolled his eyes gracelessly and stood. He walked up the three small steps from the pool to his wife and reached out his arms. She helped him place his right arm into the right sleeve and quickly pushed his left arm into the left one before he realized that the robe was no robe, but a net, a trap, an ambush. The sleeves had no ends, they were sewn shut and attached to the body of the garment, so once his arms were inside them he was pinned. He clutched at the fabric with his fingers but she had sewn layer after layer into the sleeve ends, so there was nothing he could grip. She spun him off balance, and tied the strings at the back of the robe into a quick knot.

'What are you doing?' he shouted. Angry now, not afraid. Not afraid until he saw the sword glinting in her left hand. He had not noticed a sword, propped up against a pillar in its shadow. He did not recognize it: it was a short womanish weapon. Where could his wife have found such a thing?

She drove the sword into his gut, above his paralysed arms, and he screamed. She wrenched it back and drove it in higher, splitting the gap between two of his ribs on the right-hand side. He screamed again and fell forward onto his knees as she drew the sword out a second time.

His screams were deafening, but no one came running to help him. No one came.

She stood above him now and drove her sword down, through his ribs once more. He felt the air disappear from his lung as she sliced into that, too. He opened his mouth to make a sound but his voice had left him. He looked down to see his innards spilling out onto the ground, the purple of his viscera lost in the purple of the treacherous robe.

His widow stood over his body and smiled. Everything was going according to plan. She watched his blood taint the water red. How typical of Agamemnon to despoil something even after death, she thought. She felt warm and flushed with a savage joy, as if she, too, might dance on the roof, licked by black fire. This reminded her that her revenge was not complete and she walked calmly to the altar room.

The priestess was still there, kneeling on the floor, calmly awaiting her fate. Clytemnestra hesitated for two beats of her racing heart, but she knew that she must kill again. Nothing of Agamemnon's could remain, except his blood running through her surviving children. Cassandra had foreseen it and her god demanded it. Clytemnestra stood behind the girl, and raised her sword to draw it across her neck. She must die, but unlike Agamemnon, there was no need for her to suffer. As she was about to bring the blade across Cassandra's vein, the girl opened her eyes and stared up at her murderer. 'I'm sorry,' she said. 'I'm sorry for what will come.'

And in later years, when Clytemnestra thought about this moment, she was always sure it must have been her who spoke these words. Because what could the priestess have to be sorry for?

*

Up on the palace roof, the Furies ceased their dance. They looked at one another, nodding excitedly. Their work was done; their will had been carried out at last. It was the longest they had ever waited anywhere, dancing through the halls and across the warm stone floors, warming their bare feet and their cool snakes as they went. But after a year or two they had grown bored. They had clambered onto the roof to try and spot the guilty man returning, so they could scream into his ears as he woke or tried to sleep, and drive him from his senses. They had waited and waited and waited for his return. They did not speak of all the other guilty men who had gone unpunished in the years that they had spent on the roof of the palace of Mycenae. The Furies would catch up with them soon enough. In this moment, they felt nothing but exuberance at the final settling of matters here.

And yet – one of them turned her head, as if she had just caught the edge of a sound but wasn't quite sure. The snakes paused their writhing and the flames shrank away. A second sound, and then a third. The Furies said nothing, but they began to climb down from the roof, all vipers and fire and elbows and knees. Where was it coming from? They scurried along the outer walls of the palace and the sound grew louder. A hammering noise was emanating from the storeroom. The door was made of thick wood, banded with blackened metal, but as they stood outside they heard someone pounding on the door, begging to be let out. Electra had been locked in there for hours and she was no fool. She knew by now that her father was dead, killed by her mother. Had the slaves told her? Had Aegisthus? The Furies neither knew nor cared. All they heard was her fists pounding on the locked door, and her tears as she begged to be allowed to see her father's corpse.

The Furies did not concern themselves with doors or walls. They appeared beside her and wreathed her in their black fire. Their snakes nestled in her hair, and although she could not see the women who encircled her, or the snakes which writhed around her, Electra felt their fiery warmth and knew what she had to do. She must find her brother, find Orestes. And then they must avenge their father.

40

Penelope

Beloved goddess Athene,

I raise to you my prayer of thanks. I compose it in the last hour of darkness, before the rosy dawn streaks across the sky. Odysseus is upstairs, asleep in our bed, something I never thought would be true again. My husband, in Ithaca, after twenty years' absence. Telemachus is asleep, too, safely back from his travels. They have only just begun to tell me what happened and how they both returned to me on the same day, from who knows where. But the stories will come. I already know that it is you I have to thank.

It is you who has protected them. I know you always did like Odysseus: so clever, just like you. I don't think it can be hubris to point that out, can it? Forgive me, Athene, if it is. The long years without my husband have made me sharp-tongued. I imagine you know how that feels. And I know I have you to thank for persuading the nymph, Calypso, to give him back. They say you entreated Zeus himself to intervene. That you summoned a council of the gods to demand that Odysseus be freed to return home. They say you compelled Poseidon to let him sail unharmed and coaxed the Phaeacians to give him safe harbour. Without you, my husband would assuredly be at the bottom of the sea.

He came back in disguise, of course. Typical Odysseus. Never approach a problem directly if you can come upon it sideways. And I'm sure we have you to thank for the efficacy of his disguise: his own mother would have struggled to recognize him. His own wife could not be certain it was him. Even when I looked him in the eyes, I could not be sure.

But before he came to me, he hid himself away for a day or two with the swineherd, Eumaeus. The bards sing of the great homecomings of all the Greek heroes (some of which, let's be honest, went rather better than others). But I feel sure that only in my husband's story will pigs play a crucial role. If his men aren't being transformed into them, he's sleeping next to them, all rather than coming home to his wife. I presume word had got back to him about Agamemnon, and how Clytemnestra welcomed the old coward home. They say she cut him down like an old tree as he stood beside his bath. They say she felled him with an axe or pierced him with a knife – the details vary depending on who does the telling. But one thing is certain: those daughters of Leda are a plague on their menfolk. Did Odysseus worry that he would receive a similar welcome here on Ithaca? That I, the devout Penelope, would treat him as Clytemnestra had treated her husband? The idea is preposterous. My name is a byword for patience and loyalty, no matter which bard sings it. But that is my Odysseus. And your Odysseus. Always finding things out the hard way.

So it was at Eumaeus' hut that he received his home-coming. Not at first (this last part of the story is all I have heard so far). At first, he was almost torn apart by dogs. He had forgotten – of course he had – that the swineherd's dogs were not the same ones that had barked at strangers when he was last on Ithaca. Dogs cannot wait as long as wives: these hounds were the pups of the pups of the original dogs, I should think. When they saw a strange man approach them, they snarled and barked and threatened to rip him apart. Only when Eumaeus placated them did they agree to allow the stranger to pass. Odysseus assumed the hounds were vicious, until the following morning when he heard the quick footsteps of a young man coming towards the hut. The dogs did not bark or growl, but emitted a single joyful yelp to welcome home their friend, Telemachus. Odysseus is not always a man to reveal his thoughts, as you know. But I believe this moment – when his son was acknowledged by the Ithacan dogs which did not know their old master – was upsetting for him. It was still more distressing to see how his son greeted Eumaeus, as a son might greet his father. His own child, fully grown, a young man, embracing another man and sharing with his old servant the stories a boy would tell his papa. Odysseus is the master of discretion when he chooses. But on this occasion, the tears spilled from his face and collected in his beard. His son thought of another man as his father. Odysseus could conceal his true identity no longer. He wanted to be embraced and welcomed home. So he revealed to Telemachus what he had yet to reveal to me. This – I might add – is absolutely typical.

He asked Telemachus questions all night long: how were things in the palace, had the queen ever remarried, who were the suitors of whom Eumaeus spoke who courted her night and day? The swineherd said they were drinking all the queen's wine and eating all her pigs, one by one, day by day. Was it true? How many were they? How strong, how well armed? He was already planning his revenge on the men who had dared to think of marrying his wife. There are some who will say this was cruel and unjust. Odysseus had been gone for twenty years: who didn't think he was dead? I doubted he lived, his father doubted, his mother had died doubting he would ever return. And I know his son, Telemachus, doubted too (although it would be ungracious of me to mention this). It is no wonder the young men of Ithaca wanted a chance to become its king: how much reverence could they really have for a ruler they had never seen?

If anything could have happened differently (and I hope you don't mind me mentioning this, Athene), I wish that Odysseus had felt able to take me into his confidence earlier. It is one thing to know that your husband is fighting a war across the wide, dark sea. It is another to know he is delayed by monsters, gods and sluts at every stage of his journey home. But it is one last twist of the knife to discover that he would reunite himself with his child before his wife. I know what he will say when I raise this with him one day. He will say he had to be sure of the outcome before he embarked on the battle. He was always such a cautious man, always testing his options. But here he was, so near to me, and yet I was completely alone. The one person I might have looked to for comfort was our son, and Odysseus kept him from me, too. Only for a day or two, I know. But Telemachus was and is my only child. My chance to have any more sons or daughters was taken from me when Odysseus set sail for Troy. And he must have known – they both must have known – that after years of waiting for a husband who didn't return, the loss of my son as he adventured around Greece trying to find his missing father was an injury too far. I would forgive my son anything, of course: what mother could not? But of all the things Odysseus did in his absence, I will find this last little cruelty one of the hardest to forgive. I know – again – what his defence will be: it was only a few days, it was for the greater good. Easy for him to say, when he had not spent twenty years waiting. I cannot shake the sense that Odysseus was more concerned with a successful revenge than with a successful reunion with his wife.

And that is the second reason for my prayers, Athene. I do give thanks to you for bringing him home. But who is it that has returned? My husband: the clever, conniving, desirable, paternal, filial man? Or a broken warrior, so bludgeoned by bloodshed that he sees every problem as one to be solved with a sword? Because the man I loved twenty years ago loathed the prospect of battle. He pretended to be mad to avoid sailing to Troy. Does he even remember that? I do. And he was never a coward: you know that as well as I. But still, he shunned the war for as long as he could. And I heard all those reports of his wily ambushes, his tricks and guile, and I thought – every time – that's my man. That's my Odysseus, always coming up with the cleverest scheme, always saving the

day with his wits. At some point, did I stop noticing how
many people died with each of his plots? Did I think that
was an incidental consequence, when actually it was the
whole point? When he lost all his men on his journey
home, was that even an accident? What if – Athene, I
wish I didn't have to voice these thoughts, but they will
plague me until I put them into words – he jettisoned his
men, rather than losing them? What then?

Forgive me, goddess: I broke off my prayer for a moment.
No disrespect was intended. Where was I? Oh yes.
Odysseus' disguise fooled every person he saw. Even those
of us – like me – who knew him best of all. The one
creature he could not trick was Argos. Is that because –
with all your cleverness assisting him – you forgot the dog
might remember who he was? I don't mean to suggest it
was your fault, of course. But Argos had been a puppy
when Odysseus set off to Troy. He had trained the little
hound and made it obedient to his commands. And then
he left and the puppy became a dog and eventually the
dog went grey around the muzzle and began to trot more
slowly. It is a rare mutt that lives more than twenty years.
But live he did, so that when Odysseus walked past him,
on his way from Eumaeus' hut towards our palace, his
scent caught in the old dog's nose. Argos hasn't barked
for a year or two now, and he did not bark then. Instead,
he wagged his tail – once, twice – and dropped his ears,
as if waiting for Odysseus to reach down and scratch
between them. My husband saw the tail and the ears move
and he knew – in that moment, he knew – that this elderly
mutt was the puppy he had left behind. He wanted to pet
the animal, but feared giving away his true identity. And

a moment later, it was irrelevant because Argos – who was so old and frail and unused to shock – breathed his last. It is manifestly absurd that in this whole horrific saga of war and tragedy, it is the death of his old dog which has upset me almost more than anything. But it has, and there is no denying it. The dog waits a lifetime for his master's return and then dies when his wish is fulfilled. Even the bards would think it too sentimental to include in their songs.

Odysseus arrived at the palace – at his home, at last – still disguised as a beggar. I welcomed him as I welcome any stranger who needs a meal and a roof over his head for a night. You know better than I do, Athene, that it is our duty to the gods to receive every stranger as a guest. The suitors made him as welcome as they have made any vagabond. They jeered at him and threatened him. Antinous threw a stool at him, which hit him in the back. Interestingly, not one of them noticed that this seemingly battered old man did not flinch when a wooden stool bounced off his shoulder. It had been thrown with some force and yet he shrugged it off. I will not claim that I recognized my husband at this point. How could I, when he was shrouded in your concealments? But I did notice this: for an old man, he carried himself remarkably like a warrior. An unseen missile did not hurt or alarm. And when Eumaeus introduced him as a wandering Cretan with news of Odysseus, I did wonder who this vague description might be hiding.

The suitors, of course, behaved exactly as I had come to expect over the years. It was not just Antinous, but Leodes, Eurymachus, Agelaus and all the rest of them.

They were not bad men individually, I don't think. Not all of them, anyway. They certainly did not behave so viciously to begin with. They arrived at the palace in twos and threes: shy, at first, quietly competitive with one another for my affections. It took months, perhaps even years, before they became the aggressive gang of men Odysseus finally met. I used to wonder what had happened to them, and why they were so anxious to stay somewhere they were not wanted. Pausing their lives, refusing to marry girls who would have them, failing to start families. Instead they preferred to be together as men, under the guise of wooing me. It took me some time to realize that this was in fact their war. Too young to sail to Troy, they were children when their brothers and cousins and fathers joined the greatest expedition that Hellas had ever seen. They had missed their chance to be warriors in the great war. And so they waged war upon my storerooms, and upon my virtue, because they had nothing else to fight for. In a way, I pitied them.

But when they gathered together, all better instincts were soon lost. Each one of them became as bad as the worst of them. It was this which made it so easy not to be seduced by them. Not even Amphinomus. And oh, he was handsome. Did you ever notice him, Athene? Or were your owl-grey eyes on my husband the whole time? If you had looked across the room, you would have seen a tall young man, broad-shouldered and strong-limbed, with a kindness in his eyes that the others did not have. You would never have seen him shout at a beggar or hurl insults at a stranger. He had a soft, low voice that was lost in the melee of other, louder men. He had dark eyes and thick brown curls that a woman could twist her fingers into. I imagine.

But like all the other suitors, and the maids who Odysseus believed had conspired with them, he is now dead. And I will never know if that was your design, or all Odysseus' choosing. What I do know is that I welcomed a stranger into my halls, and he was abused. And he paid back his abusers with arrows and a sword.

The arrows were probably my fault. I could not shake the idea that something needed to come to a conclusion. The self-styled Cretan was in my halls, and there was something familiar about him. The suitors were behaving like a pack of wild dogs. I knew I needed to make a decision, so I offered them a trial of strength and skill: to string Odysseus' bow and shoot an arrow through twelve axe-heads. It takes real strength to string this particular bow. It has an individual design which most men would not recognize. And it takes skill to shoot an arrow from such a weapon, let alone fire one with the accuracy and force required to traverse twelve axes. Honestly, I doubted any of them could do it. I just thought it might keep them quiet for a while so I could rest. The noise of all those young men could be deafening.

Was I testing the Cretan to see if he was really my husband? Telemachus believes that I suspected it was Odysseus all along. Certainly, I knew that my husband would be able to string the bow and fire the arrow: I had watched him do it countless times in our youth. I don't believe that was my motivation, but perhaps you – or one of the other gods – put the idea into my mind. It had certainly never occurred to me before, to test my suitors like this. Of course they all failed, and of course Odysseus prevailed. Not only did he prevail, but now he was armed with a weapon and the suitors were not. And he was armed with precisely the sort of weapon that might even the odds between one man and many.

It was not quite one man fighting alone though, was it? My son fought alongside him, and they paved our floors with blood. My husband had revealed himself to Telemachus, to Eumaeus and even (I later discovered) to his old nurse, Eurycleia, before he revealed himself to me. And when he finally did so, he was drenched in the blood of the men who have made my life miserable, and the blood of one man who did not. He had killed Amphinomus with an arrow to the throat, leaving his lovely face unharmed. The boy's eyes stared at me blankly from beside Odysseus' left foot.

My husband, meanwhile, stood knee-deep in the suitors' blood and before the twitching bodies of my maids – each one hanged from the same length of rope – and that was when he told me he was mine. In all my dreams of his homecoming, I never imagined it would be so violent or so cruel. I never thought it would take so long to clean up. And I don't suppose he gave a moment's thought to how we are to apologize to the families of these obnoxious young boors. Or indeed, how I am supposed to find a new set of maids, given what happened to the last lot. And so, Athene, the prayer I offer is this: thank you for bringing my husband home, if that is what you have done. If the man who sleeps upstairs in the bed he once carved from an old olive tree is an impostor, I suppose I will find out soon enough. He knows the old stories of our marriage, of that I am certain. And Telemachus is devoted to him, which is fortunate. So perhaps it does not matter if he is the man who left, or a changed man, or even another man altogether. He fits in the space that Odysseus left.

Your devoted Penelope

41

The Moirai

It was the same scene every day: Clotho held the spindle, Lachesis watched her with hungry appraisal in her eyes, and Atropos sat in the darkest corner, her stubby blade almost invisible in the gloom. Clotho fed the thread through her right hand and flicked the spindle with her left. She could not remember doing anything else for as long as she had ever known. She would take a clump of fleece in one hand and twist it into a thick rough string. Once, she might have plucked thorns or burrs from the soft fuzz, but she had long since given that up; they only scratched her hands. The thread was so fragile at this point, almost still fleece, scarcely thread at all. The fibres would pull apart with the slightest pressure, so she had to be careful. Lachesis would not forgive her if she shortened the lifespan of a single mortal through her clumsiness. It was her task to spin the thread of life but it was for Lachesis to decide how long the thread would be. Clotho had once suggested that they swap jobs for a while, so she could rest her cramping fingers. But neither of the others would consider it, which just proved what she had always known: that she had the hardest task of the three of them and it would never change. No wonder she felt so little sympathy for the mortal lives which flitted between her fingers.

The grease in the fibres kept her fingertips soft as she rubbed them across the puffy strand. Once it became a little firmer, she would hook it around the spindle and the weight pulled it longer and thinner still. Only then would Lachesis focus her attention on the thread. She used no measuring stick, only her sharp eyes. At the crucial moment, she would nod and Atropos would slash her short blade into the space between Clotho's hands. Another life measured and complete. Sometimes they misjudged: Lachesis did not always nod with the vigour required, and in the gloomy light, Atropos missed it. Who had that man been, Clotho tried to remember, who had lived so long after the Fates botched his mortal span? She could not recall his name, only that he had been so ancient when he died that he had looked like a pile of autumn leaves. Occasionally Atropos sliced too low or too high and cut the thread at the wrong point. And sometimes Clotho could not get the thread to form properly: her hands were dry, the fleece was not greasy enough, and the fibres simply fell apart before Lachesis could find anything to measure. She felt no sorrow for these souls, because if she thought at all about the consequences of her actions, she would become paralysed and never spin again. But she did prefer it if one of the others made a mistake, because that led – as often as not – to a longer life rather than a shorter one. When the thread would not form, it could only mean a grieving mother, standing over a cradle, howling at the unhearing sky.

42

Andromache

When Andromache looked up at the mountains that towered above Epirus, she wished they reminded her of Mount Ida, but they did not. Mount Ida rose to a perfect point, so high that often in the mornings it was shrouded in mist and she and Hector had been unable to see the top of it. She had watched the sun chase the mists away and each time the highest point was visible again, she felt calmness flood through her, like a child who can finally make out her father coming home in the distance. She missed the mountain, but when she thought of that instead of everything else she had lost, she found she could keep herself from weeping.

But Epirus was no Troy. The peaks lacked the kindly parental nature of Ida. Here, there were mountains on all sides, so that Andromache felt as though she were trapped at the bottom of a well. She had been taken from her beautiful city, with its thick walls and high citadel, for what was scarcely more than a village. Well, a collection of villages. Epirus nestled in the northernmost part of Greece, so its mountains were always covered in snow and Andromache was often cold. She had never worn a woollen tunic in Troy, or in Thebe where she had grown up. But in Epirus it was a necessity.

When they landed here – she blurred the details of that period of her life as much as she could, but this part she did remember – she had woven a cloak for herself in a matter of days. She had little choice if she was not to die from the vicious north wind that whistled down from the mountains. Neoptolemus had ordered her to spin the wool (a gift from his none-too-loyal subjects) and weave. And she had obeyed him. But although she began the task resentfully (a princess of Troy reduced to slavery) she had completed it eagerly, keen to have the thick fabric to wrap around herself in the cold evenings. It had been the realization of this – her desire not to be cold – that made her accept she might not wish to die after all.

She had spent the voyage from Troy like a dead woman. She could not rise from her pallet, she could not eat, she could barely drink wine unless it was diluted almost down to water. She watched with mild interest as the bones in her wrist grew more pronounced, and once or twice she traced her fingers along her clavicle and felt the hollows on each side of her neck growing deeper. Only on the fifth day, when he shouted, screamed really, a hand's breadth away from her face – his stale-wine breath making her queasy in a way the choppy sea never had – demanding that she ate and stop damaging his property, did she manage to swallow a small quantity of thin soup. The sailor who brought it to her looked sorry for her, when he watched her retching as she raised the too-large spoon to her lips. But he was afraid of Neoptolemus, too. Rumour had it that he had hurled one of his own men over the side of the ship on the voyage to Troy, because of some slight misdemeanour. The sailors would not run the risk of being set adrift, of watching their comrades sail off into the distance while they tried desperately to keep afloat for just a moment longer. Neoptolemus was not known to have expressed regret for any cruelty he had perpetuated against anyone – man, woman or child.

Andromache felt her mind begin to travel down the road she could not allow it to take. She focused on the spoon in front of her mouth, and tried to keep it level, so the soup did not spill on her filthy dress. The sailor nodded slowly in encouragement, as though she were an invalid. He waited for her to finish eating and quietly took the bowl away.

But eating alone did not bring her back to life. Her eyes could not focus on anything but the horizon, she did not hear anyone speak unless he screamed in her ear, and she could not bear any touch or taste. The material world repelled her because (she was sure) she should not be in it any longer. The Fates had made a mistake when they let her be taken aboard Neoptolemus' ship. She should have died on the shores of Troy, instead of her son.

She wove the cloak poorly, although she had once been a fine craftswoman. The last cloak she had woven had been for Hector – dark and bright for him to wear into battle – and it had been exquisite. It was slashed in two by Achilles when he drove his fierce blade into her husband's body, and then she had watched it stretch out on the ground behind him like a pool of blood as Achilles dragged his corpse three times around the walls of the city.

In Epirus, she was careless with cleaning the wool, so

the finished fabric scratched her skin. She did not spin a
fine thread, so the cloak was covered in lumps where the
wool was too bulky to sit flat. And she did not keep the
threads taut, so the garment had an ugly puckered edge.
But sometime during the process of weaving it, she found
herself wanting to finish it so she would not be cold. And
although she did not understand it immediately, this was
the first sign of her life after death.

But when Andromache had finished the cloak and
wrapped it around herself, she still felt cold. She remembered one day near the beginning of the war, when a
young Trojan fighter had been carried back to the city by
his comrades. He had been shot in the back – a lucky hit
from a distant archer – and his suffering was terrible to
behold. It was not the pain which was distressing: he was
in less pain than virtually any other Trojan or Greek she
saw injured. It was the gap between what had happened
to him and what he could perceive. He lay on his side
unable to feel the arrow, or his spine, or his legs or feet.
All sensation had deserted him below the chest. When
asked by the healers to describe his symptoms, he said
simply that his body felt cold. This was his only complaint
for the next three days, at the end of which he died. And
that had been what filled Andromache's mind as she
submitted to Neoptolemus.

She was not quite sure how long she had been living
in Epirus before she realized she was pregnant. She said
nothing to Neoptolemus for a while, because she could
not find the words. She felt too many things at once and
it took her many careful hours at the loom (now weaving
finer garments once more, though nothing in comparison

to what she had made for Hector) before she could isolate some of them and give them names. She felt fear, firstly. Neoptolemus rarely spoke to her other than to bark orders. She had no idea if he wanted his slave to bear him a child. He had no son, as far as she knew, and he had not yet a wife. What if she told him, or he noticed her body changing shape, and he punished her? Would he kick her in the stomach until the baby was dead? Andromache felt a wave of sickness that did not come from her child. Or rather, it came from her first child, from Astyanax. It had been Neoptolemus who killed her boy, hurling him from the walls of Troy before snarling back to his ship to bring her here to Epirus. How could she trust that a man who would murder her first child would not murder her second? She could not.

She moved her shuttle up and down through the warp-threads, pulling the weft gently so she did not stretch the edges, pushing each completed row up so she did not leave any gaps. The steadiness of the work, the feel of the threads beneath her fingers, the enforced calm of feeding the shuttle through: these things made her able to keep breathing, and naming. So fear, that was the first feeling: both for the baby and for herself. Then came revulsion. Her blood would be mixed with the blood of the man who had killed her son. And Neoptolemus was son of Achilles, who had killed her husband. To be enslaved by this vicious clan of murderers was terrible enough, but to produce a new scion was worse. She felt tainted by the infant inside her and had no confidence that the feeling would pass when the child was born. Anger, that was the third. For everything she had once told Hector had now come to pass: don't keep going out to fight on your own, she had said. Don't take so many risks. Fight among the Trojans, not ahead of them. Your honour is already assured. Catch the eye of Achilles and he will cut you down and then what will become of your wife and son? We will be enslaved with no one to care for us.

There was no pleasure in being proved right, of course, only a slowly unfolding dread. Why had Hector not listened to his wife's wise words? How could he have abandoned her, abandoned their son? Everything had come to pass as she had predicted, but worse. And if only . . . She broke her thoughts. She could not begin to consider if only, or the sun and the moon would come crashing down upon her.

So fear, revulsion, anger. Guilt, that was next. She felt a terrible pressing burden of guilt. Because in spite of all this, she felt a small flame of inexpressible joy. Her body, so long not her own, was providing her with comfort at last. She had nothing to love but her memories and those were too painful to think about. And now she had something. And in spite of the fear, the revulsion, the anger and the guilt, the flame kept burning inside her.

*

Andromache never came to love Neoptolemus, because that was asking too much even of a woman like her. His actions could not be forgotten, nor did he ever show the slightest contrition for the terrible toll he had exacted upon her and the women she had once called her family. But nor could she maintain the visceral loathing she had felt when he first took her from her home. It was not possible to keep hating a man with whom she lived in such close proximity: the aversion had to die, or she would die. And although his temper was fierce, and she sometimes found herself shrinking back from his anger, he was not as cruel as she had feared he would be. When he saw his son for the first time, she could not breathe. The wet-nurse held the child for him and she saw a soft smile transform his petulant face. He was not a good man, but Andromache suddenly saw that he might nonetheless be a good father. He named their son Molossus.

She did not resent his wife, when Neoptolemus married Hermione, the young daughter of Menelaus and Helen. Anyone could see there was no affection between them. And although he visited her bed for the first month or two, her youthful attractions quickly paled and he returned to Andromache for comfort. She lay in the darkness beside him, no longer sickened by the faint sourness of his breath. She heard his breathing slow but she knew he was not yet asleep. And still she was surprised when he spoke.

'I killed her as painlessly as I could.'

She felt her limbs stiffen. 'Who do you mean?'

'Your sister,' he said. Polyxena. Neoptolemus had killed her sister-in-law (she did not correct him) on the shore, to appease his father's ravening ghost.

'Did you?' she asked. She kept her tone as neutral as she could. Tears of gratitude would antagonize him as much as tears of anger.

'The Greeks had decided,' he said. 'They would not sail without the sacrifice. They sacrificed the general's daughter at Aulis, they needed to sacrifice your king's daughter to sail home again.' It was a peculiar quirk of his, to refer to men by their role rather than by name. Always the general, never Agamemnon. Your king, rather than Priam. And then in a rush, 'She was no coward. She died nobly.'

In the dark, Andromache nodded. She knew he felt the movement of her head. 'She was always brave,' she replied. 'Always.'

'She is the one who torments my sleep,' he said. Andromache drove her nails into her hands. Not Astyanax, a baby. Not Priam, a helpless old man. Only Polyxena had wakened the conscience of the man she had once thought a monster. Would still think a monster, if circumstances had not forced her to find something else in his character that she could tolerate.

'Why?' she asked.

She heard a muffled sound and he moved his hand swiftly across his face. 'I don't know,' he said. 'She was so—' This time he felt her go rigid. 'You should not hear this,' he said. But she found that although she could not think of these events on her own, for fear that the grief would split her asunder, even now, she was comforted to hear the words from him. The shock came first, but she could feel the consolation travelling just behind it.

'Tell me.'

'She was so willing to die,' he said. 'She did nothing to resist. She offered me her throat to cut. Why wasn't she afraid?'

'She was afraid,' Andromache replied. 'But she was more afraid of slavery. More afraid to be torn from her homeland. More afraid to belong to a man she did not know or choose. Death was not frightening to her because she preferred it to a worse fate.'

There was silence as he considered what she had said. 'Would you have been afraid to die then?' he asked.

Andromache winced as though he had slapped her. 'No.'

'Coming to Epirus was worse for you than dying?'

'I thought so.'

There was a further silence. 'Do you still think so?' he asked. She heard the unmistakeable note of hope in his voice and almost laughed at the absurdity of it. Her captor, the murderer of her son, craving her approval. And yet, she found she could not withhold it. 'No. I have Molossus now.'

'When I die,' he began, and then broke off. She did not interrupt, knowing that he sometimes needed to think his way into his words and would become annoyed if she distracted him. 'When I die, you will marry that Trojan prince.'

'Helenus?' she asked. Cassandra's brother was one of the few Trojan men whom the Greeks had allowed to live. He had performed some service for them, betrayed the Trojans in some way – that much was clear to Andromache, but she knew no more than that.

'The brother of the mad girl,' he agreed. Cassandra's reputation had extended to every part of the Greek army, even before she was slaughtered by Agamemnon's wife.

'Very well. But why would you think about this now?' Neoptolemus was silent. 'Has someone threatened us?' Andromache asked. She felt his arm reach over and his hand came to rest on her cheek.

'They will,' he said. 'They will.'

*

When they came for Neoptolemus, he was not in Epirus, but in Delphi, several days' ride away. He was killed in front of the temple of Apollo by men from Mycenae. He was heavily outnumbered. Orestes, the prince of Mycenae – Agamemnon's son – demanded Neoptolemus' wife Hermione as his bride. He claimed to be avenging some impiety Neoptolemus had committed, but Andromache knew this was a flimsy pretext. If someone was going around Greece righting every impiety shown towards Apollo during the Trojan War, there would be no Greek left alive. Had Apollo not visited a plague upon them all for their crimes? So why would Neoptolemus deserve a greater punishment than the rest? The worst excesses against Apollo had been committed by the former king of Mycenae, Agamemnon himself. What right did his son have to take vengeance on any other man? He should have been making offerings and prayers himself, in penance for his own wrongdoing, his and his sister's. Hadn't they killed their mother to avenge their impious father? How did the Furies let him go unpunished?

When Andromache heard that Neoptolemus was dead, she did not grieve. She could not weep for him. She wept instead for herself, cast once again into the world with no one to protect her, and she wept for her son, though her love for Molossus was tainted. Love had come so easily to her when she was young: she had adored her parents and her brothers. And then Thebe had fallen to Achilles, and her father Eetion and her seven brothers were slaughtered in a single day. This tragedy – the shock of which killed her mother shortly afterwards – had not broken her of the habit of loving. She had opened her heart to Hector and his family, delighting in their numbers, all those new brothers and sisters. She had been as dutiful to Priam and Hecabe as she had been to her own parents. She had found it a pleasure, had never understood the sly remarks other women made about their husbands' mothers. Losing her own family had made her all the readier to love another. Then when Hector died she had grieved as a widow should and she had found consolation in his family: her loss was also theirs.

But the death of Astyanax had changed her and she had known she would never love anyone in the same way thereafter. When her child lay smashed beneath the city walls, she knew that something inside her was broken and could not be repaired. Like any mother, she had found that her love for Astyanax was bound up in fear. When he was born, she worried with every fever: even a slight illness had her scurrying to the altars to placate the gods and beg their assistance. She cared equally for Molossus: she would have sworn it before the statue of Zeus with no fear of retribution. But she did not spend her days or nights worrying that her Greek-born son would fall ill or injure himself. She had nothing left to give to the quotidian business of motherhood. She could only trust that the gods would protect him (as they had not protected Astyanax) because she now knew that if the worst should happen, there was nothing she could do to save him. She had failed her first son, and she had no more resources now than she had had then. Instead, she had an intimate knowledge of the depths of her powerlessness: there was no possibility of self-deception. She had loved Astyanax as though she could swaddle him in blankets and keep him safe from the world. She loved Molossus as though they both lived on a cliff edge from which either or both of them might fall at any moment.

So when the message came to her from a slave, that Neoptolemus was dead and Orestes sought to make Hermione his wife, she felt the customary shudder of alarm, but it did not occur to her to flee. Where could she go, friendless as they were in Greece? And who would give her shelter from Orestes? Neoptolemus' grandfather might be of some assistance, she supposed, since he had lost his son Achilles and now his grandson, too. Molossus was all that remained of the noble house of Peleus. Andromache found herself sending the slave on to Peleus, in the hope that he could do what she could not and protect her boy. But she did it with little expectation, and was astonished when the old man appeared, brandishing his walking-stick like a cudgel and demanding that she and Molossus accompany him home.

*

As Neoptolemus had once promised, she married Helenus. The Trojan prince had a knack for making friends rather than enemies, and they were soon able to found a small settlement of their own. At Andromache's request, they began to build a city which resembled their lost home: a new Troy, less grand and imposing, but with a high citadel nestling beneath a mountain. Sometimes, when the mist took a while to clear in the mornings, she could imagine herself home again. Helenus bore a slight resemblance to his long-dead brother, Hector. Sometimes she found herself looking at his profile and seeing the features of her first husband leap from the face of her second. She never knew if Molossus resembled Astyanax as he grew up. But as she grew older, she found the two boys merging in her mind and when she saw the silhouette of Molossus returning from a day's hunting in the forest, she also saw Astyanax treading in his footsteps. Her later life was lived amid a set of shadows and reflections of all that she had lost in the catastrophes of her early life. And if the shadow of happiness fell short of happiness itself, it was more than she had ever expected to find when she lay prostrate on the shores of Troy, weeping for her beloved child.

43

Calliope

Sing, Muse, he said, and I have sung.

I have sung of armies and I have sung of men.

I have sung of gods and monsters, I have sung of stories and lies.

I have sung of death and of life, of joy and of pain.

I have sung of life after death.

And I have sung of the women, the women in the shadows. I have sung of the forgotten, the ignored, the untold. I have picked up the old stories and I have shaken them until the hidden women appear in plain sight. I have celebrated them in song because they have waited long enough. Just as I promised him: this was never the story of one woman, or two. It was the story of all of them. A war does not ignore half the people whose lives it touches. So why do we?

They have waited to have their story told, and I will make them wait no longer. If the poet refuses the song I have offered him, I will take it away and leave him silent. He has sung before: he may not want it and does not need it. But the story will be told. Their story will be told, no matter how long it takes. I am ageless, undying: time does not matter to me. All that matters is the telling.

Sing, Muse, he said.

Well, do you hear me? I have sung.

Afterword

The inspiration for this novel comes from across the ancient world, in both time and place. Some of it was literary, some was archaeological. Some chapters are entirely my own invention, and some borrow from source material which you might already know. The texts which I returned to throughout this book were Euripides' *Trojan Women* (also his *Hecabe*) for the Trojan Women chapters; and Homer's *Odyssey*, for the Penelope chapters. In addition, I turned to Virgil's *Aeneid* for Creusa's chapter (though it gave me a lot more on the burning city and the sibilant Sinon than it did on Creusa. Which isn't to say that Virgil doesn't write amazing women: I couldn't fit Dido into this novel, which was a real blow. But when something doesn't fit, it doesn't fit); Ovid's remarkable *Heroides* gave me the first insight into Laodamia, and also persuaded me that I could write Penelope's story as letters to her absent husband; Clytemnestra's chapter owes everything to Aeschylus' *Oresteia*, of course. There's not much about Briseis in Homer's *Iliad*, but the plague incurred by Agamemnon's refusal to return Chryseis is taken from there (the plague symptoms themselves are borrowed from a later author, Thucydides, who contracted plague at the start of the Peloponnesian War in the fifth century BCE, but recovered to tell the tale); Euripides' *Iphigenia in Aulis* and *Iphigenia Among the*

Taurians informed her chapter; Andromache takes her later story from Euripides' play of the same name.

There are plenty more women in this book whose stories barely exist in the surviving literature of the ancient world: Theano and Oenone, for example. Female characters are usually in the shadows or on the margins of stories even when they do appear (Euripides and Ovid are exceptional in this regard, in producing work where women are the focus and often the sole focus). Sometimes we have collectively decided a particular woman is intended even when she is not named. The *Iliad* famously begins with a line which is usually translated as 'Sing, Muse, of the wrath of Achilles'. It seems reasonable to assume he's addressing Calliope, muse of epic poetry (he would probably have hoped to find her less capricious than I have rendered her. Although if Euripides had written her, she might have been more capricious still). But Homer doesn't name her. He doesn't even use the word 'muse'. He says '*thea*', 'goddess'.

Penthesilea has suffered badly at the hands of history, unless you wish to hunt through fragments of the obscure Quintus Smyrnaeus or Pseudo-Apollodorus (which I did, but wouldn't necessarily recommend). She was a mighty warrior and had a major role in a lost epic poem, from perhaps the eighth century BCE, called *Aethiopis*. Only a few lines of this poem survive. Like many Amazons, Penthesilea was a huge inspiration to visual artists in the ancient world: Amazons feature on more surviving pots than any other mythical figure except Heracles. Also, extraordinarily, there are vases which show Greek warriors bearing fallen Amazons from the battlefield. On one beautiful pot, Penthesilea is carried from the scene of their duel by Achilles. Ancient warriors did not usually treat their dead foes with anything like this respect or affection. Sadly, when Robert Graves was writing in the twentieth century, he turned this incredible female hero into a corpse on which Achilles masturbated. This must be an example of that progress we're always reading about.

You can see a more ornate version (more monkeys, for a start) of Thetis' earrings in the British Museum. They were found on the island where she was married to Peleus in my version. If you're visiting the museum anyway, you could also track down Protesilaus, balanced on the prow of his boat, just as Laodamia imagines him in her chapter. He really does have beautiful feet. You'll have to go to Greece to see the stone lions of Mycenae, and while you're there, you could always take a boat trip and go hunting for Troy on the Turkish coast, to see if you agree with the controversial nineteenth-century archaeologist, Heinrich Schliemann, who placed it at Hisarlik in modern-day Turkey. The coastal features and plants which give Troy its detail in this book are those of Hisarlik. Apologies to those who feel strongly that Troy was somewhere else. Ithaca, home of Odysseus, has proved harder to name in the modern world (and Odysseus' route home is the source of much-wrangled discussion). I can live with the uncertainty: I hope you can too. Truthfully, I sometimes prefer not knowing things for the imaginative space it offers. I can only apologize to all my scientist friends for this despicable choice.

Euripides' version of Aphrodite and Artemis in *Hippolytus* was the starting point for the petulance of the gods in this novel. They have the emotional maturity of toddlers, mingled with immortality and horrifying power. As I moved back to the pre-Olympian gods (Themis, Gaia etc.) the petulance gets somewhat reduced and a certain loftiness is present instead. I had the most fun writing the scene where the goddesses vie with one another for the golden apple. If this book has a motif, it is that apple. Or possibly the owl which Athene refuses to hand over. I would never give up my owl to win a beauty contest, in case you were in any doubt.

Homer's *Iliad* is (rightly) regarded as one of the great foundational texts on war and warriors, men and masculinity. But it is fascinating how we have received that text and interpreted the story it tells us. I gave an early draft of *A Thousand Ships* to a brainy friend for his comments and feedback. He was funny and helpful and kind and only occasionally cross with me for not being more like H. Rider Haggard. But he questioned the book's basic premise: that the women who survive (or don't survive) a war are equally heroic as their menfolk. The men go and fight, the women don't, was his essential argument. Except that women do fight (not least Penthesilea and her Amazons), even if the poems heralding their great deeds have been lost. And men don't always: Achilles doesn't fight until book eighteen of the twenty-four-book *Iliad*. He spends the first seventeen books arguing, sulking, asking his mother for help, sulking some more, letting his friend fight in his stead, offering advice and refusing apologies. But not fighting. In other words, he spends almost three-quarters of the poem in a quasi-domestic setting, away from the battlefield. Yet we never question that he is a hero. Even when he isn't fighting, his status as a warrior is never in doubt. I hope that at the end of this book, my attempt to write an epic, readers might feel that heroism is something that can reside in all of us, particularly if circumstances push it to the fore. It doesn't belong to men, any more than the tragic consequences of war belong to women. Survivors, victims, perpetrators: these roles are not always separate. People can be wounded and wounding at the same time, or at different times in the same life. Perhaps Hecabe is the most brutal example of that.

Cassandra is the only role from all these women which I have ever performed (in a reading of Aeschylus' *Agamemnon* at school). Although her story was sometimes hard to tell, I have missed her the most since I finished writing.

Acknowledgements

This book was a man-eater and there were times I thought it would swallow me whole. So thanks go out to everyone who kept me afloat. Peter Straus is both my brilliant agent and the most thoughtful and sophisticated reader you could hope to find. I know how lucky I am. My editor at Pan Mac, Maria Rejt, is a marvel. She and Josie Humber kept me honest and rarely allowed, 'because it's in a fragment of Quintus Smyrnaeus,' as an answer. Impossible not to agree with them. Sam Sharman shepherded the book through its latter stages with a calm which I think I probably used to have before I torched it in the ruins of Troy. Tons of other wonderful people at Pan Mac contributed to this: not least Kate Green, who tricks me into doing talks and shows by asking me how my running is going. Don't be fooled by her innocent face.

Book-writing could easily be at war with my broadcasting work. It isn't, because my colleagues at the BBC are amazing. Mary Ward-Lowery, James Cook: thank you for making *Natalie Haynes Stands Up for the Classics* with me during this book. I couldn't have done the radio series without you, and the book would be less if I weren't performing. I guess I might sleep better, but that can wait. Huge thanks also to James Runcie and Gwyneth Williams for letting us keep making the shows.

Early readers are one of the most precious things writers

can have. Thank you to Sarah Churchwell, as always, for being an impossibly acute reader, and for making time when she has none. And thanks to Robert Douglas-Fairhurst who is the person on my mind when people ask who my ideal reader is. What am I saying? He's always on my mind. Digby Lidstone read the first half and told me to take out 90 per cent of the commas, so you can thank him for that. Elena Richards went through the final draft with a fine-tooth comb, and Matilda McMorrow did the same at proof stage. If either of them decides on a publishing career, please take this as the short-form of a glowing reference and apply to me for the longer version.

Huge numbers of people kept me on track while I was writing. You all have my thanks and love, especially: Helen Bagnall, for being a miracle of positive energy in my life; I'm so lucky to know her. Damian Barr for always knowing the right time to call and the right thing to say. David Benedict for taking me out when I needed it. Philippa Perry and her friend Julianne for their continued perceptiveness and kindness. Kara Manley for being here since the beginning. Michelle Flower for moral support in animal and human form. Julian Barnes for offering the best advice (in the most patient voice) when I was climbing the walls. Marcus Bell for sending me *Hamilton* videos every day for a month to keep my spirits up. Adam Rutherford for offering unrivalled advice on the flora and fauna of the Troad Peninsula in the Bronze Age. Christian Hill for (always and still) being the voice of reason in my shifting world.

Most of all I want to thank Dan Mersh for everything, always. And, of course, my family: my mum, my dad, Chris, Gem and Kez. You can all have my owl.

About the Author

NATALIE HAYNES is the author of six books. She has written and recorded six series of *Natalie Haynes Stands Up for the Classics* for BBC Radio 4. Natalie appeared at the Edinburgh Festival Fringe from 2002 to 2006, where she became the first woman ever nominated for the Perrier Best Newcomer Award. She has been on tour with her Stands Up for the Classics shows since 2010. Natalie has written for the *Times*, the *Independent*, the *Guardian* and the *Observer*.